De

Book 1 o

Consultant' series

Sarah J. Waldock

ISBN-13
978-1466307544

Dedication
To those women who find yourselves deceived and
abused; may you find the strength to escape

Other books by Sarah Waldock

Sarah writes predominantly Regency Romances:

The Brandon Scandals Series
The Hasty Proposal
The Reprobate's Redemption
The Advertised Bride
The Wandering Widow
The Braithwaite Letters
Heiress in Hiding

Wild Western Brandon Scandals
Colonel Brandon's Quest

The Charity School Series
Elinor's Endowment
Ophelia's Opportunity
Abigail's Adventure
Marianne's Misanthrope
Emma's Education/Grace's Gift
Anne's Achievement
Daisy's Destiny
Libby's Luck

Spinoffs:
The Moorwick Tales
Fantasia on a House Party

Rookwood series
The Unwilling Viscount
The Enterprising Emigrée

The Wynddell Papers
Lord Wynddell's Bride

The Seven Stepsisters series
Elizabeth
Diana
Minerva[WIP]
Flora [WIP]
Catherine [WIP]
Jane [WIP]
Anne [WIP]

One off Regencies
Vanities and Vexations [Jane Austen sequel]
Cousin Prudence [Jane Austen sequel]
Friends and Fortunes
None so Blind
Belles and Bucks [short stories]

The Georgian Gambles series
The Valiant Viscount [formerly The Pugilist Peer]
Ace of Schemes

Other
William Price and the 'Thrush', naval adventure and Jane Austen tribute
William Price sails North
William Price on land
William Price and the 'Thetis' [wip]

100 years of Cat Days: 365 anecdotes

Sarah also writes historical mysteries

Regency period 'Jane, Bow Street Consultant 'series, a
Jane Austen tribute
   Death of a Fop
   Jane and the Bow Street Runner [3 novellas]
   Jane and the Opera Dancer
   Jane and the Christmas Masquerades [2 novellas]
   Jane and the Hidden Hoard
   Jane and the Burning Question [short stories]
   Jane and the Sins of Society
   Jane and the Actresses
   Jane and the Careless Corpse

Spinoffs:
The Armitage Chronicles

'Felicia and Robin' series set in the Renaissance
   Poison for a Poison Tongue
   The Mary Rose Mystery
   Died True Blue
   Frauds, Fools and Fairies
   The Bishop of Brangling
   The Hazard Chase
   Heretics, Hatreds and Histories
   The Midsummer Mysteries
   The Colour of Murder
   Falsehood most Foul
   The Monkshithe Mysteries
   Toll the Dead Man's bells
   Wells, Wool and Wickedness
   The Missing Hostage

Children's stories
   Tabitha Tabs the Farm kitten

A School for Ordinary Princesses [sequel to Frances Hodgson Burnett's 'A Little Princess.]

The Royal Draxiers series
Bess and the Dragons
Bess and the Queen
Bess and the Succession
Bess and the Paying Scholars
Bess and the Gunpowder Plot [wip]
Bess and the Necromancer [wip]

Non-Fiction
Writing Regency Romances by dice
The Regency Miss's Survival Guide to Bath

Fantasy
Falconburg Divided [book 1 of the Falconburg brothers series]
Falconburg Rising [book 2 of the Falconburg brothers series]
Falconburg Ascendant [book 3 of the Falconburg brothers series, WIP]

Scarlet Pimpernel spinoffs
The Redemption of Chauvelin
Chauvelin and the League

Other Baroness Orczy spinoffs
Lady Molly – Married

Sarah Waldock grew up in Suffolk and still resides there, in charge of a husband, and under the ownership of sundry cats. All Sarah's cats are rescue cats and many of them have special needs. They like to help her write and may be found engaging in such helpful pastimes as turning the screen display upside-down, or typing random messages in kittycode into her computer.

Sarah claims to be an artist who writes. Her degree is in art, and she got her best marks writing essays for it. She writes largely historical novels, in order to retain some hold on sanity in an increasingly insane world. There are some writers who claim to write because they have some control over their fictional worlds, but Sarah admits to being thoroughly bullied by her characters who do their own thing and often refuse to comply with her ideas. It makes life more interesting, and she enjoys the surprises they spring on her. Her characters' surprises are usually less messy [and much less noisy] than the surprises her cats spring.

Sarah has tried most of the crafts and avocations which she mentions in her books, on the principle that it is easier to write about what you know. She does not ride horses, since the Good Lord in his mercy saw fit to invent Gottleib Daimler to save her from that experience; and she has not tried blacksmithing. She would like to wave cheerily at anyone in any security services who wonder about middle aged women who read up about gunpowder and poisonous plants.

Sarah would like to note that any typos remaining in the text after several betas, an editor and proofreader have been over it are caused by the well-known phenomenon of *cat-induced editing syndrome* from the help engendered by busy little bottoms on the keyboard.

This is her excuse and you are stuck with it.

And yes, there are two more cat bums on the edge of the picture as well as the 4 on her lap/chest

You may find out more about Sarah at her blog site, at:

http://sarahs-history-place.blogspot.co.uk/

Or on Facebook for advance news of writing

https://www.facebook.com/pages/Sarah-J-Waldock-Author/520919511296291

Or particiapate as a beta reader and get an advanced look at Sarah's work in draft form at

https://mywipwriting.blogspot.com/

Chapter 1

Mrs. Jane Churchill knew she should not feel relieved that her husband was dead.

She should definitely not feel relieved when she was being told that he was not only dead but that he had been murdered. She stared at the man who had brought the news, who seemed to fill the whole room with his presence. Maybe it was just the news that was filling the room.

"My husband is *dead?*" she repeated the words, trying to take it in; hoping perhaps that by saying it out loud it would really make it so. . She clenched and unclenched her fists in the folds of her golden brown kerseymere morning gown.

"Yes ma'am; I'm sorry for your loss."

He was remarkably well spoken for a Bow Street Runner; she had heard they could be rough men.

He was clean too.

The indeterminate blondish hair had no grease to it; the colour not quite pale enough to be blonde was natural, not a patina of dirt on naturally lighter hair.

He was tall and looked faintly uncomfortable, as though he felt too big for her little parlour, standing there, favouring one leg. Yes, he had limped as he came in.

"Won't – won't you sit down and tell me all about it?" she indicated a chair.

He looked surprised.

"Well…. It is remarkably civil of you Ma'am," he said, sitting gingerly on the edge of the chair. There was a passing flicker of relief across his face.

His aquiline nose had been broken at some point and his eyes were very blue, she noticed, now he was at a level for her to see better.

"Does it not impede your work?" she asked "Your leg?"

He grimaced.

"Only when it's been a long day, ma'am; it's a little reminder of Corunna."

"You were a soldier?"

"Yes ma'am; invalided out. They said I'd never walk without crutches again," there was pride in his voice that he had proved them wrong. "About your husband…."

"Who killed him? Why? How did it happen?" the questions came tumbling out.

"Ah. That's why I've been sent to talk to you, ma'am; to see if you knew any enemies he had," he said.

Jane stared.

"My husband was a charming man; I believe everyone he knew liked him very well," she said.

"One of them didn't," said the runner, dryly.

She flushed.

"No. Apparently not," she stared at her hands, clasped in her lap. "I suppose if you see violent death regularly you learn to treat it with a degree of levity."

He flushed.

"I beg your pardon Mrs. Churchill," he said.

She nodded.

"I understand that it makes your task easier to look upon it lightly. I have not taken offence; some might."

"Begging your pardon ma'am, few would have picked up the slight levity of my reply."

She considered.

"Perhaps you are correct; my reading of nuances of tone has always been acute….. in most cases. I can think of no enemies my husband has made; I know that one of his father's friends does not like him; but that had a degree of reason now defunct."

"Perhaps you will tell me about it Mrs. Churchill?"

She gave a slight shrug.

"My husband was raised by his aunt and uncle since his father was widowed when Frank – Mr. Churchill – was a baby. He took their name. His aunt was opposed to him marrying; we held to a secret engagement. To cover our intimacy he flirted with a girl living in the same village as his father, and where I had grown up for some of my life. The man who disliked him is now married to that girl; a

2

straightforward story."

"I see. That seems hardly relevant; but thank you for your candid explanation," he said.

"Are you in charge of finding out who killed him? What is your name? And should I not ask to see your occurrence book?" asked Jane.

"I am; my name is Caleb Armitage; and you are indeed a peevy mort – I mean an astute lady – to ask," said Mr. Armitage, removing a notebook from his pocket and showing her his name on it.

She nodded. The words 'Occurrence Book' were printed on; possible for someone to duplicate but hardly worth bothering. His name was filled in with block capitals and a signature beneath them. The brief description 'height: six feet three inches; hair: light brown; eyes: blue; complexion: fair' described him well enough. There were no comments under 'any other remarks'; presumably his leg was not noticeable enough unless he was tired. It would be a lot of trouble to go to for anyone to match so tall a young man with a stolen occurrence book; and what would be the point? It was wrong to be suspicious; though Mr. Armitage seemed to approve as she checked the details with care.

"Anyone after all might say they were from Bow Street; and anyone might then ask for access to the house when they could pilfer in the guise of searching," said Armitage as he retrieved his small notebook from her "As well to always check. Did you want me to sign my name to compare signatures?"

","That won't be necessary," said Jane "I think it would be hard for anyone to forge your inches."

"I am a distinctive height," he admitted. "I expect you have questions for me too?"

"Where was my husband found and how had he been killed?" she asked.

"In the Serpentine miss – uh, Mrs. Churchill; and at first it was thought suicide, as so many drownings there are; excepting he was not drowned; and very few suicides hit themselves on the back of the neck first."

"How do you know he was not drowned? Might he not have been assaulted for his purse and fell into the Serpentine where insensibility caused him to drown?" asked Jane. "There are so many desperate lawless people with these dreadful Corn Laws forcing the price of bread up; why one cannot get a quartern loaf for less than two and sixpence.... I am sorry, I did not mean to babble. But is it possible?"

Caleb Armitage scratched the back of his neck.

"Well I don't say that he might not have finished up the job of dying with a spot of drowning after the blow, Ma'am, but the surgeon as looked at the body said that such a blow would have finished him off in any case. Excuse me ma'am, I ain't never broke news to nobody before and I don't mean to use words as cause offence."

She gave him a thin smile.

"I am not offended; you have to tell me as it is. Frank is – was – tall; so that means a tall strong man must have been his assailant. Do you not think that robbery is a motive then that you ask about enemies?"

A man as tall and strong as this runner.

"As his purse was still on him and a roll of rather damp soft in it I believe that precludes the motive," said Armitage dryly "For no thief would hesitate, even if he fell in accidentally, to fish about for a purse. Besides he did not fall accidentally; the drag marks tell that he was pulled unconscious or dead to the side of the lake and pitched in."

"How extremely curious," said Jane, frowning. "Mr. Armitage, I can only suggest that I shall have to go through my husband's papers and see if there is any clue in them."

"I could go through them for you, ma'am," said Armitage.

A curious look crossed her face; it looked like shame. Colour rose to her pale face.

"I would prefer that you did not," she said. "I believe there may be .....personal correspondence .....in his papers that it would be unseemly for anyone else to read."

"Ma'am, I have to say this," said Armitage. "If you believe he was keeping a light o' love, and she was seeing anybody else, that is a possible reason for a quarrel."

Jane stiffened.

"I see," she said quietly. "Then if I furnish you with the name of any such, will that do? I do not wish to be humiliated by having a stranger read any intimate letters my husband may have received."

"That will do very nicely ma'am," said Armitage, relieved. She had taken it very well. Too well? Might *she* have hired someone? Yet the quiet dignity of the woman impressed him; he did not want to believe that. "Might I call again tomorrow morning? Will that give you time to examine his papers?"

"Indeed yes; at ten. That will give me ample time. I should like something to keep me occupied," said Jane.

When Armitage had left she stared at her hands. What did she feel? Primarily a numbness; and that relief. She and Frank had not been married long before the little attentions started to be eroded; before the year was out he was ordering her about, often shouting at her for being clumsy, not as svelte as she had been before the weight of pregnancy robbed her of her lithe step and worked upon her indifferent health. He had been jealous too as soon as the baby was born; little Frances. And angry that Jane had been sorely pulled by the birth.

She had worked hard to get her figure back though it had tired her, to try to regain his regard; but when she found the letter from the Female that Frank was maintaining, and discovered by a reference in the letter that he had been seeing her at least since they had been married but three months she had stopped bothering; and took a perverse pleasure in answering Frank in as few words as possible in the colourless tone she had used to others to cover their secret engagement.

He had suspected an *affaire* and had beaten her; which in light of his own infidelity Jane considered unfair in the extreme.

But one was not supposed to be glad that one's husband was dead.

It must indeed have been someone big and strong to fell

him. There could not be many tall enough to make such a blow; did one suspect the one who broke the news? Somehow Jane could not see the straight-looking Mr. Armitage as an assassin with a false blow from behind; there was that to him that recalled to her Mr. George Knightley, the man who had married Emma, with whom Frank had flirted. Mr. Knightley could never do anything underhanded like hit a man from behind; and somehow instinct said nor could the runner. There were plenty of tall men in London who had been in the army until it was disbanded.

She must therefore do all she might to help this Caleb Armitage to uncover who had killed Frank, and why, in order to assuage the guilt she felt for being grateful that someone had freed her from a petty and unkind husband whose charming façade was as false as some of the handsome Georgian façades on sixteenth century buildings.

And the sooner she got down to work the sooner the shame and humiliation of reading any letters would be over.

Chapter 2

Jane regarded the five documents she considered most significant; her thin hands shook slightly as she straightened the creases nervously, arranging them on the table. Mr. Armitage really needed to see these; and he would need to see Frank's account book written in his own hand. None of the documents was very pleasant to contemplate and together they told a sordid story that did not reflect well on Frank at all

The whole business was revolting and humiliating. However better to have found these things for herself than have some stranger do so. Jane sighed and looked them over again to see what inferences she could draw; and what things still remained unfathomable.

The first letter was from Mr. Churchill, Frank's uncle and was written some four months into their marriage. It read,

"My very dear Frank,

It is with sadness that I read your request to have more of your capital forwarded to you; I am sorry indeed that you find yourself unable to manage on a very generous income as well as the wages you receive as clerk at Chorleigh, Wright and Jekyll's where Mr Wright has been so kind as to find you a position. It surprises me that dear Jane should be such a poor manager as to fail to manage a household on what must be around twenty pounds a week; a sum on which many families manage yearly. It appears to me that if you are exceeding your income perhaps you should do better to practise economy; surely you do not need more than three servants, a maid, a man for yourself and a cook-housekeeper? And I concede a nursery maid in the future when you begin a family.

Yet I know that you keep in addition another maid and a groom and a footman. It is quite impossible for me to break the entail on Enscombe; the allowance of one thousand pounds a year that I pay you and your wage should be more than sufficient.

There is moreover the legacy of your Aunt; you surely did not spend it all in purchasing a house? Had you been

satisfied with a less fashionable part of London than Kensington, or had rented rather than buying it would have been far more economical. I fear you show signs of being as financially unsteady as your father and your poor mama, my sister, who lived above their means. It is for your own good, my dear Frank, that I must refuse your outrageous request for such a sum as two thousand guineas.

I remain your most affectionate uncle, Jasper Churchill."

Jane sighed. She loved their tall narrow white terrace house on the south side of Pembridge Square; though she had questioned Frank's wisdom in purchasing such a place. It was on the less expensive side of the Square for facing north, but with the extensive servants' quarters in the half-basement, four floors above that and the attic level for the maidservants to sleep in, it was a big house. And they employed a footman, Fowler, a housekeeper, Mrs. Ketch, her own abigail Ella, Frank's man Emerson, a maid called Juliet, Annie the young nursemaid to little Frances and Annie's young sister Molly, the tweenstairs maid. In addition there was Palmer the groom who saw to Frank's horse. It was too much; and really Ella and Emerson had been quite unnecessary as they were not society people needing to dress in a hurry and requiring aid. But Frank had his own ideas of what was due to what he saw as his own consequence. Sometimes Jane had wondered if half the reason he had encouraged her to play the part of being disinterested while they were engaged was because he found playacting more exciting than reality, and perhaps even had difficulty distinguishing between the two.

Jane had already written that morning to Mr. Jasper Churchill, who had returned long since to his estates of Enscombe in Yorkshire, apprising him of the death of his nephew; and to Mr. John Weston in Highbury who would be devastated at the death of his son.

She needed to see Mr. Chorleigh who was the family solicitor to find out what her own financial situation might be; and perhaps Mr. Armitage might accompany her as doubtless he would also wish to question Frank's nominal employer. Frank went most days to the office but Jane strongly suspected that he did very little work.

Mr. Churchill had desired Frank to take a position in some respectable business since he married and had found this position as clerk at some seventy pounds a year; a good wage for a clerk just starting out, though Frank was older than most clerks at the bottom of the profession. Frank turned this wage over to Jane and a further allowance of ten pounds weekly on which she must pay for the servants' wages and have food purchased by Mrs. Ketch the cook-housekeeper. It was a struggle. Twelve pounds seven and sixpence did not run to lavish dinners; for which Frank blamed her too. She had suggested timidly turning off Ella, her abigail; and Frank had shouted at her, asking if she wanted people to think that they could not afford an abigail to give his wife respectability. When Jane equally timidly suggested that actually they could not, he had struck her and told her to find better ways to economise without compromising their standard of living. It should be easy to live on his allowance and this extra seventy pounds; the servants' wages were a little more than his clerkly wages, coming to eighty seven pounds a year; but why did he only give her half of his allowance? True he paid for his horse out of that; some sixty pounds a year; and he must have money for diversions; but more than four hundred pounds? Jane had thought that his – what had Mr. Armitage called the woman – light o' love, must be very expensive. She had not then found the worst of it which now lay before her with the proof that he had tried to raise money with begging letters to all his relatives.

The next letter was from Frank's father; and was dated a few days later than the one from his uncle.

It was terse as one might expect from a man who had been a captain of the militia.

"Frank; what is this nonsense? Where am I to raise a sum such as you ask? You have a generous allowance from your uncle; this request is preposterous. If you and Jane have been living above your means, I suggest you sell the house in London and come and live with us at Randalls for a time to recoup your finances. Your loving father, John Weston.

PS Anna blows a kiss to her big brother and your loving stepmamma sends you and Jane all her affection."

Jane sighed. She was very fond of Mr. and Mrs. Weston; it hurt to think that they might believe that she would be a party to living beyond their means; as they would not be if she had only been given all the housekeeping she needed from Frank's income. However it was like the generosity of the Westons to suggest that Frank and Jane should rusticate at Randalls for a while to recoup their fortunes; and a sensible suggestion to sell the house and do so, or at least rent it out. Had she known of this letter she would have urged Frank to take this sensible course; because renting out meant that the investment of the property remained intact.

Unfortunately it was Frank who had been living beyond his means and was not apprising her of this fact; and she had found out where such money as did not go on the mistress had been spent. She laid out the next document.

It was not strictly a letter that Jane laid down; but a scrap of paper containing her husband's vowels to that preposterous sum of two thousand guineas, with the word 'redeemed' and some initials scrawled over them.

She had thought that his expenditure had been excessive, even taking a mistress into account; it seemed that the worst of the expenditure was in the form of gambling debts; but there were other things that were also worrying – and puzzling.

Frank had given her fifty pounds in paper money to help defray the cost of household expenses not long after these letters; and where had that come from?

Up until then he had become enraged any time she mentioned a need for money; that he was worrying about his debts might have explained why he had been short with her at first; but evidently that he found consolation with a mistress explained far better his subsequent distance; even if paying for the same would scarcely help his money worries.

But how had he found the fifty pounds – and how had he paid off those vowels?

The next letter was written in the same illiterate hand as

the letter she had found that had killed any love she had left for Frank, the one she had discovered in the worn money purse she had taken to mend, just after little Frances had been born.

This one however was dated earlier, a few weeks after the ones from his uncle and father, around the time Frank had managed to provide that extra fifty pounds housekeeping. Jane read it through with some distaste.

"Frankie me darling I do love me little nook wot you have found for me! It is our own speshul nest to bill and coo in, and play pritty games. I am waring only me stockings and shemees while I rite you this dear Frankie; your little bird, Dolly"

Jane shuddered and after translating 'shemees' into 'chemise' moved, on to the final and fifth document. This letter was even more worrying; it had been thrust into the escritoire and was dated only a few days earlier, ironically on St Valentine's day. The previous Valentine's Day had brought with it a sentimental missive for her; and a heart cut from paper in the most delicate filigree that must have taken Frank long hours to do. Unless, thought Jane cynically, he had paid some poor silhouette-cutter a pittance for it. This year she had received nothing but a complaint that the toast was burned. Frank had, however, seen fit to send a gift to his mistress.

"Frankie me deer darling! You are the best man ever! Your little bird just __LOVES__ her Valentine's diymond necklass! I am waring it __RITE NOW__ Frankie, and it is so loverly that it is all I need to ware!"

Jane groaned as she read this one again with its heavily underscored emphatics. The sort of woman who would write that had to be totally cheap. And for such a woman Frank would buy a diamond necklace?

He did not buy his wife diamond necklaces. More to the point he did not provide his wife with enough housekeeping. Unless this were paste with which to satisfy a greedy mistress. But even a paste necklace that looked convincing would not come cheap; where was he getting the money?

11

She was horribly afraid that her husband might be so totally sunk below reproach as to be spending his evenings persuading the gullible into cheating games, for she could think of no other way he might be gaining enough money!

The knock on the door must be Mr. Armitage; and soon Fowler would show him in. She must remain like ice and betray no emotion about this iniquitous business.

Chapter 3

Caleb Armitage was grateful to be asked to sit; not so much that his leg pained him today but that he felt large and clumsy in Mrs. Churchill's dainty room. It was a room that suited the occupant; Mrs. Churchill was a slight, neat figure, graceful more than dainty, thought Mr. Armitage, the dark eyebrows and eyelashes more of a contrast in her pale face, framing steady grey eyes. She had put on a gown as close as she might have to mourning at short notice, a half dress of calico in dove grey print of scrolling leaves on white. Mr. Armitage thought her very composed and ladylike; perhaps cold and unfeeling, perhaps very good at concealing her feelings. Gentry-morts, ladies of the upper classes, were taught that it was ill-bred to display emotion after all.

The room must reveal something about Mrs. Churchill to give some idea about her.

It was tidy; but that might be blamed on the maids. The chairs were fashionable but comfortable; the décor was all in the combination of silver grey, mazarine blue and cream, a cool-looking combination that suited Mrs. Churchill very well. Dark blue velvet curtains were caught back from the window with a silver cord, the carpet was blue and cream, and the Florentine silk upholstery was in stripes of all three colours, the walls draped with a paper printed in ivory with darker cream and silver grey foliage forming the overall striped design. The colours were not those that Mr. Armitage would ever have thought of as going together at all but they were surprisingly lovely together. Restful. Yes, that was it. He wondered whether Mrs. Churchill was a naturally restful woman. Somehow the unusual combination made him suspect that cool as the look might be, she was not as cold as he had wondered; it did not go with an original eye and imagination. He wondered if it were she who played the beautiful pianoforte or if it had been her husband; a proper grand it was too, none of your cheaper uprights!

He read the letters she showed him, the vowels and the rather sketchy and mysterious pocket book with odd sums entered in it. He grunted once or twice, shuffling them around on the dainty table to look at one then another.

"As I see it," said Jane, "my husband tried to move with a faster set than he had means to accomplish; became heavily in debt in what I presume were gambling hells; and the IOU was a pressing need to be paid off, in order that he not be required to flee the country after the same fashion as the likes of Beau Brummel last year. He appears to have acquired sufficient wealth to not only cover that debt but also to keep a mistress in her own rooms, and subsequently to provide her with what she at least *believes* to be a diamond necklace. He provided me also with housekeeping money above the usual amount, which enabled me to pay off some of our most pressing creditors; one hates to be in debt to the tradesmen."

"Lor' love you, Mrs. Churchill, the swell coves – the nobility and the like – are always in debt to their tradesmen," said Mr. Armitage.

Jane frowned.

"Well I consider it immoral," she said.

"Yes ma'am; but when did anyone say that the gentry – the 'ote tone they call themselves – were moral?" said Mr. Armitage cynically.

Jane was faintly shocked. She had always been brought up to respect the haut ton – if that was what he had been trying to say – and this view of them was a little disconcerting.

"Does my summation cover what you are reading here?" she asked.

He nodded.

"If I may ask, what did he give you for housekeeping; and what was your understanding of his income?" he asked "I know it is an impudent question, Mrs. Churchill, but a discrepancy is always a clue; look into anyone's life, especially once they've left it as you might say, and any discrepancy can point to exactly why they left it."

Jane nodded.

"I can see that," she said. "I have nothing to hide; let me fetch my own housekeeping books," she exited through a door at the end of the room, set in an alcove, her step brisk and decisive whilst remaining graceful and feminine.

She returned swiftly; and Caleb Armitage perused the neat, fastidious hand and its careful entries.

"You keep good clear accounts, ma'am," he said in approval. "Presumably Mr. Churchill kept back a considerable sum with which to gamble; and turned out to be bamboozled by some peep-o-day boys so he outran the constable and turned out to be a real Johnny Raw. And then there's suddenly the dibs flowing; a honey fall as you might say. Reckon I might have to find out if I can who held these vowels; PDV the initials say. Well, I can't say I'm familiar with the initials from the Hells I know; but then, you have to realise, Ma'am, that the vowels of one man might be staked by another; or even sold."

"Oh dear!" said Jane. "Would – would knowing who he had lost money to help solve his murder?"

"That? Well maybe not, Ma'am," said Armitage "But knowing who he paid off; ah, now that *might* put us onto the right track. See, whilst I hesitate to tell a beautiful woman that her husband sounds a dashed shady character, up to something havy-cavy, I cannot help thinking that there's more ways to redeem vowels than cash."

"I fail to comprehend your meaning," said Jane.

Armitage sighed.

"Mrs. Churchill, if you weren't taking this so calm, I'd never be even telling you a tenth of this; but you've been good enough to be open and to search for things to help me. And I'm bound to say I see little affection for your husband in you even allowing for a swell mort – I mean, a class lady – like you to hide emotion from a fellow like me."

Jane sighed.

"Let us say that the honeymoon was swiftly over and many scales fell from my eyes," she said.

"Ah, that's what I thought," nodded Armitage. "And forgive me, but yesterday the thought crossed my mind that you might have paid to have him killed. But then I thought, Caleb, my boy, any professional wot did that would take his purse. And that was professional enough. And what's more,

15

he'd been bound, surgeon says; after he'd been on the slab, there was marks on his wrists, and marks under his nails like someone had shoved a needle up them. Oh Lord!" as Jane swayed in her chair. Caleb Armitage leaped up and pulled the bell pull hard, hearing the jangle somewhere below.

The door opened and Fowler came in.

"'Ere, Ferret, wotever yore name is," the East End emerged briefly more strongly in Mr. Armitage's alarmed voice "Go get the lady's maid and smellin' salts or somfink!"

Fowler raised an eyebrow and crossed to Jane.

"Mrs. Churchill, would you like Ella?" he asked.

"No thank you Fowler," said Jane "If you will pass my reticule, my vinaigrette is in it."

Fowler did as he was bid, fetching the ridiculous confection of silver net on the soft feet of a well trained servant. He gave the impression of despising Caleb as much as Caleb despised him for being, in his own vernacular, a man-milliner. Jane took the little filigree silver box from her reticule to inhale the pungent scent from within it.

Fowler withdrew again at a sign from Jane, now a better colour. She spoke, her voice hardly shaking,

"My husband was tortured; and you spoke of more than one way to redeem a debt. Both of those things puzzle me. I have been fearing that he has been luring the unwary into gaming hells for the consideration of having his own debts written off. But why that might lead to torture I cannot see."

Caleb Armitage nodded. She was not afraid to face the unpalatable this lady; and she had a long head on her.

"As any decent lady might be puzzled," he said. "And there's more ways to recoup that debt than being a trapan, that's someone as leads the gullible to be gulled; though it's something to keep in mind. If someone from a less than salubrious background as we might say had obtained your husband's vowels, a favour might have caused them to be signed off; working in a solicitor's office, the favour perhaps of an advance look at a brief to a barrister; or a will; or the removal of a copy of a will leaving a previous one extant; or any one of a number of such activities. And whilst a man might be upright enough to refuse in normal circumstances, a man facing social and financial ruin might find himself tempted as would be outside of his normal code."

"You are tactful, Mr. Armitage," said Jane, dryly "Though I should say from the experience of my marriage that my husband's code might prove remarkably elastic if his own image and comfort were in any wise at stake. I find your suggestions shocking but not, I have to say, wholly surprising. And in some ways not as bad as persuading poor gullible fools into debt to what I believe might be called Captain Sharps."

Caleb Armitage gave a sigh of relief. Suggesting to this bang-up swell mort that her husband might be involved in such fraud had always been the sticking point. And she had the imagination and the realism to accept that he might be even worse.

"I shall have to ask at the place he worked if anything has been moved or gone missing," he said apologetically.

"Oh quite," said Jane "Perhaps you would escort me to the place so that I might ascertain my legal position with regard to my husband's allowance from his uncle; as I have a daughter of the marriage to maintain and can therefore scarcely easily undertake work as a governess should I be entirely destitute."

"I cannot think that any reasonable uncle would cut off the allowance that feeds his great niece!" said Caleb Armitage.

Jane gave him a tight smile.

"I expect that will depend how much Frank has disgraced his name and whether his uncle will decide to cut off root and branch of an unsatisfactory heir," she said. "Frances can at least probably be reared in the nursery of Frank's father, dear Mr. Weston, and his wife; for Frances is a year and a half younger than her half-aunt. And I believe that dear Mrs. Weston will present her husband with another *petit paquet* before long too. But it would be nice not to have to be a slave to other people's children in which situation I will not be able to watch my own daughter grow up," she added wistfully.

"Well, Mrs. Churchill, perhaps it won't be so bad as that,"

said Caleb. No, this woman would not have her husband killed; too much was at stake, and though she might risk it for herself, he had never known a devoted mother who would risk her child – and he could read the devotion for this child Frances in Mrs. Churchill's eyes. It was a relief; because the torture had been nasty. He cleared his throat. "A professional murderer – such as a lady might hire to get rid of an inconvenient husband – might be told to beat him well; but this looks like something deliberate to ask questions. And I may say your husband was not badly hurt so one may presume he talked."

Jane nodded.

"He would," she said "Frank does – did not like discomfort. It is hard to imagine him dead, even now; I apologise for the wrong tense."

"Ah, and something else I've noticed," said Caleb, feeling even more relief "Someone what has done away with a party readily mentions them in the past tense; because they already started to think of them dead before even they are, and certainly by the time the news is broke."

"Fascinating," said Jane "You have read a lot from me and I have always considered myself hard to read; there is much skill in your profession concerning the reading of people."

"Well some does it more than others, ma'am," said Caleb flushing slightly. "But if you agree that your husband would rapidly cave in then whoever killed him knows whatever it is they wants to know."

Jane paled.

"Might he have hidden a will or documents of some kind *here*?" she said "The doors are locked at night but one hears terrible stories…."

"Well, Ma'am, the thought that you might be in some danger had crossed my mind," said Caleb "And if you will permit me to help you search I would be grateful; and perhaps you might find me a corner to sleep in the servants' quarters for a night or two; I'm handy with my fambles – hands that is – when it comes to a mill. A fight," he translated. "And I do have barking-irons – pistols."

"That would be a relief to my mind," said Jane "But I hardly think that sleeping with the male servants in the basement will answer; anyone who breaks in would head for the family quarters to search or – or to find out if I knew anything. And – and if they threatened Frances….. you must sleep in a guest room to be near at hand."

"It ain't proper ma'am," protested Caleb.

"You are staying in a professional capacity," said Jane, decisively, ringing the bell.

Fowler arrived in his usual silent fashion.

"Fowler, Mr. Armitage believes that the felons who did away with your master may be looking to steal something; work he may have brought home from the office," she temporised crisply. "You are to see that the bed in the blue room is made up and warmed for Mr. Armitage who will be staying over to protect Miss Frances and me from possible attack."

"There ain't no need to make up a bed," said Caleb hastily "I shan't be sleeping deep like; I'll take off me boots and lie down on the coverlet."

"If it is to be for more than one night, Mr. Armitage, you should sleep properly for at least a portion of the night or you will be too tired to do your duty," said Jane. "I would suggest that you retire early and Fowler will awaken you after he has locked up for the night. Then when the servants rise, you might sleep properly again for another hour or two."

"That would answer admirably, ma'am," said Caleb with some admiration "They won't come into a wakeful household, nowise. Whoever *they* might be," he murmured to himself by way of a parenthetic addition.

Chapter 4

Caleb procured a hackney carriage to carry himself, Mrs. Churchill and her abigail to the solicitor's premises; and by the afternoon that same abigail had finished making up a mourning gown for her mistress by rapid and clever conversion of a white muslin; new sleeves and bodice of black crepe had been cut and applied and three black crepe flounces had been added to the skirt, the lowermost mimicking the three inch hem that was customary on mourning costume.

"Are you sure it is all right Ella, to have the black on the white?" asked Jane anxiously "White is acceptable until full mourning is to be had... and my silk gown has gone to be dyed.... You have done a remarkably economic job with that old crepe cape, Ella, if you think it looks well enough...,"

"You look a treat Mrs. Jane, and as proper as could be asked with such an unexpected event," said Ella firmly "When your silk comes back from the dyer we shall send this so it is black all over; don't you fret, Mrs. Jane my dearie."

Jane sighed.

Black was *not* a colour that flattered her; though her complexion was not so pale as to be made to look washed out, the unrelieved black of her bodice did make her look paler even so. Slightly worried grey eyes looked too large in her oval face; and she sighed again. It was quite improper to be considering her appearance when she was but newly become a widow.

Well if she looked young and tragic and sufficiently attractive perhaps Mr. Chorleigh would be moved to help her by interceding with Uncle Jasper. She tripped downstairs to meet with Mr. Armitage and the Hackney cab. She was glad of the quilted petticoat she had had the forethought to put on; muslin was not a practical fabric for February, though enough young girls desirous of being fashionable braved the cold to wear it even in midwinter.

They were crossing the metropolis from Jane's home in the newer north west residential portion of London to Gray's

Inn Road, where the solicitor's firm had its office, close to the bustling centre of legal activity, the Inns of Court, so that that a barrister might readily be briefed on behalf of a client. Chorleigh, Wright and Jekyll's was not the sort of partnership that would readily encourage litigation in their clients; this was far too public and vulgar a thing for any of their clients to be involved in. However in the case of a juicy piece of tort on the part of a third party, or a suit contesting a will drawn up by some other solicitor was a situation in which Chorleigh and Partners might condescend to go to the bar. Their office was in a tall building that somehow managed to be both facelessly modern and seedy looking, exuding an air of respectable, but uninviting shabby-gentility.

"Your husband.... Ah yes, the nephew of Mr. Jasper Churchill.... He applied to me almost a year ago to see if it might be possible to break an entail if his uncle agreed.... Quite impossible I fear.... Living beyond his means I suppose; well so far as the legal situation is concerned Mrs. Churchill in the event of his death the entail passes directly to any offspring you have and will be broken on the event of the death of Mr. Jasper Churchill; have you offspring?" Mr. Chorleigh was not what one might describe as fat; but he was carrying some *embonpoint* which he swelled towards Jane after the fashion of a pouter pigeon displaying and doubtless with similar motive. His pigeon grey waistcoat did nothing to dispel this impression.

"We have a daughter," said Jane "As to any others it is too early to say. Though I believe it unlikely," she added. "Does that mean that the portion of the income that Mr. Jasper Churchill has been paying to my late husband will continue to cover the needs of our daughter?"

"That I shall have to communicate with Mr. Churchill over; but I cannot see that there would be a problem," said Mr. Chorleigh. "If you have been used, however, to high living you may find that you will need to make small economies....."

"Oh I do not believe that I shall be requiring as many

21

servants as Frank thought necessary," said Jane, "and I have not myself enjoyed any high living so I do not believe there will be any difficulties. However, there may be a few complications regarding my husband's death; perhaps Mr. Armitage here will explain."

Mr. Chorleigh had been glancing rather doubtfully at Jane's companion; he wore respectable enough clothes with a reasonably good quality wool coat and good quality buckskins and boots that had a military look. He might pass as an affluent tradesman or even a clerk; and what role he fulfilled Mr. Chorleigh could not guess.

"It appears," said Caleb, proceeding to stretch the truth for the lovely and dignified lady, "That Mr. Churchill may have been placed under duress; threats to harm his lovely wife and daughter; and this lead to his untimely death. I'm from Bow Street; an Officer of the Law. And in case he was told to remove wills or other documents from your office it is my dooty to ask you to discreetly check if any such documents 'ave been moved, misplaced or dahnright gone missink," his accent emerged again under the outraged stare of the solicitor.

Mr. Chorleigh looked mystified as well as outraged.

"But how would Mr. Churchill have any access to documents in this office? Only the other partners and clerks could see and touch them."

"But he worked here!" said Jane "His uncle insisted; he spoke to Mr. Wright about it!"

Mr. Chorleigh blinked, plainly taken aback.

"He worked here? Mr. Wright you say knew?" he rang a bell; and a young man no older than twenty rapidly appeared. He was affecting a dandy look so far as he might in the dark, unremarkable clothes of a clerk; but his collar points were so high he could scarcely turn his head and his waistcoat was a far from sober lavender embroidered in silver and purple. A spasm of disapproval passed over Mr. Chorleigh's face as he surveyed this sartorial mutiny.

"StClair,"said Mr. Chorleigh "Ask Mr. Wright to step in here please."

"Certainly Uncle William," said the youth. Mr. Chorleigh

swelled in a rather purple fashion.

"*How* often do I have to tell you not to call me Uncle William at work?" he demanded.

"Sorry Mr. Chorleigh sir," said the youth, not sounding sorry in the least. He bobbed out of the room.

Shortly ponderous steps were heard; and a jovial looking man who was inclined to the adipose stepped into the room. He made Mr. Chorleigh appear relatively svelt by comparison and his claret coloured velveret waistcoat might be seen to strain on the buttons.

"How may I be of assistance?" he beamed all round.

"Mr. Wright, did you engage the *young* Mr. Churchill to work as a clerk?" demanded Mr. Chorleigh.

"Indeed I did, indeed I did," cried Mr. Wright "His uncle felt it would have a steadying influence on him; and at first I believed it would not work for he was idle! Idle indeed! But of late he has been staying late and working keenly upon the projects that have interested him; a change, you see, a change!"

Chorleigh paled.

"Mr. Armitage will explain," he said giving both Caleb and Jane a poisonous look.

Caleb repeated his explanation; and Mr. Wright's face lost all jollity and took on an ugly look. His belly seemed to swell even more with anger and Jane wondered whether any of the buttons would pop off his waistcoat.

"If he has cheated this firm, I say we should have our dues from his uncle!" he growled "Made a mockery of me he has, a mockery!"

"Not, sir, necessarily," said Caleb imperturbably. Jane thought him rather brave to speak so calmly to two such angry men; she was only keeping herself composed by making bets with herself over which button would fail first if any did. "There is a possibility that Mr. Churchill was threatened into performing some indiscretion; it is no certainty. But for your own peace of mind and the potential solving of this poor young man's murder then you should check all the documents that you may be expected to have."

"*Murder*!" cried Mr. Chorleigh.

"*Murder*!" echoed Mr. Wright.

"He did explain," said Jane with some asperity.

"My dear Mrs. Churchill; I beg your pardon, Mr. Armitage and you also spoke of sudden demise," said Mr. Chorleigh "And I immediately assumed that if he was in debt that young Mr. Churchill had committed suicide. That puts a whole different complexion on it; a most distressing affair!"

"Quite so," said Mr. Wright resuming a more natural size and colour, to Jane's relief. "A man under threat by such ruffians as will kill has more excuse than one who has taken the coward's way out to escape from shame."

"Excellent; you will not mind then that I must question all the other clerks," said Mr. Armitage.

They minded; but there was very little that they might do about it.

There were four other clerks who worked in the office including the one who had summoned Mr. Wright. Jane perforce sat in the poky office where they did their copying of writs and other such menial duties while Caleb Armitage spoke with them. He introduced her politely.

The slight, dark, man in his middle twenties, with guileless blue eyes and the air of a schoolboy, gaped in amazement.

"But that cannot be Mrs. Churchill!" he cried "Why, I have seen Frank out with his wife; a blonde with rather…. well she filled her bodice rather well," he added blushing, "and Frank even introduced me to her as Dolly!"

Jane went pale.

"I should have thought," she said, "That if you had any pretensions to being a gentleman you might be able to tell the difference between a man's *wife* and his – his infidelities."

"Now *that's* a good name for a ladybird *if* you like," said Mr. Armitage approvingly. "Try not to act like you was born yesterday, Mr. …?"

The young man flushed.

"My name is Perrin; Kit Perrin. And – why, Frank was married barely more than a year ago; what else was I to think?

I know he is – was – spendthrift and frivolous but not that he was a deuced *libertine*! Why I have been married almost four years; we have three children, and I should *never* step outside marriage!"

Armitage hid a grin; this youth was too innocent to live!

He also stifled a comment that if there were three offspring in four years of marriage the young couple appeared to occupy themselves too fully in the bedroom for him to have time to seek elsewhere; it might offend Mrs. Churchill.

She caught his eye; and he suddenly realised that exactly the same thought had crossed her mind; and he felt a degree of heat touch his cheekbones as he gave her a sheepish grin.

Her smile was small and swift and rapidly directed towards her neat black gloves as she looked down.

"I too had not realised that Frank was so ill behaved," said an older man, who was going thin on top; it was a description that might also have been levelled at his coat which was shiny at the elbows. "Richard Pennythrift is my name; I had spoken to him about his fecklessness but he just laughed. Those of us who do not have a wealthy uncle andwho must provide for seven surviving offspring cannot afford so cavalier an attitude. But he was good company," he added. Caleb noted him down as one who might have liked to have been a bit more of a bang-up cove himself given the monetary advantages Mr. Frank Churchill had enjoyed.

A freckle faced young man laughed wryly. Like the young clerk who was Mr. Chorleigh's nephew he had pretensions to dandyism, but confined his efforts to high shirt points and a neck cloth that may have been meant to have been tied in the style of the Mathematical and was, to Mr. Armitage's way of thinking, unlikely to graduate.

"And I am glad that I have not yet been leg shackled in the parson's mousetrap," the young man said "Edward Jarvey. I'm going to mourn Frank; he was good company. Of course," he added looking boldly at Jane, "if there is anything I can do for Frank's widow, she might even convert me to considering matrimony as good for the soul."

Jane gave him a fishy stare.

She could scarcely believe such a level of brazen contumely and ill taste!

"Thank you Mr. Jarvey; I believe when this unfortunate incident has been resolved the best thing that may be done for me is that I never have anything more to do with this office and its denizens than I have to," said Jane.

"Mrs. Churchill!" cried the youngest – the youth who had been addressed as StClair "You surely do not suspect any of *us* of killing him do you? I say what a lark!"

"Be silent, Mr. Despard," said Richard Pennythrift uncomfortably.

"Mr. Despard, can you think that anyone in this office is likely to *want* to kill Mr. Churchill?" asked Caleb intently.

Mr. Despard grinned.

"Tempting as it is to picture Uncle William or Mr. Wright tiptoeing ponderously around with a knife in their hand, somehow it's too ripe a picture to swallow," he said cheerfully. "However much Mr. Wright used to complain about Mr. Churchill's lack of industry. Maybe Mr. Jekyll? He has, as the Bard puts it, 'that lean and hungry look'."

"That's because he suffers from dyspepsia," said Edward Jarvey, not crushed for long by Jane's set down "And because he believes the worst of everyone. Maybe he has dyspepsia *because* he believes the worst of everyone."

"Oh let us place the case for the prosecution in the clerks' room then," said StClair Despard

"Shut your stupid mouth," said Kit Perrin uncomfortably "Just because you have taken your law exams, and hope to join a firm of solicitors, does not give you the right to play-act as a barrister."

"The case against Mr. Perrin," intoned StClair Despard sepulchrally as though he had not heard "Disliked Frank Churchill; thought him frivolous. Disapproved of the woman he was innocent enough to think was the real Mrs. Churchill … No actually Kit, you couldn't kill anybody; you wouldn't even think about it."

"No of course not!" said Mr. Perrin. Angry colour burned on his cheeks.

"Case against Edward Jarvey," said Mr. Despard "Got on well with Frank; went drinking and to watch the gees with him; unless you owed him money no case to answer. Case against Mr. Pennythrift!"

"*Must* you make yourself look more like a chawbacon than you are?" asked Mr. Pennythrift.

"Well the officer of the law isn't stopping me; so he's enjoying it," said Mr. Despard shrewdly.

"I shouldn't say enjoying was the right word lad, but it is revealing," said Caleb. Mr. Despard smirked.

"Have I or have I not a great future ahead of me as a clever interrogator of clients?" he said. "Mr. Pennythrift! You liked Frank but disapproved of him! You killed him to save his wife from starvation when he spent all his money!"

"You are a fool StClair," said Pennythrift. "You sound like my Horace; and he's twelve."

"Now *that* was a put-down of put-downs," said Mr. Despard. "But to conclude; the case against StClair Despard. Who knew that Frank Churchill was up to something dashed havy-cavy but was not sure what sort of a may game he was playing staying late in the office, writing out documents."

"Writing out documents? Copying do you mean?" asked Caleb sharply.

"No your honour, honest as the day is long … Sorry sir," said Mr. Despard as Caleb frowned at him. "He brought in parchment of his own and sat at his desk preparing documents. Sometimes he referred to notes. Well, I saw him do this twice; when my uncle was working late and required me to run errands. And as Mr. Wright has been praising Frank's industry the last few months, saying that he has worked late on a number of occasions, I drew my own inferences as the law will have it."

"Ever nosy enough to read over his shoulder?" asked Caleb.

"He wouldn't let me get near enough," said Mr. Despard regretfully "But I *did* look at his blotting block in the mirror; and what I could read was 'with one hundred' which was no real help."

"You never know," said Caleb "You've a glib **tongue** on you my lad; and I'm surprised it's this side of the law you've chosen not the bar; but you know the value of evidence."

"That's why I've chosen this side of the law sir," said Mr. Despard "Because I know the value of evidence. Any idiot can stand up and speechify, and if parliament is anything to go by, most idiots do."

Chapter 5

Caleb sat himself gingerly down again on a dainty chair, at Jane's request, in her parlour; and Fowler, looking disapproving, laid down the tray with the tea caddy, teapot and tea-set. Jane took the key of the ornately inlaid tea caddy from her chatelaine in her reticule and looked at her footman thoughtfully.

"Fowler, this household is going to have to economise," said Jane crisply, "and I might be inclined to consider anyone with a Friday face as one of the first to go. I shall be consulting with Mrs. Ketch on the matter; I am sure she knows who are the most convivial of my servants below stairs," she added, unlocking the caddy to spoon the precious leaves into the teapot.

Fowler looked startled; a rare event for a man whose countenance had, as Caleb put it to himself, two expressions, stiff and stiffer. He managed to keep himself sufficiently contained to pass the hot water to Jane to pour into the teapot and to pass the bone china cups to Caleb and Jane. It was plain that he felt quite anguished that the precious brew was being given to a low type like a Bow Street Runner.

"I beg your pardon Mrs. Churchill; I did not intend to cause offence," he said in his cultivated voice.

"Then you will be pleased to be given a hint that you have come close," said Jane, expertly and gracefully lifting the pot once or twice to seethe the tea and pouring it into Caleb's teacup, a pretty thing of pale blue with darker blue scroll work on it and a gilt rim. Mr. Armitage had recovered enough stolen goods to recognise it as quality ware and hoped fervently not to further lower himself in Fowler's eyes by breaking the delicate cup. Jane went on "Mr. Armitage is doing his best to find out who has foully murdered the master. He is to be given due respect for that and without grudging. I have been hoping to retain your services, and those of Mrs. Ketch and either Ella or the maid of all work, Juliet."

"With due respect, Mrs. Churchill," said Fowler "Juliet is a brazen piece who would put on airs at helping you to dress as well as cleaning. It would not be a much greater outlay – since Juliet would expect her wages to be raised – to retain Ella and the 'tweenstairs maid. At twelve years old her wages are but five pounds a year in addition to her board and clothing; and she is a good willing girl of whom Mrs. Ketch has expressed the hopes of much promise. She also is the sister of the girl who cares for Miss Frances and helps her willingly."

"Thank you Fowler; I shall consider that option when I am speaking with Mrs. Ketch," said Jane. "I pray that you will explain kindly to both Emerson and Palmer that I shall have to dispense with their services and will write them good characters; with the explanation that their situation in my household has become superfluous not because of any problem with their service."

"Very good, Mrs. Churchill," Fowler bowed and withdrew on his noiseless feet.

"That fellow is first cousin to a cat I swear," said Caleb.

"He is however very efficient," said Jane, "and worthy of his hire if he will not indulge in a fit of the sulks over serving you while you stay. I will not have my orders questioned even tacitly; I may not be used to playing the great lady as Frank would have me do, but I know what is acceptable."

"He's quite right though, ma'am; I'm not really the sort of fellow a fine lady like yourself should be hobnobbing with," said Caleb "I got some respectability in the army, rose to sergeant; but I was born in a rookery; that's the worst slums in London, ma'am," he explained as she looked puzzled. "A warren of dirty narrer streets; the sun don't even shine into a lot of them they're that narrer; and the army or navy the only way to escape; maybe free or four famblies – three or four families I should say – living in a room. There's never no complete quiet nowhere; skeered me bad at first how much space I had, how quiet it could be at night in the barracks, only the tramp of the guard to be heard, and the odd challenge; a bed to meself; cor, I thought I was in heaven! Then I got took on by my officer, Sir Henry Wilton; a fine gentleman, what trained me as his batman and learned me to talk proper, when I think about it. He got me the job in Bow Street; he never believed I wouldn't walk again. 'Caleb,' he said, 'you've as stubborn as an ox with....' Well, he praised my courage, after the coarse fashion gentlemen may, Ma'am, and I couldn't let him down. So here I am; and not a fit subject to be sitting in a lady's parlour so familiar-like."

"Mr. Armitage; I think you have done extremely well," said Jane "And this is the age of the self-made man. Why in Highbury – the village in Surrey where I spent much of my youth – there is a family who have risen from relatively humble origins as shopkeepers, who are quite accepted by all the local notables, even by Mrs. Emma Knightley, who is something of a stickler," her eyes widened. "I will write to Emma; she has been a good friend and shown every kindness to me; perhaps she will be able to come and lend her support to me for a week or so, though I hardly like to ask it, for her father is ailing and too she is in an interesting condition. But I shall write; I am sure Emma will know exactly what to do and," she laughed ruefully "Will write me many pages of crossed and re-crossed lines of advice, for Emma likes nothing better than to give advice."

"She sounds a most excellent friend," opined Caleb "Assuming the advice is sound and not merely written for liking the sound of her own thoughts."

"She is; and took with rare good humour the fact that my husband – we had engaged upon a secret betrothal since his aunt was in opposition to him marrying at all – that he engaged upon a flirtation with her to allay the suspicion of others," said Jane, flushing slightly at the remembered humiliation, and secretly wondering whether Frank might have abandoned her for Emma and her fortune had Emma shown any real sign of reciprocating his apparent partiality. "And though her advice has been ill advised in the past, her maturity and her marriage have brought to a genuine good will a lot more wisdom to think through such advice as she might dispense," she added.

"Ah, that will be the lady whose husband had cause to dislike your husband," nodded Caleb. "Especially perhaps if he is a peevy cove who might see that Mr. Churchill was loose in the haft as you might say."

"Your expressions are sometimes difficult to follow but quite picturesque," said Jane.

"Well that's cant for you Ma'am; meant to confuse the swell coves," said Caleb, "and handy for an officer of the law to be familiar with, because one of our dooties is listening to loose talk in low dives to pick up clues. And if that was all there was to finding out who has killed Mr. Churchill then the task would be easy; but it's hard to see how to proceed, Ma'am; not that I should be talking to you at all about it."

"I am glad that you do," said Jane "I – I should like to help as much as I may; you have surmised that perhaps our marriage was not particularly *strong* but I should like nonetheless to know who has killed my husband."

"Ah, well, if I was a relative of yourn, ma'am, I'd be wanting to shake his hand when we finds him," said Caleb "Not having so far a very high opinion of Mr. Frank Churchill,"

"Alas," said Jane "I fear he does not appear in a good light throughout this business. I would urge you though to consider that his actions have been governed by a weakness of character rather than any inherent wicked intent. And I thank you for shielding me by shielding his character at Chorleigh, Wright and Jekyll's."

"Not sure what came over me," admitted Caleb, "but that Mr. Chorleigh put my back up."

"Where does one proceed from here?" asked Jane, glad that she was not the only one to find Mr. Chorleigh's manner offensive.

"Well strictly speaking, I should wait and see what information Mr. Chorleigh might have to give me concerning any wills that turn up missing say; but I have to say, I'm wondering if that was Frankie's lay – beg pardon ma'am, Mr. Churchill's lay – at all."

"Never mind my feelings over what it is customary to call a, er, shady character," said Jane. "Lay is business?"

"Yes ma'am; usually of the less salubrious kind and rather

smoky," said Caleb. "Mr. Despard, whose word I have no cause to doubt, spoke of him bringing his *own* parchment and making out documents that did not seem to be copying; one phrase was about an hundred of something. Now it may be that your husband has been misusing seals and purporting to be a solicitor to make out documents – say writs to serve on the unwary for a supposed offence that no true solicitor would touch, not really quite blackmail but something close; say serving a writ to someone who has spat on the highway, pretending to be an officer of the law and demanding a so-called fine. Provincials in the city are easily fooled, ma'am."

Jane flushed.

"Mr. Armitage, I am a provincial; and if anyone declared that they were an officer of the law and that I had broken some by-law I should be ashamed and shocked and pay any fine asked without thinking to check," she said. "Only in my own home would I think to ask to see an occurrence book."

"Ah, well, there you be," said Caleb "It's the honest folk these peep-o-day types target, see. And Mr. Churchill might or might not have known how serious a business he was getting into."

"But would that be enough to pay off so great a debt?" wondered Jane.

"Well ma'am look at it this way," said Caleb "If he forged a warrant to declare a man was an officer of the law for at least two supposed officers, seems to me each of those crooks could manage to touch at least three visitors to the city - and some residents at that – for three guineas each, a good sum but not enough to make most visitors grumble *too* much, for they'd pick those as looked prosperous enough, and they do that every day of the main part of the season; that's about a hundred days. That's near a thousand guineas for each so-called officer; and they can do the same thing year after year, because different people come up every year. And if you arst me, it would be more like ten or a dozen every day; more'n enough to make the outlay worth it. See that sort of enterprise would be run by a nib cove, a top man. A thiefmaster. Only I'm afeared your late husband might have been involved in worse."

"Dear G-d, there's a potential worse?" said Jane, faintly "Mr. Armitage you had better tell me the worst my husband may have been up to."

"Well, Ma'am, there's fraud on a large scale, see," said Caleb "The forging of documents for all sorts of schemes and scams. F'example; s'pose someone hires a fine town house like this. To rent, I'd suppose a place like this, and in such a location, would cost a thousand pounds for a year; or an hundred pounds a month; I know to a fairly close guess what most places in London are worth, see; that's part of my business. Now, supposing that the person who had rented it represented himself as the owner and sold the property – with a forged deed – to some poor fellow who parts with his thousands and then finds at the end of the month he is to be evicted and his deed worth nothing?"

"How fiendishly ingenious!" cried Jane. "Oh I do hope that Frank was not involved in such; for he spent the entire of his legacy from his aunt on purchasing this house, and such might quite ruin someone!"

"Yes indeed," said Mr. Armitage "And there's plenty of flats as have swallowed a spider account of how it ain't just the bridle lay as is daylight robbery. 'Cept strictly speaking the bridle culls work at night. Highwaymen," he added in explanation.

"Dear me!" said Jane "Well I suppose at least I may be thankful that it is unlikely that Frank ever indulged in being a highwayman; I doubt he would have had the physical courage. And speaking of courage I think it behoves me even more to find the *moral* courage to find out what Frank may have been involved in; and to make redress where I may do so."

"Nobody don't expect you to do that, ma'am," said Caleb, "and what he may have been up to and what I have conjectured as possible may be two different things; because conjecture ain't fact, no not by a long chalk it ain't. And I was just coming up with examples out of my head of what I have heard of to cover what a jarksman – a forger – might be

34

needed for. And I think we can safely say he was involved in some kind of forgery – knowingly like or otherwise – because working late and taking care, that's a discrepancy. It's the discrepancies that is always the clues. Now what I wants to do next is to go see this Dolly; see what *she* knew about him. Men tell their mistresses what they doesn't always tell their wives, see."

"I see," said Jane "Might you get more from her with a woman asking questions?"

He laughed.

"What, borrow a wardress from one of the women's gaols? Hard women they are; not so good at questioning as threatening."

"Actually, Mr. Armitage, I meant myself," said Jane, "and approach her in the spirit of a shared bereavement."

"*Ma'am!*" Caleb was shocked "A nice lady like you doesn't want to meet such a female!"

"Why not?" said Jane. "Had Frank not offered for me I was anticipating becoming a governess; for my portion was non-existent. I have lived on the charity of relatives and friends of my late father. Had I been so unfortunate as to have been....used.... by the paterfamilias of a household where I worked – and I have heard suppressed rumours that though uncommon it has been known to happen – then if I bore a child I should be ruined and perchance in the same situation as the unfortunate Dolly."

Caleb scratched the back of his neck.

"There's no two ways about it, Ma'am, the lot of women isn't easy," he said. "You are a brave lady if I may dare to say so; and I applaud your fortitude. And if that top-lofty abigail of yours who looks at me like I'm a slug won't go you'll take that tweenie-maid Mr. Fowler talked about."

"I'm not sure I want Molly exposed to such," said Jane. "No; Ella shall come. My own need for her is not so pressing that she can afford to offend me; because I am quite capable of dressing myself without need of an abigail."

Chapter 6

The apartment where the girl Dolly was maintained by Frank was in an unfashionable indeed rough part of the town and Jane was the recipient of many stares in her elegant black-trimmed gown and veils. Caleb took her elbow reassuringly to guide her towards the house. It was a structure of some three stories of timber framing and the wattle and daub between it pitted and damaged and darkened by grime to be almost as dark as the blackened beams. The street was filled with piles of refuse and filth, some of which steamed ominously. Caleb knew the neighbourhood well enough to know which door to take by Dolly's rather sparse directions on her letters to Frank.

"'Ere, Mister yer don' wanna go vere, mate; vere's trouble," volunteered an urchin. "Murder gwine on, shouldn't be s'prised."

"Gawdstruth," said Caleb, letting go of Jane's arm and belting up the stairs. Jane began to follow.

Shortly a large and dirty individual came hurtling down with Caleb in hot pursuit. Jane pressed against the wall to let Caleb past and wished she had only had the presence of mind to trip the man he was chasing. Ella screamed and seemed about to have hysterics.

Jane grasped her shoulder and gave her a little shake; it was no time for such displays.

"Control yourself, Ella!" said Jane.

She tripped on up the stairs and entered the rather dingily tawdry room of her husband's mistress much hung about with cheap cambric and Persian silk hangings that were uniformly too demandingly pink to be at all tasteful.

The girl Dolly was tied to a chair sobbing loudly, her rose coloured gown torn away and burns on her face and bosom. The poker, thrown down in a hurry, lay in the tatters of the torn gown smoking ominously. Jane picked up the poker and threw it into the hearth where a small fire had been coaxed to greater heat, and stamped quickly on the smouldering cotton gown.

"I shall have you out of there in a brace of shakes," said Jane firmly, reaching for her sewing scissors in her reticule. The ropes were tough but Jane persevered in cutting open the knot and freeing the unfortunate young woman. Dolly was not very old, as Jane could see at a glance, the makeup ruined by her tears of anguish making her look almost like a little girl who has been at her mother's dressing table to play at being grown up. The girl was well developed but below the line of face paint her skin had a dewy freshness to it that made it a shame to spoil it with makeup. Her blonde hair looked to be quite natural too and not bleached with caustic soda or potash lye, either of which dried the hair and could burn the skin and which produced a characteristically brittle-looking and unnatural blonde. It did rather stand to reason that such treatments were bad for the hair, since potash lye was also used by tanners to help strip the hair from hides; however those of Dolly's profession could not always afford, perhaps, to be nice about such things. The girl had big blue eyes to go with the hair, which being currently wide with fright and pain added to her youthful appearance, and Jane's heart went out to her. There might be very little behind those eyes resembling an original thought but in a way that made the girl all the more vulnerable.

Dolly swore as feeling returned to her hands and wrists; and Jane winced, but went into the bedroom to see if there was an ewer of water.

There was; and she stripped off a pillowslip to get at the underslip which was less soiled to soak in the water to lay against the young Paphian's burns to soothe them.

"Gawd bless yer, lidy!" said Dolly in deep relief "Gawdstruth, wot's a fine mort like you doin' 'ere? You ain't an abbess are yer?"

"I am not in Holy Orders," said Jane.

Dolly stared then gave a coarse laugh.

"Nar! An Abbess! A madam! One what runs a bawdy 'ouse!"

Jane flushed.

"No," she said "I am not. I am Mrs. Churchill; Frank

Churchill's wife."

The laughter was suddenly cut off.

"Then – you done this? As revenge? But lidy I swear, strite up I do, 'e di'n't never tell me 'e was legshackled! Please don't 'urt me no more, you can 'ave the ruddy necklace, if I'd known it was 'is wife's…….."

"I have *not* done this!" Jane almost snapped "I ignored his *affaire*; it was a more dignified thing to do than to take issue with him! I have come to see you because my husband has been murdered; in the hopes that you might be able to throw some light on the matter! Ah, Mr. Armitage; have you apprehended the villain who has hurt, er, Dolly?" she added as Dolly let out a screech that impacted painfully on Jane's eardrums.

"No Mrs. Churchill; the beggar went between two carriages, it weren't safe to foller; even if I could of found the, er, feller again once I'd got across the street," said Caleb ruefully. "Here, Dolly; you stubble them whids, you, in front of Mrs. Churchill!"

Dolly had been crying and swearing.

"Oh-oh- *ooooh* Frankie's dead!" she howled.

"And not much loss to the world either," said Caleb. "Nah then Dolly! I'm an officer of the law; and you had better tell me what I need to know."

"I ain't sayin' nothin' to no ruddy Runner," said Dolly sulkily.

"Nonsense Dolly!" said Jane "If you want to catch whoever killed Frank – who may be something to do with that lewd fellow who was hurting you – then you will tell Mr. Armitage and me everything we want to know. Now you gave me to believe that the man who was hurting you asked for the necklace. *That* might be significant; so if you are sufficiently recovered to fetch it, I suggest that you do so."

Dolly scowled.

"*He* didn't find it and you won't neither," she said.

"What, strung danglin' out of the window is it?" asked Caleb "Or inside the hem of a gown to seem like a weighted hem? Ah, Dolly, better to co-operate with the law you know," as her expression gave her away with his second suggestion.

"You….." she began

"*Not* in front of Mrs. Churchill!" Caleb barked in the voice of the parade ground.

Dolly stuck her tongue out at him; but went to her bedroom. Her gowns were hung behind a curtain; and soon she drew out a coruscating band of bijouterie, shimmering in myriad prisms of colour even in the dimness of the shabby room.

Caleb gasped.

"Oh Lord, Mrs. Churchill, your husband was into receiving stolen goods!" he declared in horror.

"Stolen goods? Do – is – excuse me I am not sure what questions to ask," said Jane, faintly, sitting down.

Caleb twitched the necklace from Dolly's reluctant grasp.

"This belongs to the Duchess of Avon; it was stolen last week," he said "There's a gang of high class jewel thieves who steal from the 'ote tone and we've every belief that the stones are reset to disguise them. Only this is according to description, unchanged."

"It is a beautiful thing," said Jane, "and I can understand Dolly's reluctance to part with it; but my dear girl! Was it worth being so badly hurt for?"

Dolly was holding the wet cloth to her burned face and bosoms alternately.

"It were the way 'e asked," she said sulkily "Why should I give it up? I s'pose if it's stolen I don't get no choice," she added truculently. "Frankie said 'e was onto a good fing, but nuffink about bein' a prigger o' baubles!"

"I don't think he was actually involved in the stealing of them," said Caleb. "I'll see you get the reward, my girl, for being co-operative; and at that you can think yourself lucky I don't believe you to be involved in this business or you might be before the beak for bein' in possession of stolen goods. Now go and put some clothes on; there's too much flesh on display and I feel like I'm in a butcher's shop with it poking out at me."

Dolly gave him a filthy look and went sulkily into the bedroom.

"Mrs. Churchill; I would like to get you away from here," said Caleb anxiously.

"Mr. Armitage, if you think I intend to leave that poor girl alone when that monster might come back, you can think again!" said Jane. "I am taking her home with me!"

"Mrs. *Jane*!" wailed Ella.

"Ella," said Jane "You are an excellent abigail and I appreciate your services; pray find it in your heart to extend a little charity to this unfortunate fallen creature in her most unhappy hour."

Ella blew her nose hard.

"If you insists Mrs. Jane," she said "But it isn't what I'm used to. And places like this; my pore mother would turn in her grave!"

"Your mother," said Jane firmly, "would adjure you to do whatever your lady needed; and to thank your Maker that you were not yourself in the situation that this, er, Dolly is in."

Ella nodded dubiously, not entirely convinced; but sufficiently shamed to be subdued at least.

Jane nodded her to the bedroom.

"You shall insist that Dolly packs and help her," she said. "We shall place her…..dear me. She is to be my guest but one can scarcely place her in the red room; it is *not* suitable."

"No indeed Mrs. Jane!" said Ella "She ought by rights to have that Juliet's room once the hussy goes; but…. Mrs. Jane, there are rooms suitable for elder children; might she be placed in one of those?"

"Excellent," approved Jane "I leave it in your efficient hands, Ella."

Caleb watched with a raised eyebrow as Ella stalked into the bedroom.

"You have the management of that one down to a 'T'," he said.

"Ella is a good woman; and a little too impressed by her concept of my consequence," said Jane. "She is also proud of her own abilities. Doubtless with her skills we shall soon have Dolly speaking acceptable English and dressing in such a way that I may find her a position with a mantua-maker or milliner; for I have every expectation that the trim on her gown is what she has herself added."

"You really are a most remarkable lady, Mrs. Churchill," said Caleb who had not up to that point noticed the competently executed vandyked ruffle on the smouldering gown.

Chapter 7

Dolly was reluctant at first to leave her 'own little nest' but Ella was firm and Dolly gaped at the fine town house in Pembridge Square with its gleaming white stucco frontage. It might be on the unfashionable side of the square and not so large as those on the North side but to Dolly it was next thing to a palace. She squealed with delight and hugged Jane.

"Dolly dear, you must save such effusions for our private rooms if you want me to teach you how to act in a ladylike manner," said Jane, firmly. "Come now; Ella shall issue orders that a room is prepared for you and we shall drink tea."

"Cor this beats Pimlico," said Dolly enthusiastically. "Don't you have no blue ruin instead of tea?"

"Certainly not," said Jane "I am certain that it would be bad for your complexion."

Dolly was taken firmly on ahead by Ella and Caleb murmured to Jane,

"I am amazed that you knew that blue ruin is a name for gin."

"Mr. Armitage, I had no idea," said Jane primly "But I suspected it was some kind of spirituous liquor and made the comment accordingly. That poor girl needs careful handling."

"You're a remarkable lady!" Caleb said again. "She'll find a lot of difference in this fine modern house, too, from the old timber framed buildings in the West End. Though I fancy the residents there will find themselves evicted when someone realises how big the city is growing and how close it actually is to the centre of London."

"And remarkable that she has managed to keep as clean as she is in such insanitary places," said Jane. "And she must have a modicum of conversation, albeit rough and untutored. Frank may have kept her for other reasons then conversation but he always likes – liked to show off how erudite he was and how clever and if she did not appreciate that I fancy he would have got rid of her in short order. Dear me, what a charge he has left upon me! And consider if she might also be with child! I wish I had male relatives that I might rely upon;

but I will not hang upon the sleeve of Colonel Campbell who has been so good to me; and I certainly do not wish to involve Mr. Churchill for he will surely see how much disarray Frank's affairs are in. And I must sell the horse; but I have written all my worries to dear Emma and I hope that she may advise me."

"I would do what I could, Mrs. Churchill, but I am not a man of affairs and I would not be taken seriously in undertaking any of your business needs," said Caleb, clenching and unclenching his hands in frustration.

"Oh Mr. Armitage your very offer of support is heartening," said Jane. "As a governess I should have had to manage all things for myself; and so I shall contrive to do, though I fear being cheated over the horse."

"I can make enquiries as to that if you will, ma'am," said Caleb. She brightened.

"Would you? How kind you are! Then if you will do so – when your duties permit of course – I should be delighted. Now I know you wish to get that necklace safely away; will you return in time for dinner? I shall have Dolly write out some kind of affidavit if that will help you."

"Thank you; it will. I think it will not harm you if I say that as yet it is not known how a stolen necklace came into your husband's possession; I cannot think that he would move in the right circles, either as a guest or as a servant, to be a thief."

"It must needs come out eventually that he was a criminal, however minor; how thankful I am that a wife cannot be sent to gaol for her husband's misdeeds as a man might be for his wife's!" said Jane.

It made her feel quite cold to think that had not the law stated that a woman was too incapable to undertake illegal activities without the participation of her husband or other protector she might have been held liable for her husband's misdeeds. Going to gaol for a crime she had no knowledge of – indeed was not even sure of the nature of – was a terrifying thought!

Caleb left to relieve himself of the responsibility of the Avon necklace; and Jane went in to drink tea with Dolly under the disapproving eye of Fowler after Ella had looked over the girl's wounds in a more detailed way than the perfunctory treatment at her rooms. .

"Fowler, you will share the responsibility of helping Miss…." she looked a question at Dolly

"Baxter, lidy," said Dolly.

"Quite so, Miss Baxter, to feel at home and to adapt to living here," said Jane firmly, "since it may be that she is to be the mother of a sister or brother of Miss Frances. I will not neglect the wellbeing of a half sibling of my daughter."

"Ow, you have a babby girl?" said Dolly "I love babbies! Frankie never told me nuffink about her neether."

"Perhaps, Fowler," said Jane smiling at him "You will ask Annie to bring Miss Frances down to the parlour."

"Yes Mrs. Churchill," said Fowler. "You want, er, Miss Baxter to be taught to be a lady? Have I those orders clear?"

"I believe that Miss Baxter is perfectly capable of learning a ladylike manner that we might support each other in what is, after all, a mutual bereavement," said Jane firmly. "Please also send out for a doctor to attend to her at his convenience; she has been hurt by the villains who killed Mr. Churchill and needs appropriate ointments for burns."

Fowler glanced involuntarily at the burn on Dolly's cheek and shuddered.

"Yes Ma'am," he said.

Jane induced Dolly to write in her own words how she had been given the necklace as a love token from her protector and to make a brief description of it. Dolly sighed as she regretted the necklace but wrote obediently.

Jane stiffened as she read ''undreds and 'undreds of loverly shinin dyemons'.

Hundreds. An hundred.

That might be significant.

She permitted Dolly to cuddle little Frances and play with

her – Frances was at an age where she could sit firmly and was starting to crawl and wanted to investigate everything – and smiled to see the buxom girl dandle Frances on her knee and play 'this is the way the farmer rides' with her, a rhyme that must be universal. Jane took her own daughter for a while and showed Dolly how to play 'Pat-a-cake' which Dolly laughed over.

"I fink I have played that when I were small, but not wiv my little bruvvers and sisters," she said. "Cuh, Mrs. Churchill, I 'opes you can get me a good position, 'cos I were sending back a lot of what Frankie – er, Mr. Churchill – gived me. And lucky I fort meself to be the peculiar of a classy gent like him after me bad luck!"

"What bad luck is that?" asked Jane.

"Well, see, I worked as a barmaid in an inn at Sadler's Wells – the resort just outside town y'know – and gent took my good name away by force, and I was turned orf account I had the babby in me, Well I 'ad it dealt wiv...... only I were right ill of it and landlord, he found out."

"You were lucky not to die from the ministrations of the awful old women who do that!" said Jane, scandalised. Such things too she had heard of in whispers when she had been finding out all the pitfalls that might befall a governess.

"Yerse, I fort I were going to fer a while," said Dolly. "And me away from 'ome and fambly; Bethnal Green we comes from, a long way away. But I di'n't turn up me toes, and so I come into the city and found I could work on me back standin' up as you might say round the back o' Covent Garden theatre, and that's where Fr – Mr. Churchill picked me up and offered me lodgin's and well, I been his peculiar ever since. 'E said I weren't 'ardened and 'e liked a girl what was quiet and com- comp – I forget the word."

"Compliant," said Jane. "Yes, his aunt was domineering; he picked me for my compliance."

Dolly regarded Jane and wondered whether a stiff necked lady had actually been compliant enough in the way Frankie had liked and decided not to ask. Swell morts probably did not know that gentlemen sometimes liked playacting. And she had heard stories of some flash coves who liked their playacting to include hurting so she had been well off with Frankie

It had been a kind of freedom not to be bound by the conventions, but she had been so happy as a barmaid, flirting without meaning anything with the coves who came in to drink, out in the countryside of Sadler's Wells which was right pretty, but with enough amenities not to be as inconvenient as she had heard the real countryside could be. Being respectable might be nice; and seemingly as she did not have much choice with the gentle forcefulness of Mrs. Churchill she might as well do as she was told. Poor Frankie dead!

She burst into tears.

Jane put her arms around her; and let her sob out how she missed her nice job and her family and Frankie all about as much as each other. Ella came in without knocking as a good servant must to tell Jane that a room had been prepared and Jane sent Dolly up to undress and lie down for a while. It would be convenient too for the doctor when he arrived.

She cuddled Frances for a while then handed her back to Annie to take back to the nursery; by which time the doctor had arrived and could be shown up to Dolly.

Jane used Dr Wingfield, the physician who was recommended by Isabella Knightley; and he came into the room looking grave.

"Mrs. Churchill, I cannot know where you found that unfortunate woman but the burns on her did not occur by accident; she was burned deliberately."

"Yes I know," said Jane impatiently "I was going to see her – she was my husband's mistress – and found the villain actually hurting her. Are the burns going to heal without complication?"

"I believe so," said Dr Wingfield. "Excuse me, Mrs. Churchill, why would you wish to go to see, er, your husband's mistress?"

Jane had no intention of sharing her husband's possible shame with the doctor.

"Don't you consider it civil to inform the poor woman that she too is bereaved?" she said with as much hauteur as she could muster. "Thank you; you have given a prescription to my maid to have made up?"

"Yes Mrs. Churchill I have; and I believe that the young female will soon be on her feet again and in no need of foisting herself onto you any longer," said Dr Wingfield in disgust.

"I believe," said Jane sweetly "I pay you for your medical opinion not your social judgement. Good day."

Chapter 8

Jane asked Fowler to show Caleb Armitage into the parlour when he arrived.

"Mr. Armitage," she said, as the tall figure of the Bow Street Runner entered the room, "I believe I may be able to throw some light on the documents my husband was writing – forging. It was Dolly describing the necklace for your affidavit that made me think of it."

She passed it over.

Caleb read through Dolly's laborious scrawl.

"Hundreds and hundreds…… you think he was describing jewels, perhaps to fences? – that's the name of men as can sell such stolen things?" he asked. "Why would he need parchment?"

"Perhaps you have never seen one of these," said Jane, passing him a piece of parchment.

He read it through, his eyes narrowing as he perused the contents.

"So this is the copy of a letter to Lloyds of London to insure a necklace for travelling….. with a minute description of the necklace. But surely it would be a risk to claim ownership and then subsequent theft……,"

"This is the necklace belonging to Frank's grandmother which was sent to us for me to wear on our wedding day," said Jane. "Set with, as the document says, thirty five rubies of seven carats to eleven carats in ascending order towards the centre and small diamonds numbering seventy in between them. It is a hideous thing," she added. "However I was advised that should I ever need to sell it, this insurance description may count as something called 'provenance' which is a proof that I have the right to the necklace; and Lloyds also require, should I have it reset, that a description of the reset piece be appended to the original document," she went on, adding thoughtfully. "There was also much made of the fact that Mr. Churchill has a letter from his ancestor who first gifted it to the first ancestress to wear it in 1687. It would appear to me that if there were false provenance for newly reset pieces that had been made up from stolen jewels so that the original owners themselves would not recognise them, then this might constitute a means by which higher prices might be commanded for pieces sold to regular jewellers who can see what appears to be proof of ownership; where surely if the ownership is unconfirmed and the seller seems in a hurry to sell, as must often be the case with stolen items, any jeweller is going to be wary of giving a full price."

"Mrs. Churchill; you are prodigious clever," said Caleb.

"I also recall Frank asking me what became of the Lloyds' documentation because he wanted to check something," said Jane "Which is a discrepancy; you said discrepancies are clues. Frank never bothered himself with paperwork; he threw all correspondence that was not personal unopened into the escritoire; and bundled in personal letters on top too. Bills that he found that I had not dealt with he dealt with by throwing on the fire. I believe that his aunt dealt with most of the matters arising in their household before her death and Frank had very little experience of undertaking any kind of record keeping. It surprised me at the time that he should want to actually deal with anything pertaining to paperwork. ,"

"Well I already knew he was useless and feckless," said Caleb. "How's the girl Dolly?"

"Grieving more than I," said Jane with a sigh that might have been regret; whether regret on behalf of Dolly, or on her own behalf that she felt no urge to mourn, Caleb was unable to divine . "Perhaps I am deficient in that I have shed no tears of grief for Frank; though I cried enough bitter tears when I found out that his affection for me was never more than superficial and that I may as well have been a superior kind of housekeeper to whom he might also boast of who he had seen and to whom he had spoken in town and that he had......," she paused. "I was considering that I was making a cake of myself speaking out so but he said that he had made a friend who would see him right-and-tight for life," she said "I took it for a social acquaintance, a potential patron; but it was when he gave me the fifty pounds. He laughed a lot and said that you could not call his new friend a Tulip of Fashion but that he was onto a better thing than the original tulipmania and that Holland had plenty to give with two lips that might whisper promises. He liked word plays like that," she added.

"I should of said it was a little forced meself," said Caleb "I would've thought rather than labouring the connection if he wished to be obscure he'd of done better to hint at 'two lips meeting in financial gain across the north sea' if he wanted to say without saying that he was speaking of a Dutchman."

"Why Mr. Armitage, that is extremely subtle!" said Jane. "You are a much cleverer man than your speech suggests if I may say so without causing offence."

"I take no offence, Mrs. Churchill," said Caleb "And right glad I am to be able to speak as I think and have my love of words and wit appreciated; for I have not lost my rough Soho accent nowise and most expect me to be stupid. Which has its advantages."

"To be underestimated must be an advantage," agreed Jane "So too was I underestimated when Frank and I courted secretly; though often I was angered at the lengths to which he went to disparage me in public, yet I hid it.. I do not know why I tell you this; I have never been so forthcoming to any."

"Bless you, Mrs. Churchill, you may have learned indifference to Mr. Churchill, but you still grieve for the love you once held for him; and you will be shut of me when we have uncovered who has killed him so you may speak freely without worrying about what a neighbour or friend might later think," said Caleb heartily.

Jane gave a small smile.

"I fancy, Mr. Armitage," she said, "that perhaps it is more that you are a man who is big and safe and good at listening who thus elicits confidences from people that they might not give were you not good at just sitting."

Caleb gave a shy smile.

"I do not say that the same does not happen," he said, "but there are those as talk and those as are good at keeping close mouthed whether it is for their own good or no; and I fancy you are used to concealing all within, even from yourself, and a shock has brought it out before one who you do not have to consider as important in your world. For you cannot talk to a servant as there is no better way of letting out a secret. The most loyal servant may be induced to talk if they may be made to boast of their gentleman or lady."

Jane was startled.

"That I had not considered," she said. "So how much have you learned about Frank and me from my household?"

"That he kept you short; but demanded perfection. That he demanded near slavery from you; that he hated the baby and was jealous of her especially as she is a girl not a boy; that he beat you when you rebelled and would not submit to tyranny by becoming monosyllabic towards him – not that your servants know such a word – and he accused you of having a lover which the servants knew well that you had not, but declared that his mistress had expensive tastes in perfume and was blonde. From the scents and hair on his laundry you understand," he added.

"There are apparently *no* secrets in any family!" cried Jane, shocked.

"No Ma'am," agreed Caleb. "The only ones who can keep secrets do not keep servants; and they are generally of the estate that live so close to others that the neighbours know instead."

"I find I am quite cast down," said Jane "And not a little humiliated."

"Mrs. Churchill," said Caleb earnestly "Not one thing have I learned from the servants that in any wise might diminish any one's opinion of you who are a patient and kindly lady, never taking out your feelings on the servants and speaking douce words even when your husband has beaten you – and I *do* want to shake the fambles of whoever turned him off," he added "And it is only *he* what shows deficient in all that I have heard."

Jane flushed.

"It gives you more reason to think that I may have had a hand in his death," she said.

"If you had had a hand in his death, Mrs. Churchill you would have been more readily able to deal with such matters

51

as turning off his servants, and disposing of the horse because such details a meticulous lady like yourself would have considered ahead of time," said Caleb. "You may not be saddened by that blasted rascal's death if you pardon my French, but you are plainly quite shocked. Even though I am most impressed by how quickly you can think out details and implications. And I am certain that you have the truth of the matter that he was forging provenance for reset jewellery to hide its origins. Maybe even with several pieces having their stones mixed and matched. The price would not be top sovereign but it would as you surmise be higher by far than without any provenance at all, and if done systematically then two thousand guineas is a small price to pay off a forger *and* a salary into the bargain. It is my belief," he added excitedly "That we may be onto the greatest jewellery robbing ring that London has ever known!"

"Why did they kill him?" asked Jane "If he was of such use to them?"

"Because he cheated them!" cried Caleb enthusiastically. "He took the Avon necklace – and before it was reset too, so that if anyone had seen it, he could, unless his tongue was silenced, lead the law enforcement officers right back to the thieves! They tortured him to find out what he had done with it – and they went to retrieve it from Dolly who showed a remarkably venal and stubborn streak in not giving it up. Had we not arrived when we did I make no bones about it that I believe they would have killed her too."

Jane shuddered.

"I think it is less venality on her part than sentimentality," she said "The girl is inclined to an excess of sensibility; though she has her reasons. I had thought that I should hate a woman of such a kind but actually I feel nothing but compassion for her. And she is scarce more than a child; though she is so," she blushed, "well grown; I cannot think her more than fifteen years, little older than our nursery maid."

"More than likely," said Caleb. "And as you have not fainted for the thought of her being turned off by these rogues

I fancy you are like the excellent Elinor in the novel by 'A Lady' called 'Sense and Sensibility'."

"I should prefer never to be like that silly widgeon Marianne," said Jane. "So might this help to catch the jewel thieves? That will surely enhance your career?"

"It had crossed my mind," said Caleb "And the fact that there is a substantial reward for information leading to their capture would benefit you too if I make it clear that your help was essential."

"But would not the reward be yours?" asked Jane.

He shook his head.

"We are not permitted to partake of rewards, bribes or other remuneration outside our salaries bar the reward for a conviction," he said "And I don't say bribery don't go on because it do. Does I mean. But it ain't supposed to."

"It does seem unfair that you should not benefit," said Jane. "However," she brightened "If all goes well and I may help you to catch these precious villains and avenge my foolish and weak husband and if there *is* a reward, there is nothing to stop you partaking in it so far as dining with me regularly."

"Now Mrs. Churchill that's generous right enough but not wise," said Caleb.

"I have tried to be wise so long," said Jane "It has cost me the love of a husband, his life, and possibly financial security. Perhaps the time has come to be a little foolish. Disregard my distempers, I pray you; let us go into the dining room, it is time for dinner for I hear Fowler making discreet noises with the cutlery."

Chapter 9

Dolly was subdued eating, and surreptitiously watched Jane to see how she managed her cutlery. Jane smiled at her.

"You are doing very well," she murmured.

"Ta," said Dolly looking pleased. "What you gwine ter do if I am pregnant?"

Fowler almost dropped the plate of potatoes he was carrying.

Jane flushed.

"Here, Dolly, me gal, not at the meal," said Caleb. "When you ladies withdraw, that's the time to talk lady stuff; we men is too delicate to cope."

Dolly subsided with a muttered apology. Jane mouthed a thanks to Caleb who – she could hardly believe her eyes – *winked* at her. Nobody had *ever* winked at her before.

It was most reprehensible that it made her want to giggle. She looked down quickly at her plate.

Caleb was dismayed; he had somehow broken etiquette. Her chin was wobbling; surely he had not made her cry? No – that little single dimple of hers was popping in and out, such a tiny, half hidden dimple, hardly a dimple at all in a face that should have more colour, be less thin and drawn….. she was laughing. He heaved a sigh of relief.

"Gawd Mr. Armitage you do have your uses," murmured Fowler as he served Caleb "That ruddy girl will be the death of me straight up she will."

So Mr. Fowler had the tones of London beneath his carefully cultivated nob voice, thought Caleb. Well if he can do it, so can I.

"Comes of being in the army… I was a sergeant," he breathed back.

"Mr. Armitage! If you'd only let me know earlier you were respectable I shouldn't have taken snuff at you," said Fowler and straightened up to move on to get the next dish.

Caleb gave a silent whistle. That top-lofty footman had unbent seemingly! Well as an ally he was easier to take than as an undeclared enemy. And he was loyal enough to Mrs.

Churchill; and Molly the tweenie had told him that it was because Mr. Fowler had been sent by the Mistress to pawn her *own* necklace – not the family one – to pay the wages of all the servants before the master got plumper in the pockets because Molly had overheard it with her own ears while she was cleaning under the table. Fowler knew where he was well off.

Caleb resolved to tell him that the Master was involved in something that might bring the mistress a reward; without going into unnecessary detail he could get the immobile-faced servant as an even closer ally for Mrs. Churchill's sake.

"So what *does* happen if I'm in the family way?" persisted Dolly when she and Jane withdrew, leaving Caleb looking dubiously at the bottle of port.

"Well I should think that it would be best for you and the child if I adopt him or her to grow up with Frances," said Jane "Of course if it is a boy he would not inherit; illegitimates are barred from inheritance, though I should think if I have any rights over my husband's estates I could make a fair provision. And you shall then be an aunt; will that suit you?"

Dolly looked wistful.

"It wouldn't be no life for a nipper wiv no da wivout a swell ma like you," she said. "Couldn't we make like you 'as a posthumous child?"

Jane looked startled.

"I – I do not know if I could carry off the imposture," she said. "Besides, I cannot be certain that I do *not* have a posthumous child; Frank continued to enjoy marital relations with me."

Dolly shuddered.

"That don't sound too friendly," she said.

"Frank disliked me having a child," Jane decided not to go into detail "And it meant that we were not…..friendly."

The jeering remarks about the changes childbearing had wrought upon her body – *his* child conceived in, at the time, love for *him*. His comments about udders because she wanted to feed Frances for herself……. His jealousy because she would leave him in the night to feed the baby. His insistence on marital rights before her body had recovered enough to make it anything but painful; and continued exertion of those rights on her regularly; her revenge to lie passive and unresponsive. Oh her revenge had been petty; but then Frank made her feel petty. She had always been the one who had to give; somehow to make him take was a bittersweet revenge.

"I ain't a gentleman to be drinking Mrs. Churchill's port," said Caleb to Fowler "But sit down a moment; I want to tell you somethink,".

"It will only spoil if it isn't drunk," said Fowler pouring Caleb a glass full. "Maybe just this once I'll join you; it's a shame to waste a fine port."

He poured himself a modest measure and recapped the decanter. Caleb nodded in approval. This was no man tippling when the master's back was turned but a genuine appreciation of the wine and a desire not to see it go to waste. The liquor smelled rich and expensive; and Caleb told himself to be careful with a drink that was likely to be somewhat stronger than the heavy wets he was used to. The similarity in name between the malted porter he was used to and this fortified wine was a coincidence and the effects of the two should never be confused – or the unwary drinker of port would be the one to become confused!

"It's like this," said Caleb "Mr. Churchill was into something havy-cavy as I expect you have surmised."

"Well if you ask me, and since it's the mistress who pays my wages now, he was a dashed loose screw," said Fowler "And I don't need military language to explain it! Bless the lady, she has no need to take on his Cyprian!"

"The girl was attacked by the ruffians who killed him thinking that she knew what they couldn't get out of him," said Caleb "Which is how I come to be staying here, account of worrying that they might turn up to torture Mrs. Churchill, or the babby to make her talk."

"You don't say!" Fowler was deeply shocked and actually showed it in a spasm of emotion across his wooden face.

"Well then Mr. Armitage, I'll fettle Mr. Churchill's pistol then and sleep with that aside me just in case!" said he grimly. "Pretty deep stuff he was in then?"

"I think deeper than he realised; which was how come he did something to annoy them; and I don't *know* nothin' so I shan't be whiddling the scrap to you right now," said Caleb. "But if it leads to catching some other precious villains, there's a reward in it for missus; which means she'll be able to feel that she can keep on the house and her servants and you my lad as secure as her."

"Well I hope you manage that, Mr. Armitage…. Lawks but you do manage that hussy well!"

"Oh I think she'll be amenable to you dropping her a hint too, Mr. Fowler; especially if I put it to her that she's to listen to you. Give her a burst of the *old* tongue if you know what I mean."

Fowler flushed.

"It took me long enough to lose it," he said.

"Oh but a wise man knows 'ow to be bilingual," said Caleb "I learned some swell-cove words in the army and how to pick up me aitches most of the time; but I'd be no end grateful if you'd give me a few tips," he added artfully. A few tips would be useful; and so would consolidating his position as an ally to Fowler by letting the man feel that he could show Caleb a thing or two.

"It's all in the accent," said Fowler "See when I started learning – teaching – myself I started off talking with a round pebble in my mouth to make me mince my words out. Getting the grammar right – that's just book learning that you can do in a library. But the voice now; that's the hard bit. Different vowels."

"You don't say!" said Caleb "Well I call that downright ingenious I do. Here, put that decanter out of the way, lad, before it looks too tempting-like back at us both."

"You're right," said Fowler, moving the decanter firmly onto the tray and standing up. "Well, Mr. Armitage, time for me to ask Maggie Ketch to put on water to boil for you and the….Mistress and her guest. Thank you kindly for letting me know what's what. And an army man is always respectable; my brother was in the army."

With which pronouncement he swept out as silent footed and majestic as usual.

Caleb went through to join the women and found Frances had been brought down. She crawled over to him and took a hold of his boot. Caleb stooped and picked her up without thinking, and threw her up.

For a moment her lower lip wobbled ominously; then she decided that she had liked the experience and gave a gurgle of delight. Caleb threw her up again so that she was giggling and gave her firmly back to young Annie who was watching him in some trepidation.

"Have you children of your own, Mr. Armitage?" asked Jane, a wistful look on her face.

"No ma'am; a few nieces and nephews. Never married," said Caleb.

"You look as though you are quite natural with babies," said Jane "I cannot imagine Frank doing that."

She did not mention – she did not have to, for Caleb could guess – that Frank had never even held his daughter. It had been irresponsible of him to pick the baby up; why with no contact with her father any man might have terrified her! But small Frances seemed to have her mother's courage not her father's cowardice.

Caleb smiled shyly at Jane.

"She is a bonny baby," he said, "and you must be so happy that she is so healthy!"

"I am," said Jane "I do not know how I would bear it if anything happened to her!"

"I am sure she will be glad of such a devoted mother," said Caleb.

Whatever it took, whatever it cost, he swore to himself he would never let these faceless villains take Fanny and even threaten to hurt her. Had it occurred to Mrs. Churchill that they might do so? He hoped not; that extra sick fear she could well do without. But on the other hand.....on the other hand, Mrs. Churchill was a very level headed woman and if she were prepared for any such act she would be perhaps ready to take precautions.

"Mrs. Churchill," said Caleb, "it might be wise not to let Fanny go to the park for a while."

The grey eyes dilated in terror. Then Jane nodded.

"Certainly Mr. Armitage," she said. "An ounce of precaution is worth a ton of cure."

Caleb gave a silent whistle. She was worth a score of such as her late fool of a husband!

Chapter 10

When Jane arose in the morning it was to have a note handed to her by Fowler.

"Mr. Armitage had to go out," said Fowler. "He said the note explained."

"Why thank you Fowler," said Jane. "Then I shall spend the morning writing the characters for the servants we shall not be keeping; they may work out their month but I shall not keep them if they find another situation before the time is up if they may start immediately. Tell me, is there anything positive I may say of Juliet?"

Fowler considered.

"She is honest," he said, "and clean in her own person if not too scrupulous about those portions of the house that do not show; Mrs. Ketch has had occasion to speak to her about dusting the tops of doors and cornices."

"Ah well, honesty is a virtue," said Jane. "Thank you Fowler."

She took herself into the book room to peruse Caleb's letter and to write.

The letter ran,

"Dear Mrs Churchill,

I have gone to find out what I may of Dutchmen in London. It is my belief that if we may find the identity of Mr Churchill's accommodating friend we may be much closer to the puzzle. I have not forgotten the disposal of your horse but I feel this is more important as you have already fodder in the mews. I do not know how long I shall be gone; Mrs Ketch has kindly agreed to keep me a bowl of stew and some bread so I beg you do not await nuncheon for my presence.

Your obedient servant,
Caleb Armitage."

"He is such a thoughtful man," murmured Jane.

Jane had finished writing the characters for Juliet, Emerson and Palmer and took them down to the servants' quarters to hand them over personally.

She had learned from Mrs. Campbell that having the mistress arrive suddenly in the servants' hall was a good way to keep servants on their toes; and a little judicious and unladylike eavesdropping before walking in often highlighted any problems in the household. As Mrs. Campbell had said, a military wife learned the tricks her husband had learned as a junior officer to help maintain discipline in the ranks, and nothing destroyed discipline like discontentment.

Jane tripped lightly down the stairs to the basement and listened accordingly; the door to the servants' hall being pushed to but not shut.

The talk was of Mr. Armitage.

Fowler was holding forth.

"If you ask me he's a bleedin' gent, whatever his birth might be; learned it military fashion. And he's devoted to the mistress' interests. Wouldn't mind betting he's half sweet on her. And gawd help us he can keep that fancy piece in order! Not that she's as loud and brazen as I was afeared she might be mind," he added.

"Ar, you'm a fair man, Mr. Fowler," said Mrs. Ketch "Pore little body, I took her up her supper account she retired early and she said I reminded her of her ma; she's hem cut up about the master's death."

There was a giggle from Juliet.

"Well he knew how to kiss a girl," she said. "Any girl he paid attention to would miss him."

An awful silence ensued.

"You, my girl, are no better than you ought to be," said Mrs. Ketch majestically.

"And a disruptive influence and a bad example to young Molly here," said Fowler. "It's just as well you are getting your marching orders. Oh, don't look so worried; the mistress asked if there was anything positive she might say about you. It's my belief she don't miss nothing; and she knew about you making eyes at the master."

Jane, feeling slightly giddy, wished she did not know now; but a reputation for omniscience with the servants was always good.

She withdrew and made something of a noise descending the stairs a second time.

The servants all rose respectfully as a body as she walked in and she smiled kindly.

"You all know that I shall be cutting down my household," she said "Fowler will have explained to you that I do not need so many servants; Palmer, I shall be selling the horse, and I hope you will stay until I have done so even if you get a position rapidly. Here are your characters; which of course you are at liberty to read. I should consider it improper to seal them. And may I offer, Juliet, a word of advice; making obvious overtures to the master or a son of the house is going to be your fastest way to fail to keep a position. Otherwise I wish you, as I wish Palmer and Emerson, the best of luck in finding good new situations."

The three who were to leave murmured thanks and took their written characters with becoming humility; though Juliet concealed impudent anger.

Jane lingered long enough outside the door when she left to hear Fowler say

"Told you so, you scheming hussy!"

She had to consider the implication of something else Fowler had said; that Mr. Armitage might be, in his idiom, sweet on her. Well, Fowler had been incorrect in his summation that she had known about Juliet flirting with Frank; so it was entirely likely that he should be incorrect in this also.

It was a little unfortunate that her reiteration of her own supposed omniscience also boosted Fowler's reputation as an oracle; but something that she, and Mr. Armitage, would have to live with.

Jane was sitting in the Parlour trying to read – she felt very unsettled – when a carriage pulled up outside. She glanced out and gasped.

Why it looked like Mr. George Knightley's carriage – had Emma come after all? It was most injudicious of her if she had, for Emma was surely at an uncomfortable stage of being in an interesting condition!

Jane looked out of the window shamelessly filled with curiosity.

Yes, it was James, the Hartfield coachman driving; and Mr. Knightley who alighted first, turning to hand someone else out... not Emma, but *dear* Aunt Hetty!

Jane felt quite overwhelmed; of all the people in the world who could help her to feel better, it was Aunt Hetty, that mainstay of her childhood, a loving constant in an inconstant world. Jane ran downstairs to go to the door for herself, etiquette and proper behaviour forgotten in her joy to open the door and, as Miss Bates opened her mouth in surprise at the door opening before she had rung the bell, drew her in to embrace her warmly. Fowler had heard the door open and came up looking faintly disapproving.

"Oh Fowler, such a wonderful surprise; this is Miss Bates who has stood in the place of a mother to me, my dear Aunt Hetty!" she said "Please bring in her baggage, and any of Mr. Knightley's who has driven her here and have Palmer show James to the mews; Miss Bates must have the red room. Oh I suppose that should go to Mr. Knightley...."

"I wasn't planning on staying overnight," said Mr. Knightley, following Miss Bates in. "But I thought perhaps to render you assistance in any business matters you need a man's hand for. I will not stay away from Emma or Mr. Woodhouse more than a day however."

"No of course not; how *kind* you are!" cried Jane. "Oh but what of grandmother?"

"Oh my dear Jane! How peaked you look!" said Miss Bates "But indeed, Mr. Knightley is all kindness; he and dear Emma, Mrs. Knightley I should say, arranged it all between them when you wrote to Emma; you are a kind girl not to want to worry *me* but I must scold you for it nonetheless, my dear Jane, for who is to help you bear problems but your own family? But I was telling you, Emma had a wonderful idea that mother should stay with them at Hartfield, is that not *generous* of her? Such a gracious house, a *pleasure* and an *honour* for my mother to spend time under its roof; and Mr.

Knightley has volunteered his services to bring me to you in your *hour* of *need* my *dear* Jane, and to be a *support* to you!"

"Oh Aunt Hetty, nobody could be a better support than you!" cried Jane, embracing her aunt again and drawing her into the parlour. "We shall drink tea; you must be cold!"

"Oh not in the least; for though it was a long journey Mr. Knightley made sure I had a hot brick at my feet and wrapped me well with rugs; it may be a drear February outside but I assure you the coach was *quite cosy* – why thank you," said Miss Bates, throwing a grateful look at Mr. Knightley as she took off her wrap and her old hair-brown pelisse to hand to Fowler with her thanks. Unlike Jane Miss Bates had mourning clothes laid away, and if the style of her black worsted gown was some ten years out of date it was at least refurbished since she had first made it up for her sister, Jane's mother, more than a decade before that. There was no sense after all in wasting a good wool gown.

"And if I may, Mrs. Churchill, I should like to ask if there is any commission I might carry out for you," said Mr. Knightley, passing his beaver and greatcoat to Fowler with a nod of thanks.

"Oh Mr. Knightley! If you would, I should like to see the horse sold; and if Palmer might go with you, it may be that a situation for him might be found with its new owner," said Jane "Mr. Armitage was going to see to finding someone who knew horseflesh but he has his duty……," she flushed at the raised eyebrow "It is nothing improper, Mr. Knightley; Mr. Armitage is a Bow Street Runner; he is investigating Frank's murder and is staying here in case the villains who killed him should also stage an attack upon my person for there is reason to suppose that they might. But he has too to follow up clues. Oh dear; and there is someone else staying here, who is sleeping late; and though it reflects badly on Frank, *dear* Aunt Hetty I beg that you not judge *her* too harshly for she did not know that Frank was married when he took her under his protection…,"

"Jane, am I to suppose," said Mr. Knightley in some shock, "that you are entertaining Frank's *ladybird*?"

Jane flushed.

"She is scarce more than a child and she too was in danger," she said. "Oh I cannot tell you in a hurry what Frank was involved in; but it has put anyone associated with him in danger. And I cannot leave that poor helpless girl to fend for herself; she has had to do so more than enough."

"Your generous nature as always does you credit," said Mr. Knightley "And I hope you will not regret it. Perhaps I may speak to this young person later and make my own judgement."

"You can speak to me now, Mister swell cove," said Dolly coming in the door. "And you ain't got no call to be so top-lofty; Missus Churchill is right down nice and I won't stand to hear you call her down fer bein' good ter me."

"Oh you poor child," cried Miss Bates; for dressed in a simple muslin round gown with her hair loose and no makeup on her face – Ella had refused to pack any – Dolly looked very young and the wound on her face livid and painful looking added to her air of vulnerability.

Mr. Knightley gave her a smile.

"Why your loyalty to Jane – Mrs. Churchill – is a credit to you; though I should like to know more about you."

"Awright; though I told Mrs. Churchill my story," said Dolly. She told it again; baldly as before with no embellishment and Mr. Knightley nodded, believing that straightforward tale, compassion in his face.

"An unfortunate tale," he said, "but I am sure that Mrs. Churchill will look after you well. I shall go now to Tattersall's to see about selling your horse, Jane; do not set luncheon for me, I shall eat out. There are some excellent ordinaries about the town where I may get a good meal. I hope to be back for dinner and then I shall set off. Is there anything more I may do?"

"If you would drop in to Chorleigh, Wright and Jekyll and ask them how the matter progresses over my continued income I should be grateful," said Jane "Having a gentleman to conduct business does tend to mean it is actually conducted."

"I shall be glad to do so," said Mr. Knightley. Jane did not exaggerate in suggesting that letting the solicitors know that a gentleman took an interest in her affairs would be likely to make them take her business more seriously than if they thought her a lone woman to be palmed off with excuse and roundaboutation. He would also drop a word in his brother's ear; Mr. John Knightley being in the legal profession himself and more than capable of holding his own with any lawyer.

Chapter 11

Caleb Armitage arrived just as Jane had finished giving Miss Bates a somewhat edited version of what had been happening; she loved her Aunt Hetty dearly, but the garrulous woman might be expected to spread everything she knew to anyone she took a liking to, not to mention all around Highbury on her return home. Jane had her pride. That Frank had a mistress was an unavoidable thing to mention; Dolly was, after all, ridiculously ingenuous for a girl in an Unfortunate Profession and would cheerfully tell Miss Bates everything about her relationship with Frank; but as Dolly was herself rather hazy about what Frank had been involved with, Jane might readily tell Miss Bates that he had been foolish and had become mixed up with some jewel thieves who were threatening him into doing some illegal work for them and they had killed him for not doing all that they wanted; and that Mr. Armitage was trying to find out who 'they' were.

If indeed, she thought there was more than the one man who had been harming Dolly. Though Dolly had said he had spoken of a boss, reflected Jane, trying to recall all that the girl had sobbed out, saying that the boss wanted to know where the necklace was.

Jane rose when Fowler announced Mr. Armitage and held out a hand to him; which he clasped with polite minimum lightness.

"Fowler, will you bring tea for Mr. Armitage and myself in the book room? We shall repair there to discuss his findings," she said "Mr. Armitage, permit me to make you known to my Aunt; Aunt Hetty, this is Mr. Armitage. Mr. Armitage, Miss Bates, who brought me up."

"Enchanted," said Caleb taking Miss Bates' hand in a greeting clasp "And if it is not bold, may I say Miss Bates, that Mrs. Churchill is a credit to your rearing; the finest lady I have ever met and I have met a few swell morts – I mean fine ladies – in my time."

"Oh Mr. Armitage! She is the *finest* lady in the world; and so clever and accomplished!" declared Miss Bates, perceiving only recognition of her darling and failing to see any compliment to herself, being a modest woman.

"Oh Aunt Hetty!" said Jane, flushing. "Mr. Armitage you are an outrageous flatterer but I am most pleased that your flattery extends to my Aunt who is worthy of the greatest praise; to bring up her dead sister's child without thought for herself is something for which I am eternally grateful! But I hear Fowler with the tea tray, for you have been looked for; let us retire to the book room."

Caleb followed her and waited for Fowler to pour boiling water on the tea. When the footman had left he said quietly,

"It wasn't flattery you know, Mrs. Churchill; I have met many ladies of higher birth and lower gentility than yourself both serving my gentleman in the army *and* since I have been sent to deal with the gentry out of Bow Street – account of my superior accent," he added with a rueful smile. "Many have been rude to me for my subordinate position; you, like a true lady, are as polite to low as to high."

Jane flushed at his look of admiration.

Could Fowler have been right? Well right or wrong, the best course was to behave in the same way; as any lady should.

"Mr. Armitage, I cannot see that I have any reason to be anything but civil to you; even if you fell into the mistake of believing me responsible for my husband's death, I should consider it ill bred to curse you for a natural error. When you do your best to aid me, how can I be anything but pleased and filled with gratitude that there is an organisation to undertake this unpleasant but necessary work? And to be grateful too to you."

"There is no need to be grateful," said Caleb, "for it is my work; my duty and, when there is so fine a person as yourself distressed by lawlessness, my pleasure to do all I may."

"Then I shall feel no personal gratitude but merely pleasure that you are here to aid me," said Jane. "And on that score, you may be relieved of having to deal with finding a purchaser for my husband's mount; for Mr. Knightley, a long time friend of my dear aunt and grandmother, has driven my Aunt Hetty and has undertaken to dispose of the beast and too to make representation to Mr. Chorleigh concerning my income."

Caleb felt and looked a little chagrined; whilst his common sense acknowledged that this was probably for the best.

"This is why I am most sincerely sorry that I am not a gentleman to help you," he said. "Though Fowler has told me the secret of an upper crust accent!"

"Fowler has the most upper crust accent of anyone I know," said Jane and gave something akin to a giggle, " and I have often wondered if he was the side issue of some aristocrat."

"No, he can slip to the tones of Southwark if much moved; he recommends that I practice speaking with a rounded pebble in my mouth. It occurred to me that a glass marble or one of true marble stone such as small boys play with might do just as well, one of the big ones. Fowler is living proof that it works very well."

"A fascinating insight into him!" admired Jane "Are you going to do so?"

"Yes ma'am, I am; it can be useful being able to pass as a gentleman. And perhaps your good offices will advise me in matters of dress; for I have some savings. And moreover though I am not permitted to take a reward from private persons – such as this reward that has been set up by those who have been robbed of jewellery – we are paid a reward for successful convictions of any we apprehend, and to have more versatility means I would then have a greater ability to support that appearance as a gentleman for I should take more thieves."

"It seems to me, Mr. Armitage," said Jane, "that you have overcome the greatest hurdle of seeming – indeed becoming – a gentleman in your delicacy of feelings and politeness and chivalry which cannot be readily simulated. Though I fear, alas, you are correct in assuming that most will interpret speech and appearance before even considering your manner. I hope you may succeed; but please be aware that I consider you a gentleman in all those things that are important. And be assured I will advise you to the best of my ability; though perhaps again the indispensable Fowler might also be knowledgeable on gentlemen's attire."

Caleb flushed feeling suddenly bashful.

"You are very kind," he muttered. "Here, let me tell you what I have found out," he went on hastily. "I have obtained as full a list as I may of all Dutchmen living in London; it may be incomplete. I have discarded all those who are employed as artisans in trades other than jewellery businesses; and labourers too. I cannot see that Mr. Churchill would refer to anyone as a 'friend' who could not at least go to those places where he could rub shoulders with gentlemen and support the apparent position AS a gentleman. There are places where any might meet – milling kens, that's houses where fights are arranged – and at fights, at cock fights, at the races, at dog fights and the like. And our job to break up pretty much everything but the races for being illegal. But still…the way you described it I think the Dutchman we are looking for is at least wealthy appearing."

"I do agree; my recollection of the way Frank spoke of him is of a man he would consider within his social sphere," said Jane. "With a little contempt for a foreigner. Frank would have spoken more disparagingly – and with a bitter overtone – had he been beholden to one he considered a definite inferior. He made a joke about him not being a tulip of fashion – that is, it would not be someone of really acceptable social standing according to the Ton; but he said nothing more disparaging than that – one infers a wealthy tradesman with whom Frank would be prepared to take a meal, or to greet in the street."

Caleb nodded.

"Thank you for confirming my view; you know Mr. Churchill and his reactions as of course I do not. I have narrowed down the list to three master jewellers, two journeyman jewellers – who might be involved though I doubt either might be the one Mr. Churchill spoke to - a gentleman, and an importer of Dutch bulbs. I have included the last because he has much traffic with the continent; and that means that the passing of jewels back and forth might be possible, perhaps hidden in packets of bulbs. It is perhaps fanciful but I did not wish to ignore the idea."

"Far better that you should consider every possibility," said Jane. "What of their initials?"

"None directly agree," said Caleb "So I thought it best to include all; and it is a very rounded and flourishing signature of initials; and I felt I had to consider I had read the initials wrongly – or indeed that the Dutchman *loaned* your husband the money to buy back his own vowels from whoever actually held them, rather than having bought them out for himself. Moreover the Dutch in England often make small changes to the names they use in business whilst signing themselves by their true names; anglicising the spelling, leaving out a 'de' or 'van'. Here is the list."

He passed it to her.

"And the name of the importer of bulbs, being Piet-Dirk Vandervalk is interesting in light of his initials being PDV," said Jane.

"Yes; though I have wondered if the P might be a D or an R; which is why I left on those two lesser artisans, Ruud de Witte – a V might be a very close W – and Dennis Voeteli who might be de Voeteli; or have two Christian names and use only one save in signature," said Caleb.

"The second letter is surely a D; if the first were, we should not mistake it for that, having another D to compare it to. An R I grant you though," said Jane. "And these other, Master jewellers; Poul, also called Paul Vries, Pim Van Diemen – yes, the order of the initials we might have misread in the florid monogram of initials – and Joost De Bruin. He is there just because he is a Master Jeweller and Dutch?"

"Yes," said Caleb "Because of the tentative theory about Mr. Churchill having a loan from his mysterious friend."

She nodded.

"And the gentleman, Maarten Van R-I-J-N – *how* do you

pronounce that?"

"As I understand it you say it 'Ryan'," said Caleb "These Dutchmen seem to use their J as an I or a Y. Rum language but there you are; not so heathen to hear spoke as what French is."

"Ah, but I have learned French and so do not find it so strange," said Jane "I find these names quite odd to look at. What are Dutchmen doing in London?"

"As I understand it many of them – or their parents – fled as émigrés when France occupied their homeland in 1796 I think it was; and any who might be reasonably supposed to be accused of being aristos by those murdering Frenchies did the sensible thing and got out."

"I suppose that would be the sensible thing to do," said Jane "I fear I am somewhat ignorant of foreign affairs; I am well acquainted with Geography and globe work, for such things I should have been required to teach as a governess. But a girl is not of course trained in the understanding of politics."

"I think, Mrs. Churchill, you have a superior understanding of so many things that a small deficiency is easily overlooked – though I fancy most men of your own class would consider it an advantage not to have a woman who understood politics and foreign affairs, for then she does not know enough to find that most statesmen are but risible creatures," said Caleb.

"Why Mr. Armitage! What an interesting reason that men should prefer to keep women in ignorance! Are they so afraid that we might spoil their games of political intrigue by applying the common sense of a good housewife?"

"Why, yes ma'am, I fear you have the sad truth of it," laughed Caleb "Though I wish the common sense of the good housewife might find some way we might now reasonably proceed."

"The best thing seems to me to be to get a look at all of these jewellers," Jane said.

"Easier said than done; if I question an innocent man, then I shall be in trouble," said Caleb.

"Why Mr. Armitage; we shall employ subterfuge," said Jane gaily. "After all, shall I not require mourning jewellery for the next year?"

"Mrs. Churchill, you really are an amazing woman!" said Caleb fervently.

Chapter 12

Jane was glad to introduce Caleb Armitage to George Knightley; she thought that there was much about each that was alike, an instinct for mannerly behaviour and an objectivity that transcended social prejudices of all kinds that led to a degree of tolerance that was quite remarkable. Mr. Knightley had been so kind, for not only had he managed to find a buyer for the horse, and at a fair price, and found Palmer a position, he had also arranged the selling of the spare fodder through an arrangement he had made with Mr. Chorleigh who was to arrange to rent the mews to someone in the neighbourhood who might be looking for extra stabling.

"I have also had Mr. Chorleigh organise the funeral arrangements for Saturday; he will take care of the expense too. In light of the unfortunate and violent way that Frank met his death he has agreed with me that a simple funeral should take place without the body returning to the house but picked up from Bow Street by the undertakers. The least you have to do the better; the mourners must return to your house of course but a simple light repast will be all that is called for; many just serve wine and biscuits," said Mr. Knightley.

"You are very good," said Jane. "I should not have known how to begin to organise a funeral in London! And I cannot think that a body already immersed in water should travel to Enscombe the way Mrs. Churchill's body was transported; the putrefaction would be untenable even at this time of year and in such inclement weather. Indeed it is not impossible to fear late snow; and it would be unreasonable to expect any carrier to be snowed up with a body of some considerable odour."

"Quite so," said Mr. Knightley. "As Mr. Churchill is aware of his nephew's death, if he set off the moment he heard he may be in time for the funeral if he travels post; but to be quite honest, Jane, I should say that a rapid interment is more important than his feelings. I expect that Mr. and Mrs. Weston will wish to travel up to London; but Mrs. Weston will not wish to be away from her daughter too long and will doubtless wish to return the same day. You will be put to no trouble putting the Westons up."

"It would be no trouble; they have been all that is good to me," said Jane, "but I would not wish to leave Frances overnight so I quite enter into dear Mrs. Weston's feelings. Thank you for all that you have done!"

Jane hardly had to make conversation at dinner, because Mr. Knightley drew Mr. Armitage out to talk about his work; though Mr. Armitage glossed over a few aspects that he said were not fit subjects while people were eating – what a delicacy of feeling and nice appreciation of the feelings of others he had! thought Jane warmly.

Even Miss Bates was more interested in listening than talking; Mr. Armitage had a fund of stories, most wittily told and generally very funny about law enforcement; though Jane could see, as Miss Bates did not, that there were a few where he missed points out that were likely rather more dark than funny. Mr. Knightley nodded approval as he lightly skipped over the deeds performed by a highwayman to tell how he had been discovered not by betrayal or clever work but by sheer bad luck on his part, and good luck on the part of the officer of the law who took him up, in that a hole in the highwayman's greatcoat pocket led to a few small trinkets leading a glittering trail to his hideout; and when he demanded to know who had given him up was told by the laconic runner, 'your tailor'.

Jane laughed out loud at that.

"Oh my dear, what will the servants think that you laugh and poor Frank scarcely cold?" asked Miss Bates, who had herself laughed.

"The servants know well enough that our marriage was almost a sham," said Jane. "Mr. Armitage will tell you himself there are no secrets in a house with servants."

"Indeed," said Caleb, "I actually came upon one household where the chamber maid was selling copies of the poems her mistress' paramour sent, to all the young men in the locale to send to *their* inamoratas. The matter came to light – and this is where we came in – that one young man was too innocent to read the rather....explicit .....allegories and was shot by his beloved's brother. He did recover; but he felt injured enough to lay a suit against the brother for assault. I was involved in that case and I had to mark it unresolved – in law that is; because I managed to bring all parties to negotiate and showed how the young lover was too callow to know what he was plagiarising so happily. They sent me a piece of the wedding cake which I thought very civil," he added.

"And so I should hope!" said Jane. "For you missed out on the reward for an arrest to sort out their lives for them; and reconcile all parties rather than pursue the vigour of the law! I am very impressed that you are permitted leeway to pursue justice rather than the law!"

"Oh strictly we are not," said Caleb, "but I, er, failed to find any evidence. And as the wounded youth withdrew his plaint, there was no more to be said. Silly cub!"

"Did you also warn the chamber maid?" asked Mr. Knightley.

"Oh yes," said Caleb. "*she* had no idea of the classical references either so I rang a peal over her head about how strictly speaking the selling of such material made her in law a fallen woman and suggested that if she did not know enough to recognise the contents she should not be continuing to sell it."

"I wager that chastened her," said Mr. Knightley who had a shrewd idea that Caleb would have put the matter more bluntly to the foolish maidservant. "You have acquired a classical education?"

"A rather indifferent one, sir; I had some instruction from my gentleman during the times that the war was tedious, which was, as you might say, better than when it was altogether too exciting; and I have pursued other reading since. I have small Latin only but I have read translations of the myths and legends of Greece and Rome, and a rum lot some of them were and that's definitely not a fit subject in front of ladies," he added.

"There are a few rather, er, warm stories in the classics," agreed Mr. Knightley.

"I appear to have missed the more interesting parts then," said Jane mildly.

"You don't want to read any nasty stories about heathen gods, dear Jane," said Miss Bates. "I cannot think that it is in any wise seemly; and it would fret your delicate constitution too to study too much you know! Why when you were a little girl I always worried to see your nose always in a book, and such a poor pale little thing you were! You should know, Mr. Armitage, she took every cold going, poor little thing, and had to be lying down inside too much, without wanting to stay in to read when she was well! And she is looking quite ill over this business of Frank; we must go for a walk tomorrow in a park my dear!"

"I must go shopping for black fabric, Aunt Hetty," said Jane "And black jewellery; perhaps Mr. Armitage would loan us his protection and presence?"

"I should be delighted," said Caleb.

Mr. Knightley shot him a look; and Caleb closed one eye in a slow wink and gave half a nod towards Jane. Mr. Knightley nodded almost imperceptibly. This was Jane's play; and within Mr. Armitage's duty, he interpreted.

He did not like the idea of Jane being mixed up in the enquiries over her husband's death; but Jane had always been quietly, secretively stubborn and headstrong. And perhaps it would help her to *be* involved; for though Jane might manage to sit, like patience on a monument, if one might borrow from Shakespeare, he knew it irked her.

"Will you play for us before I leave, Jane?" he asked "We have missed your playing in Highbury."

"Cuh, Missus Churchill, do you play real music?" asked Dolly, who had listened wide eyed to Caleb's anecdotes without any interruption.

Jane smiled.

"I love to play," she said, "though I have not touched the pianoforte for a long while; I have not had the heart before."

She reflected that another of her little rebellions had been to refuse to play anything but 'Greensleeves' for Frank when he told her curtly to play for him; a song about betrayal of love.

She sat down at the grand piano, an extravagance at quite thirty five guineas and bought to assuage Frank's pride that would not permit an upright in the parlour where those who saw it might think he was cheap.

Lovingly she touched the keys; and then she was lost in Mozart's 'Eine Kleine Nachtmusic' and then Beethoven's 'Fur Elise' and Bach's 'Toccata and Fugue in D minor'; the music she had loved before Frank's courtship had drawn her to play lighter, more frivolous pieces. The music transported her and she quite forgot the company and the reason that they were there.

"Delightful," said Mr. Knightley sincerely as she paused to collect herself, "but it has tired you; I apologise for asking."

"No Mr. Knightley; it was time I rediscovered music," said Jane, "thank you for urging me to make the effort."

"You are just so ... brilliant!" sighed Dolly who had been about to add a qualification until Caleb glared at her.

"That was sublime," said Caleb soberly. He had never heard anything like it; he was not someone who generally would have considered attending concerts even if he was likely to be welcome at the more prestigious ones; the nearest he had come was hearing a band play in Vauxhall gardens, which might be good, bad or indifferent. It was the feeling in Mrs. Churchill's playing that set this aside; as though she had set all her soul into this. As, he reflected, she probably had; and he wished that Frank Churchill were not dead that he might have the pleasure of knocking down one who had trammelled and almost extinguished the spark of this lovely and talented lady.

Miss Bates was busy telling him how talented Jane was, and how she loved to play, between adjuring Jane to go early to bed for Mr. Knightley would not mind for she was done to a cow's thumb.

And Jane meekly said good night and took herself off, Dolly slipping an arm into hers and talking nineteen to the dozen about how wonderful Mrs. Churchill was in so many ways and begging the privilege of helping her to bed.

"I beg you, Miss Bates," said Caleb, "draw that little ninny away and let poor Mrs. Churchill rest; can you perhaps find her some small task for you that you might say you would have asked your niece to aid you with – untangling embroidery silks say, tangled by the journey? I cannot but feel that she will fatigue Mrs. Churchill who is too sweet natured to repulse her."

"Oh! How *wise* you are, Mr. Armitage!" declared Miss Bates. "Yes, the poor silly child wishes to be helpful but does not understand how she is tiring poor Jane; I shall go immediately!" she leaped to her feet with alacrity to follow the two younger women.

"Will her determination to help you place Jane in danger?" asked Mr. Knightley straight out, once the gentlemen were alone together.

"She is already in danger – as is that girl Dolly – while these murdering villains are uncaught and while they do not have the necklace that Frank Churchill stole from them," said Caleb, "that I fancy they may suspect Dolly has still, hidden from Mrs. Churchill. Which is why I am here. Being involved keeps her from worrying as much; and she is a shrewd and clever lady who has helped me a great deal. I do anticipate an attack upon her; and I am on my guard, Mr. Knightley, and Fowler too is carrying arms at night. I will guard her with my life."

Mr. Knightley nodded.

"Then I shall commend her and her household into your hands, Mr. Armitage. May I say that you should proceed in other matters slowly and with great patience. Jane has a lack of openness to her character that I hold to be her only flaw; but as you enjoy word plays, may I say too that a degree of Franklessness may lead to an increase in frankness. However I can see that she considers you a friend; and whatever else happens I shall hope that you continue to be so."

"Gawd you ain't half a peevy cove," said Caleb shocked

into blushing.

Mr. Knightley chuckled.

"You know too much cant for me to do more than guess at your meaning; but if I surmise that you mean I can see further than my nose, well I cut my eye teeth long since! I have stood in the same shoes as you with as much hope and as little expectation; so I wish you well. An honest man with the compassion to have that poor little hussy diverted rather than dash what was meant as a kindly gesture on her part tells me more about you than anything else. I bid you good evening; I shall try to get over to town again in a couple of weeks, but all depends on when my anticipated heir decides to make his or her appearance."

"Oh don't you worry about leaving your lady," said Caleb. "I'll take care of Mrs. Churchill as tender as any."

"Yes Mr. Armitage; that you will," said Mr. Knightley.

Chapter 13

Jane awoke refreshed next morning until she arose; when waves of nausea swept her.

She swallowed hard as a temporary measure and leaned over to pull the utensil from under the bed hurriedly so that the heaving of her stomach could empty itself safely. She rinsed out her mouth with the glass of water she customarily kept by the bed, since she was a poor sleeper much of the time.

She rang for Ella.

"Mrs. Jane, my dear, what is it? I hoped to see you better this morning with a good sleep; but you look that queer!" said Ella.

"Ella I pray you, empty that," Jane gestured to the utensil, preferring not to look at its contents, "and bring me a piece of dry toast and some weak tea."

"Of course I will, Mrs. Jane my love!" said Ella, not usually given to endearments. "Are you ill or is it…."

"I have not had my flux that is usually so monotonously regular," said Jane. "I would not have wondered seriously though for another day or two; but this seems fairly conclusive. Perhaps you will arrange to have me brought weak tea and dry toast daily ere I rise."

"That girl Dolly might as well make herself useful in organising that," said Ella.

"Unless she turns out to be in the same interesting condition," said Jane dryly.

"Well until or unless she is, she may as well do what she can," said Ella firmly. "Lie in bed all morning she shall not; for if she is to have the training of how to be a dressmaker she may as well begin with care of clothing and she shall help me make up your blacks my dear Mrs. Jane and I shall help her to make up her own mourning if you've a mind to buy the fabric for her."

"I did plan to; it is an excellent idea, Ella; most clever of you that she shall have some gain from her early lessons. But please, just take that away."

"Of course; I am sorry," said Ella whisking off with the offending article. The tween maid Polly returned it in a few minutes with a curtsey and Ella herself followed bearing a cup of weak tea and dry toast cut into fingers to dip in it. Jane grimaced; she disliked this valetudinarian breakfast but she acknowledged that it settled the queasiness very well.

And then she might rise and even partake of a little proper breakfast with Aunt Hetty and Dolly and Mr. Armitage before sallying out to purchase both fabric and jewellery.

"Are you too fatigued from yesterday to go out, Mrs. Churchill?" asked Mr. Armitage sharply.

"Oh, not really," said Jane "You may as well know; I shall have to inform Mr. Jasper Churchill through Mr. Chorleigh; it would appear that there will be a posthumous child as a sibling to Frances."

"I am hardly sure whether congratulations or commiserations are in order," said Caleb dryly. She gave him a thin smile.

"I fear that at the moment I could not engage to answer accurately as to that myself," she said. "My feelings are somewhat mixed; though I try to remind myself that a sibling for Frances would be pleasant for her. The awkwardness however of bearing a posthumous child does weigh somewhat on my mind however."

"And the fact that there will be those who will spread unpleasant gossip," said Caleb. "You should tell your aunt; for I believe that the news that you are definitely with child so soon after your husband's death precludes the possibility of any whisper that the happy event was concluded after he was, as you might say, out of the way."

Jane flushed.

"Bluntly put, Mr. Armitage; but your words are wise. I shall do as you suggest. Aunt Hetty will write to grandmother who will require the letter to be read by Emma and as she – grandmamma – is deaf, half of Highbury will know by the day after tomorrow," she grimaced slightly, "and Augusta Elton will be making spiteful comments that I should get with child again so quickly like some brood mare," she added. "But at least I shall not have to listen to her snide comments dressed up as caring concern."

"She sounds a singularly unpleasant female," said Caleb.

"She is," said Jane. "She is also a vulgarian; and her family money was made in the slave trade which I despise; why we do not, in my Grandmother's household, even drink coffee, because it comes from the labour of slaves; and we use only maple sugar not plantation sugar, or German root sugar when it is to be had."

"I had wondered that you never served coffee," said Caleb, "but now I see; it had not occurred to me that it was produced by slaves."

"I who expected a slavery of the spirit as a governess am alive to the more awful truth of enslavement of the body as well," said Jane. "And in answer to the question of whether I am fit to go out, I am as fit as I shall be until this matutinal nausea passes; and that may be several months. I will not faint to cause you embarrassment."

"It would distress me, Mrs. Churchill; but would never embarrass," said Caleb. "Though I should be relieved if you did not wear your stays too tight if you pardon my mentioning such."

Jane blushed.

"Thank you for practical advice, Mr. Armitage," she said "I shall take it."

Shopping was always an exciting experience, at least for Jane, who so rarely had managed to shop for much more than remnants. Frank had required her to be well dressed, which was another budgetary difficulty and had required much juggling and retrimming; but she was armed with an advance from Mr. Chorleigh that Mr. Knightley had induced the solicitor to give her in order to purchase suitable mourning wear. To be known as too nipcheese to provide blacks for a widow would not be a good advertisement for Mr. Chorleigh; and as Mr. Knightley's brother was a senior and well thought of clerk of court Mr. Chorleigh knew fine well that the more fashionable barristers might be persuaded to pass him over when taking briefs which would not be disastrous but would be a dent in his firm's income and also sufficiently embarrassing that he might even lose other custom too.

Thus Jane sallied forth with a lump sum far more than she believed necessary; but that was all to the good, for she might then save enough to actually purchase, if it became necessary, the odd piece of mourning jewellery to convince the jewellers that she was truly interested.

Oxford Street was the street for drapers' shops; and Jane intended avoiding fashionable places such as Layton and Shears in Leicester Square, or any of the shops in Bond Street for the less modish shops where one might actually get service from one of the men who served in the shop rather than having to deal with a crush. In Oxford Street too there were haberdashers and glovers, fringe and trimming sellers and plumassiers; so that she might purchase all the trimmings and feathers necessary for hats and gowns all at once.

Dolly was in transports of delight.

"You must remember to be temperate in your expressions of joy," said Jane. "And I believe too we should call you Dorothy, since that is what Dolly derives from; it has more dignity. Dolly is too juvenile a name."

"Me ma allus called me Doroffee," said Dolly wistfully "She said it's what she named me and what she intended me to be called. Lawks, I'd almost forgot!"

"Then we shall respect your mother's wishes," said Jane, thankful that her suggestion had met with so positive a reaction. Dolly was a good name for a baby, a.... well a female of Dolly's profession; or a sheep.

Mr. Knightley had a sheep called Dolly, a prize beast which produced healthy twin lambs year after year and had a tendency to wander and get into trouble. Perhaps there was something in a name.

It was not so cold as it had been the year before, the year without a summer; but Jane was glad that they might purchase heavy fabrics for mourning. Bombazine was always serviceable – and might too be given to an upper servant to wear out once out of mourning – and kerseymere would be warm. Black crepe was de rigeur and might too be an over-gown on a plain white muslin for its fineness which would do on hot days. Five and three quarter yards per dress length would be almost thirty shillings for the bombazine, but less for the other fabrics; really by making up the dresses herself there was so much saving over a modiste; indeed if she and Ella cut the gowns out, then Ella could take the pieces to a girl she employed for a modest sum whose sewing was fine enough so long as she did not have to design or finish a garment. Ella and Jane had made with her help on plain seaming and hemming many a garment that it pleased Frank to believe had come from a modiste on Bruton Street.

How he might imagine she could, on the allowance he gave her, pay in guineas what the gowns she wore had cost in shillings had never ceased to amaze Jane; Frank was so unobservant. And really too so utterly ignorant about money.

But Frank was not here to spoil her enjoyment of the fine fabrics; and she might dress as she pleased not worry about the latest kick of fashion whether it suited her or not that Frank always insisted his wife should wear.

Aunt Hetty too was greatly enjoying herself, for Jane insisted she should have a new gown too; Aunt Hetty already wore sober cotton prints most of the time, or plain drab; but a pretty length of lavender crape and a deeper shade of kerseymere to put with it was something Jane was determined she would purchase to add to the plain worsted gown; and would make a pretty half mourning gown so that Aunt Hetty might proclaim some familial association but not so much as wearing black, and then she might be stylish too. Aunt Hetty had taught Jane to sew and to keep house and to make a shilling go further; and she deserved pretty things. And lavender might be acceptable as half mourning but it was also a pretty colour to wear at other times too if worn with white gloves not grey. And with kerseymere at quite seven shillings a yard it would be a sinful waste not to use it again after Frank's funeral when Miss Bates would no longer really need mourning.

The cost of bombazine – a dress length was ten guineas –

could not be helped; and Jane would be in mourning long enough to make it worth it.

Gloves they needed too; grey for Aunt Hetty – who had really had no need to go into full mourning at all – and black for her and for Dorothy, in which fashion she must get into the habit of thinking of the girl; and black gloves too for all the servants to attend church in, and an extra pair for Fowler to answer the door. And Frances should wear only half mourning too; black for a baby was too impractical to readily launder. Some more of the deep lavender kerseymere and otherwise white cotton would be quite sufficient. Black ribbon trims on white lawn was sufficient.

It was not as though Frances actually knew her father to miss him; she had so far had more contact with Mr. Armitage.

Armed with Jane's purchases, Ella and Dorothy were to be sent home in a hack, while Jane, Aunt Hetty and Mr. Armitage went on to seek jewellers. However, there was a delay while Mr. Armitage went in search of a Hackney carriage; and Dorothy was hailed by a girl clinging to the arm of a dissipated looking gentleman. His clothing was that of a gentleman but it sat decidedly awry, and his heavily veined nose spoke of too much fondness for too much liquor. He wore a moustache which may have been intended to give him a military air but somehow gave the impression of having grown with the same haphazard carelessness that he appeared to have put on his clothes.

"'Ere, Dolly, waddya doin' dressed as a swell mort?" demanded the girl, pretty enough in a rather coarse way, her face over-rouged and her lips redder than could be achieved without artifice; her white and coquelicot striped gown was a masterpiece in its way in managing to both display and yet somehow not lose from its tenuous control her aggressive bosoms.

Dolly looked to Jane for guidance.

"Would you call her friend?" asked Jane almost inaudibly, her lips scarcely moving.

"Nah," said Dorothy "Specially not dressed like a ruddy barber's pole!"

"Then I would suggest cutting her," said Jane "And leave this to me."

Jane looked the female up and down.

"Excuse me sir," she said to the girl's escort, "but apparently your … *chere amie* … has poor eyesight. I believe that it is possible to purchase spectacles that might be more suitable adornments for her features than her makeup. I pray you take her away."

"Sorry ma'am," he said, fiddling with his collar in embarrassment.

The man might look dissipated but he was still a gentleman and recognised a lady when he saw – and heard – one. He raised his hat and hustled his companion away, remonstrating with her.

"But I tell yer, strite up guvnor, I reckernised 'er; she landed a live one wot work fer… someone I knows," said the shrill voice of the youthful *hetera*, doubtless of the community who haunted Covent Garden; and who had, reflected Jane who knew some at least Greek legends, more in common with the *Eriynes* than with the Graces.

"Clementina is a buttock and file," said Dorothy. "She steals," she added to translate for Jane's confused expression. "Give uvver girls a bad name, her sort."

"She sounds like the sort of girl you would do well not to know," said Jane. "A friend of course one must be civil to, and be prepared to be pleasant towards."

Dorothy stored that snippet away. Being a lady was not then a case of pretending not to know the people one knew before.

"So you treats people like what they've treated you?" she asked.

Jane considered.

"Anyone who is ladylike will speak in a pleasant tone and be prepared to be polite to all. If they have been unpleasant or rude, there are ways to be rude back politely without raising voice or using unpleasant words. But it is important to remember those who have done kindnesses and repay kindness with kindness. It is a trifle ill-bred to repay unkindness in the same coin; it is more dignified to ignore it. Unless by acting you may stop them hurting others."

Dorothy digested; and as the hack arrived with Mr. Armitage nodded.

"So them wot took me in, I gives 'ouse room to, if they're on their uppers; and them wot laughed at me fer bein' new on the game I mince past wiv me nose in the air and they chew on their own liver," she said.

Jane stiffled a sigh.

"That is more or less the way it works," she said.

It was close enough; and the girl had the instincts to repay kindness with kindness. And the desire to make disparagers chew on their own livers – colourful phrase – was one she knew very well and it generally was associated with Mrs. Augusta Elton.

And she was eager to share with Mr. Armitage that this girl Clementina had said that Dorothy's lover had worked for someone the light fingered Paphian knew.

Caleb listened with interest.

"It ties in very well with the idea of a whole gang of jewel thieves," he said. "From the casual diver – pickpocket – like this Clementina – to ken crackers and jumpers – that is to say, house breakers and those who climb in windows, all bringing their goods to a clever fence who has employed your late husband to sort out provenance as you suggested. Peevy cove that fence. Clever fellow I should say."

"I am starting, I fancy, to make some shrewd guesses as to some of the terms," said Jane. "It may be that by the time you have uncovered the whole of this startling business you may not even need to translate any more."

"I hope we might find out the whole before you become fluent in cant, Mrs. Churchill," said Caleb. "I wonder if it is worth bothering to find this Clementina and see if she will talk? Better perhaps to leave her be – a diver is never high up on the pecking order, she is unlikely to know much and the risk of revealing our hand by arresting her is too great for the possible returns."

"I bow to your superior knowledge, Mr. Armitage," said Jane.

"A matter of experience," said Caleb with a deprecating shrug.

Chapter 14

Pim Van Diemen was a pink, smooth man whose white satin waistcoat was inevitably as shiny as his face; he smiled with as much display of ivory as Jane's pianoforte and had a patronising manner of speaking to a new young widow that irritated Jane from the first.

"Of course your dear husband would want his beautiful young wife decked out as finely as is possible within the strictures of mourning; you must look your best for his memory," he said oleaginously, rubbing his pink, smooth hands together. "Perhaps I may show you our finest black amber? Boy, fetch me out a tray!"

"Yerse Mr. Van Diemen," said an apprentice more in the tones of Bermondsey than those of the Low Countries.

"He means jet Ma'am," said Mr. Armitage dryly as Jane was raising an eyebrow, "sounds better as black amber see."

"I see," said Jane.

"Oh I have an excellent mourning brooch for your dear mother, dear Jane, carved out of bog oak," declared Miss Bates "Such a *pretty* thing in the shape of a rose and with a silver mount that has a lock of her hair plaited around it. But we have not had Mr. Churchill's body returned to us yet, so we have none of his hair."

"Never mind, dear aunt," said Jane, "we shall say goodbye at the funeral tomorrow; I cannot like the sensibility of the habit of keeping locks of hair. It does not suit me. I wish only to look my best for Mr. Churchill always liked me to look my best and wear fine jewels."

"Well the finest jet is certainly elegant and stylish enough for anyone," said Van Diemen as the boy came with the tray of pieces on display on oyster coloured silk that reminded Jane how much she hated oysters even when she was not feeling generally somewhat nauseous. She fought the urge to gag. Van Diemen had not noticed and beamed expansively. "Here you are, some very pretty pieces as might adorn a pretty lady."

"I cannot think though," said Jane "that I have much

business to do with one who is ambiguous in the nature of the jewels that he would display; for so ambiguous a description of jet as black amber might also lead to ambiguities of pricing; so I shall bid you farewell Mr. Diemen."

The Jeweller looked irritated but bowed over her hand as she held it out in farewell.

"I gather his method of gaining custom was not to your liking Mrs. Churchill," said Caleb.

"No," said Jane "It was not. I disliked him intensely; which is no reason to consider him guilty. He made me feel as though any jewellery he had a hand in making would somehow sully me to wear."

"Oh my dear, you are fanciful!" said Miss Bates.

"Quite possibly, Aunt Hetty; but a man who misrepresents one thing will misrepresent another," said Jane. "So I do not discount him, Mr. Armitage."

"He made no reaction to your name or your husband's liking of jewellery; but a canny fellow would not," said Caleb. "You know it occurs to me that we might have someone join the mourners tomorrow to slum the ken – to look over the house – and it is worth while watching out for any who should show an interest where it might not be expected to be shown."

"I will ask Fowler to watch too then," said Jane. "We have hired extra footmen and we are serving a cold collation prepared in advance since those who wish to get back home need more to travel on than biscuits; and we have too confections ordered from Gunter's; so Fowler has only to make sure that the hired footmen do not run off with the silver, which is his current gloomy prediction. I am of the opinion that any who did would not be kept on the books of those ingenious people who arrange such hirelings at short notice."

"Fowler is a pessimist," said Caleb, "and probably wise to be so; there are suggestions that there may be those who hire out in such a manner who do so purely for the slumming of kens for thieves though they may not steal themselves."

"Well that we may look out for," said Jane. "Where do we go next?"

"Mr. Poul or Paul Vries," said Caleb.

Poul or Paul Vries was a man in his forties who looked sleek and successful. He had a workshop full of apprentices and underlings.

He appraised Jane.

"Ah, my dear lady; doubtless you have come for mourning jewellery?" he asked. The guttural tones of Holland were almost completely suppressed.

"I have come to look in any case," said Jane. "What would you recommend?"

"I have some pretty pieces in jet; some call it Black Amber, for it may exhibit some of the same odd properties of lifting hair or small pieces of paper if rubbed as amber may do," said the Jeweller. "Some prefer stained horn or bog oak for economy; I can show you some ready-made pieces or if you prefer to order any pieces, perhaps incorporating a loved one's hair……,"

"That will not be necessary," said Jane, "as my husband, Mr. Frank Churchill, was a man who loved to see me well dressed and he would have wished me to have attractive jewellery to attend his funeral. Show me one or two pieces."

The proprietor waved a hand and an apprentice ran up with a tray. This was lined – practically rather than decoratively – with green baize.

"These are the best pieces Mynheer de Vries," he said.

The Jeweller laid them out reverently before Jane; he obviously loved his craft.

"These are all too heavy," said Jane. "I should prefer simpler pieces."

Another tray was brought. Jane sighed.

"Nothing takes your fancy Ma'am?" asked the jeweller.

"I quite like this brooch carven in the shape of ivy leaves," said Jane, "but I have to say nothing else quite suits. Still, I shall take that."

"Oh that is very pretty, Jane," said Miss Bates "What about that collar though?" she indicated an intricate collar wrought of jet beads, some faceted spheres, some faceted bugles.

"Oh no Aunt Hetty; it is definitely in the Egyptian style," said Jane "That is not at all the thing these days. I may not be concerned about being the *dernier cri* but the mode has been out of date for quite three years; it would be positively deedy to be seen in such an old style."

"I am afraid, Mrs. Churchill, that I do not have the sort of clientele that permits me to make the sort of jewellery that your husband must have liked," said Vries with a snap to his voice "Or that evidently pleases you; but the choice in mourning jewellery will always be limited for the more normal stones like emeralds or diamonds are not acceptable."

"Oh it is not the stones that I am concerned about; merely the style in which they have been set," said Jane sweetly.

She paid for the purchase and they left.

"Joost de Bruin next," she said. "Dear me what a depressing array of carven sensibility that was!"

"You liked him very little more than Pim Van Diemen," said Caleb.

"Perhaps it is merely that they feel that they should put on unctuous airs when dealing with a widow," said Jane, "but I found both false, patronising and annoying. And this one was positively poisonous that I did not wish to be outmoded."

Joost de Bruin, another middle aged man, was richly clad in a coat of superfine with rings on his long bony fingers; but that he did not have the figure for a well cut coat did no credit to the tailor's art. He wore a jewelled fob to presumably be his own proclaimer of fine wares; and his eyes glittered with mean suspicion as he took in Caleb's rougher appearance; and mentally contrasted Miss Bates' simple printed cotton gown with Jane's dyed silk morning gown. He made a sign to an underling who came out ingratiatingly but obviously watching Caleb's hands at all times.

Jane frowned, angered; but Mr. Armitage looked frankly

amused. Since he was a Bow Street Runner, she reflected, he probably had every right to be. But it was not funny.

"I wish to see mourning jewellery," she said "My husband liked me turned out well; for his funeral I need something suitable. He liked jewellery. I do not know if he ever purchased any here – Mr. Frank Churchill was his name."

"I cannot say I have heard it," said de Bruin indifferently. He made another sign to one of his underlings who went to fetch a tray of jewellery; this lay on a soft dove grey cloth, less ostentatious and more tasteful, Jane felt, than oyster coloured satin. "Put it down boy; don't hover!"

"Sorry Mr. Broon," muttered the youth.

"*De Bruin,boy*!" screamed Mr. De Bruin. The boy cringed, muttered an apology and fled thankfully back to his work.

Jane examined jewellery.

"I think this is some of the best I have seen so far," said Jane. He might be suspicious and unpleasant but he also had a light touch. "This necklace will do very well I believe; it is not so heavy as some I have seen. I like the use of silver Indian beads amongst the jet; it is plain and simple and stylish. I shall have it."

The beads were similar to those in the outmoded collar in the previous shop but had been set in a more modern style, definitely lifted by the inclusion of the few silver beads.

They left after she had paid.

"Well he was not unctuous!" laughed Caleb.

"I still did not like him," said Jane. "Will we visit the workshops where the two journeymen work?"

"No; I shall make enquiries," said Caleb, "asking questions about them is less likely to cause problems than questioning master jewellers."

"I cannot think of a way I might seek out the bulb importer," said Jane, "nor yet the gentleman."

"Ah, Mr. Maarten Van Rijn, gent, I have received some information about," said Caleb. "And I believe we might discard him as a suspect; in light of Mr. Churchill's comment that he were *not* a tulip of fashion. Mr. Van Rijn is said to be a very smart gentleman when in town though of ruddy complexion not universally admired; but he is not in town at the moment as he is overseeing the ploughing of his lands. He is married to one Madelaine, daughter of Sir Richard Cribbins who is said to be a most respectable man. I am certainly not about to anger someone who is on friendly terms with judges and other mighty people to ask questions about his son-in-law: who has not been in town for months. He is on my list for maintaining a small town house. I would, by the way, point out of Mr. de Bruin that those who see dishonesty in others may often be less than honest themselves."

"You question Fowler's integrity for his comments about the silver?" asked Jane.

"No; that is merely common pessimism born of a man who has seen too many dishonest servants," said Caleb. "He does not stare with suspicion at all times. That de Bruin was continually darting glances at the leathers attached to the boards at which his underlings worked, that catch the filings of gold, to make sure handfuls did not disappear from them."

"Perhaps that was how he saved enough to set up in business himself then," said Jane. "Dear me! I cannot say I would willingly exonerate any one of them!"

Jane rested for the afternoon while Caleb made further enquiries; she might sit at the dining room table directing Ella piecing her pasteboard pattern pieces onto the new cloths. Her own gowns were to be made full to allow for an expanding figure; and pieces laid aside to place gussets in the bodice should her milk make her heavy. Dorothy was trying hard to help; and Ella only spoke sharply to her once.

"If your mother could see you now, Dorothy, she would surely wonder that she had birthed a monkey not a girl!" said Ella. "Adone do with your fidgeting; stand still on both feet at once and pull this cloth straight and help me fit these hem pieces on without acting like something out of the menagerie at the Tower of London!"

Dorothy muttered an apology.

"Ma said I was born fidgeting," she said. "Pa said I was his quicksilver girl," she sighed. "they'd not want to see me I suppose," she said mournfully.

"You could write," said Jane, "and tell them that you are now overcoming the misfortunes that precipitated you into an unfortunate profession."

"Well, Mrs. Churchill, where's the good in that?" said Dorothy. "They couldn't afford to pay for the postage when it arrived and wouldn't bother for who's to read it?"

"I apologise for making assumptions," said Jane. "As you read and write I thought perhaps your parents would do so too."

"Nah, I was learned out at Sadlers Wells; landlord at the inn wanted his barmaids and barmen literate; we was sent to the parson to be learned our letters," said Dorothy. "That way he could leave messages about what was to be done if he was away in town and we di'n't have no excuse not to do it. Nipcheese old…..man," she amended her vituperation.
"I swear he set me up with that…fellow….who took my reputation; he sent me to the barn where the….fellow…..was waiting anywise; and then said why hadn't I worn armour. Well I ha'n't never even heard of it then, had I?"

"I have to ask Dorothy," said Jane, "you are not talking about metal plates to prevent the passage of musket balls are you?"

"Well that's what I allus fort armour was 'til I was out Covent Garden," said Dorothy "It's a thing you put over a man's – you know – it's made of sheep gut. They're awful expensive but they say they keep out disease as well as stopping unwanted pregnancy. I ain't never had one."

"Well really!" said Ella.

"How enterprising," murmured Jane. "Dear me; one should be glad that some at least may try to avoid the unfortunate diseases that must be a hazard; a shame they are not more readily available at a low price. It would doubtless prevent much misery."

They were interrupted at this point by the emergence of Miss Bates from a post-prandial nap; by mutual consent

Dorothy stayed well away from controversial topics in the hearing of the sweet natured Miss Bates, whom Dorothy thought just about as kind as Mrs. Churchill and one of the best people she had ever met.

Chapter 15

Caleb arrived in time for dinner and went to change into his rather limited evening wear. Jane appreciated that he bothered; for it must have irked him.

"Mr. Armitage I shall not be offended if you do not change," she said to him.

"Mrs. Churchill, it is good to be out of the day's working clothing; I hope you do not mind that I have only pantaloons not smallclothes," he said. "Having lighter shoes on too is a relief I do confess."

"Then I am glad," said Jane, "and I am not concerned in the least that you do not wear breeches and stockings; I must say pantaloons look vastly more comfortable."

"Well ma'am they are," said Caleb. "My everyday buckskins are comfortable enough too; but leather needs care to keep it nice for longer and a bit of treatment over the evening prolongs the life of it no end. And bless the wench, young Molly's taken on the task for me." He grinned "These pantaloons were spoils of war; I acquired them from a Froggie who had obviously prigged them from a Black Brunswicker cavalry officer – they were named for their uniform. Saved our bacon at Waterloo the Brunswickers; good old Blücher! Never had a better pair of netherclothes; when they fall apart reckon it'll be worth my while to pay out to have them copied. But I didn't ought to discuss inexpressibles of any kind with a lady," he said suddenly aghast and blushing.

"Mr. Armitage, I do not take offence," said Jane. "Alas that my education did not include tailoring; for only men may understand how to make men's clothing set properly! Otherwise I should gladly offer to sew a new pair for you. I had always believed that most of the trousers worn by soldiers were baggier and less stylish."

"Ah, that's the boot cut for the cavalryman," said Caleb, "and they looked hem ridiculous on the Frenchie with his skinny legs that were too short for them; all hung in wrinkles. Y'might say it was my sartorial duty to relieve him of them and give him a pair of slops wot looked no worse on him than

98

on any."

Jane laughed.

"Mr. Armitage that is a casuistry," she said. "Ah, a word I have caught *you* out with? It means a sophistry to explain away less than exemplary behaviour."

"Guilty ma'am," said Caleb.

After dinner Jane and Caleb repaired to the book room as had become customary, drinking tea there.

"The two lesser jewellers both work under the eye of well established jewellers who did not think that there was any way their men might be involved in any shady work," said Caleb getting directly to the point, "and I took the chance of talking to the bulb importer. I decided to take the tack that his employees might use the careful packing to send out other things. Well the good news and the bad news is that he unpacks everything himself; but there's nothing he sends across the channel except an agent with a moneybag once a year to purchase in advance those bulbs that promise well; the agent looks them over in the spring when they're in flower, makes an advance order – seem odd to me to pay for stuff you won't get for a while, the other is more often true – and then the bulbs are sent before the winter frosts. Mr. Piet-Dirk Vandervalk has some land to plant them on but mostly he sells on immediately what he has had sent. That comes from a number of bulb growers and not sorted out by any one agent over there. So stuff coming in seems unlikely; and if you arst me, it ain't nowise feasible to send it out once a year. No, he's nothing to do with jewels; they're being reset here like you said, and sent about with new dockiments, docUments I should say."

"Back to the three unpleasant master jewellers then," said Jane.

"Well for various reasons I have my suspicions," said Caleb.

"In light of both the way he spoke and the way in which he was addressed?" asked Jane.

"Quite so," said Caleb. "I fancied he might have been looking for a reaction from you when he spoke; but you might of been unaware of anythink that was going on; I was that proud of you if it is not impudent to say so!"

"Why thank you Mr. Armitage," said Jane "I confess I left most of the noticing to *your* eyes and ears that I might concentrate on playing the part of a foolish woman looking for jewellery and just dropping my name into the conversation. It did not occur to me until we had left the shop that he had actually said anything significant."

"You are very clever, Mrs. Churchill," said Caleb. "You played the part perfectly."

Jane flushed. It had been fun playing a part; she had enjoyed that aspect of concealing her romance with Frank. Looking back the intrigue, the acting had been more of a thrill to the senses than the thought of being in love at all; it had enhanced her rosy image of Frank to enter into a conspiracy with him. But Frank had taken it as read that she would play her part; indeed had seemed to take a cruel delight in trying to make her angry enough to reveal the truth in his sly and cruel asides to Emma and others and in his obvious flirting with Emma. She should have realised then – had she not been besotted! – that he had a cruel streak that liked to humiliate. If she ever re-married she would be careful to choose a man who would be kindly and who spoke to her always as though she were important to him; someone who was always there to help and who noticed if she felt ill, and who cared enough to consider *her* feelings. Someone who was ready to give her praise – not hollow compliments, but true praise when she did anything well.

She suddenly flushed even darker!

It did not do to unfavourably compare Frank to someone who was, after all, only doing his duty. Whatever Fowler might imagine!

There was a knock on the door of the book room and Mrs. Ketch came in, a sulky looking Juliet by the arm.

"Excuse me troubling you, Madam, Mr. Armitage, but I should like to turn this trollop out first thing in the morning if you will give me permission," she said.

"What is the reason, Mrs. Ketch?" asked Jane.

"Well, Madam, you have given permission for the girls to have followers on their day off, which is generous; but loitering and flirting *in the area* is not decent behaviour in a decent household!" said Mrs. Ketch indignantly. Jane winced. Juliet was taking a chance if indeed this was what she had been doing; any of the neighbours might have seen her behaving improperly in the area; deep though the stairs and area that led to the servant's door might be, and narrow such that one might be almost invisible in the crepuscular gloom of incipient nightfall; but one might be heard. The narrow area created echoes very often.

The door to the kitchen and half basement opened under the steps up to the front door off the sunken area railed off from the street; the kitchen and its half windows on one side of the front steps, the chute to the coal cellar on the other side. The narrow sunken area seemed quite secluded when one was in it, but the plain walls of it could act like a sounding board, and it was amazing how much might be heard up in the street from what loose chatter servants might make when taking the air or hanging up dishclouts to dry when the washing lines at the back of the house were full of family washing.

It was not unknown for the servants of adjacent houses to gossip with only slightly raised voices from one area to the next, though generally they would come up the steps at the end to meet and exchange news and views almost on street level, where they could converse more discreetly but be ready to fly down the steps to their proper subterranean regions if there was a danger of being caught by their mistress or worse, the housekeeper or cook.

"Juliet I should like to hear your side if you please," said Jane crisply. She would not be unfair.

Juliet scowled.

"Well Mrs. Churchill, I don't see as you can say nuffink

when you got yore paramour livin' in," she said nodding at Caleb.

Jane, white with anger, mastered herself before slapping the girl quite hard but not as hard as her first inclination had dictated.

"You are both impudent and inaccurate," she said coldly. "Mr. Armitage is not my paramour; and you are obviously a very stupid and unobservant girl not to realise that. You are fortunate not to be turned off with your reference torn up out of hand just for such impudence! I will hear of this follower if you please. I, unlike you, do not make judgements without facts."

Juliet put her hand to her face, scowling; then shrugged.

"Well it didn't mean nuffink," she said sulkily "It weren't no follower anyways; just some bloke what's coming to 'elp out wiv the funeral termorrer wanted ter know wot sort of employer you are, see if 'e wanted to apply for a permanent job an' I put 'im right on that account of you turning some on us off. I didn't let 'im kiss me or nuffink."

"You let him come halfway down the steps and put an arm around your waist and you were giggling enough, my girl, to let anyone know you wanted to be kissed," said Mrs. Ketch.

"Well whaddya expect you old baggage where the Mistress looks at 'im wot ain't her paramour like *she* want to be kissed?" said Juliet "And her pore husband not even buried yet!"

Mrs. Ketch slapped her on the other side, harder than Jane had done.

"Juliet you will apologise to Mrs. Ketch and to me immediately," said Jane icily "Or you will not merely be leaving tomorrow morning but it will be without a reference at all because I will rescind it; and if any ask I will tell them that I prefer not to discuss your morals."

Juliet went white.

Servants were plentiful; a good position was dependant on a good reference.

"I'm sorry Mrs. Ketch; I'm sorry Madam," she said.

"If I hear any lying rumours about me," said Jane, sweetly

"I will take out a classified advertisement in all the papers explaining that you are of a loose nature. Do I make myself quite clear?"

"Yes'm," said Juliet almost inaudibly.

"Good; you are relieved of all duties for the rest of the evening; you will want to pack. I should like you out of my house before breakfast. Fowler will give you your wages to the end of the month," said Jane.

"Thank you Madam," said Mrs. Ketch. "And don't you forget to leave your work clothes my girl; they don't belong to you."

She hustled the girl out.

Jane was shaking.

"First serious servant problem?" asked Caleb.

"I dislike confrontation," said Jane. "Oh *how* I wanted to slap that impudent hussy into the middle of next week! I tried to make it a judicious blow however; it could not be permitted to pass."

"No it could not. I am sorry that my presence here has caused such a nasty little piece to make up tittle-tattle. It must be very humiliating and embarrassing that she should even think of linking your name to mine," said Caleb.

Jane burned scarlet.

"It – it is not the personage linked," she said in a low voice "But that she would think I would be so improper when – when Frank is not even *buried* to consider…..any emotional entanglement; it would hurt those who did not know of Frank's deficiencies or were blind to them."

Caleb changed colour several times.

"Is – Mrs. Churchill; can it be that you are not indifferent to me?"

"Mr. Armitage I have been so blue devilled and wrung as well as the – the condition I am in making me ridiculously mawkish that in truth I cannot say what my feelings might be," said Jane "You have been a tower of strength; I would not wish to make any mistake in my feelings a second time purely because I have met someone who seems to my eyes to be everything positive that Frank was not. I have not known you a week; though we have been thrown perforce into close proximity. I should prefer not to throw my cap over the windmill. This does not mean that I should be in anywise averse to you coming calling once this business is all solved."

He bowed.

"I apologise, Mrs. Churchill, for permitting my feelings to rule me to ask so improper a question," he said.

"Ah, you are all delicacy; thank you for understanding," said Jane. "Now I pray you that we will not speak of it again."

He bowed acquiescence.

Chapter 16

Mr. and Mrs. Weston's coach arrived at half past eight the next morning; Jane had scarcely risen from her light and unappetising breakfast in bed to settle her nausea. They must have been on the road before dawn!

Jane embraced Mrs. Weston and offered her cheek to Mr. Weston to kiss.

"Oh my dear Jane!" said Mrs. Weston, "we should have come earlier only Mr. Knightley so kindly offered to come in our stead and bring Miss Bates; Anna has been fractious of late."

Jane held the older woman's hands.

"Oh my very dear Mrs. Weston, it is good to see you today; I know you will wish to be back to Anna, for I should hate to leave Frances. And you must take great care of yourself!" she glanced at the gentle curves of Mrs. Weston's gravid figure.

"I had to come however; poor dear Frank!" said Mrs. Weston. "What can you tell us? Mr. Knightley was unable to say much. You look tired, my poor dear!"

Jane flushed.

"I must break to you the news that only in the last few days I have become certain that I had become with child before Frank died," she said "I have written as much to Mr. Jasper Churchill. I do not know if he will come for the funeral or not; it is rather short notice, but even in this weather it is wise to get a – a waterlogged body underground rapidly."

"Dear God! Did Frank then *drown*?" demanded Mr. Weston, who looked haggard; as well he might, thought Jane, over the death of, as things stood, his only son.

"Oh my dear papa-in-law! Let me have tea sent to us and I will tell you all I may," said Jane. "It is a painful story I fear; for Frank was induced by who knows what threats to engage in less than honest practice; and as Bow Street believe that I may be at risk also I have an Officer of the Law – they do not themselves like to be called Bow Street Runners –

staying here to protect me."

Mr. Weston looked grave.

"They may be rough fellows; many used to be professional free-lance thief takers and they can be unsavoury," he said

"Oh, no, Mr. Armitage is perfectly gentlemanly in his manner," Jane assured him hastily. "He was invalided out of the army; he was wounded at Corunna. I have nothing whatever to complain about him and he has been very good in lending me escort and I believe he has also seen to reassuring tradesmen that when probate is sorted out all will be paid; Fowler you understand just damns tradesmen for impudence, being used to a household that ran on credit. I dislike it intensely but….. there have been problems."

"Frank outran the constable by a long measure soon after you were married; care to tell me about it dear Jane?" asked Mr. Weston.

Jane flushed.

"I believe he had been gambling," she almost whispered, "though he seems to have sorted that out. Oh *dear* Mr. and Mrs. Weston, you must be told about Dorothy; she is a mere child under the makeup, but she grieves most sincerely…,"

"Jane, dear, are you saying that Frank had a mistress and she has foisted herself on you?" asked Mrs. Weston gently.

"*Hussy*!" said Mr. Weston.

"Oh no, it is *not* like that!" said Jane. "I do not know in what way Frank found her more congenial then I; but I went to her lodgings and brought her back here for she was under foul attack by one whom Mr. Armitage believes may have been involved in killing Frank; but who unfortunately used the heavy traffic to escape. She is rough of speech and a trifle vulgar but not in any ill natured way; I should be less ashamed by far to claim friendship with Dorothy than with certain of those who might be accepted anywhere in Highbury," she added with some spirit.

"Well if such is true, my dear, we shall greet her and make up our own minds; will we not, my dear?" said Mrs. Weston appealing firmly to her husband.

He grunted.

"If you say so," he said.

Jane filled the Westons in on the edited story that showed Frank in the light of being more sinned against than sinning; it did no good to unnecessarily hurt his father and stepmother. Explaining away a mistress was hard; but perhaps he had been persuaded that all smart young men needed a mistress as well as a wife. So Jane put it to the Westons.

Dorothy looked such a woebegone and frightened child over the idea of going to a funeral that Mrs. Weston warmed to her; Miss Bates had taken the young Paphian under her wing and Dorothy looked nothing like the Westons' expectations. Her rapidly sewn plain black morning gown in a serviceable wool, trimmed with a few bunches of black ribbon was just as one might expect of a young girl's gown; and it might readily be assumed that she was a relative of the family.

The funeral was to take place in that society church, St George's Hanover Square, being the parish church of the neighbourhood; and the funerary procession would then go to St George's Fields for the interment. The funeral having been arranged by Mr. Chorleigh, Jane expected no hitch; the purpose of hiring solicitors to organise things was to ensure that there would *be* no hitch.

Certainly the coaches with their magnificent black horses decked out with black plumes arrived in plenty of time for the mourning party. All the servants were to go to the funeral; returning to the house during the interment to make sure that all was ready for the mourners in the big ground floor reception room that was rarely used since Jane had set out a smaller room on the first floor as a dining room.

The procession trotted sedately to the big Palladian church where so many society weddings took place; it seemed large and intimidating as they alighted by the six soaring Corinthian columns of the frontage. With so classical an array of architecture it was hard to think of it as a church so much as a temple to the wealth of the upper classes, now combined with being a gateway to Hades. Jane thought unbidden of some of the little Latin poetry she knew, an ode by Horace, beginning '*Eheu fugaces, Postumus, Postumus, labuntur anni*'; 'alas, Postumus, the fleeting years fly past'. Who Postumus might have been she could not begin to guess but the whole poem was about how death came to all and all must travel through the depths of the underworld. It was as grand and depressing as the exterior of St George's seemed to be to Jane.

The interior was very plain; and more beautiful for permitting the architecture to be seen, the barrel vaulted roof a pure and simple soaring arch. The altarpiece was a painting of The Last Supper by William Kent; though it was hard to see from the high box pews. At least it was more plainly a church on the inside; there was something about the impersonally classical exterior that revolted a granddaughter of the manse used to the traditional stone churches of the English countryside. Jane was glad to be hidden away in a pew, with Miss Bates on one side of her, Dorothy on Miss Bates' other side, and Mr. and Mrs. Weston on Jane's other side. Caleb had gone with the servants; but was loitering outside a pew. He wanted to see who else might turn up; on the offchance that Jane or Dorothy should be under observation by the murderers.

The service was not to be conducted by the rector, Robert Hodgson MA, who was also Dean of Chester; a man of great importance. As there was some impropriety concerning the manner of Frank Churchill's death the great man had asked another man of the cloth, one Martin Ferry, to be his vicar for the occasion. Jane could not blame him; and it was some relief not to have to listen to the usual eulogies from a great man like a Dean.

The main obsequies passed over Jane's head almost as if it were happening to somebody else; she made the correct responses at the right time and stood or kneeled when she was supposed to stand or kneel but had she been asked to describe the service she would have been hard pressed to do so. Dorothy was sobbing quietly into a handkerchief; Mr. and Mrs. Weston and Miss Bates all made resort to their own kerchiefs from time to time; but Jane felt nothing. All she could think was that she hoped it was the correct coffin and that they were not praying over a stranger. Or – a fantastic and whimsical thought! – that Frank had somehow been used one last time and his coffin be used to store and hide stolen jewellery!

I am become too fanciful, Jane told herself severely. It is akin to hysteria and unladylike.

She composed herself firmly; and was ready to go with the others, now joined by the clerks and solicitors of Chorleigh, Wright and Jekyll, to go to the graveside.

And Caleb was there to give her a reassuring smile and to shake his head; he managed to whisper, as he handed her up into the carriage,

"Nobody more suspicious than those Friday-faced word mongers," nodding at the solicitors.

Jane bit back a hysterical giggle. Trust Mr. Armitage to be able to make her smile with an irreverent description!

The day was cold and wet with sleet in the rain; and Jane was glad that she had a dark pelisse to wear and that she had an older one too for Dorothy. Miss Bates was bundled well up in shawls as they stood at the graveside for the final obsequies. The coffin was lowered on ropes by the four hefty pall bearers; the time honoured words were at last all spoken; the first handful of earth thrown in as the appropriate words were said by the parson; and then the mourners might leave and let the sexton do his job of filling the grave in.

Again Caleb's strong arm was there for support, not just for Jane but for Dorothy and particularly for Miss Bates.

"We want to get Miss Bates in swiftly," said Caleb. "Here, Dorothy my girl, you're a good gal; you sneak Miss Bates up to the parlour in front of the fire and get her some rugs and a hot toddy; Molly will help you in the kitchen. She don't need to do the polite to them fellows from the office."

"'Course I will, Mr. Armitage," said Dorothy.

Jane reflected again how thoughtful and how clever he

was; Aunt Hetty was fagged to death and frozen and needed taking care of – that the widow might not do for needing to be on display. And that kept Aunt Hetty looked after and too placed Dorothy out of the way where nobody might upset or embarrass her by asking too much about her. She smiled at Caleb in pleased gratitude for his thoughtfulness.

Caleb reflected ruefully that when a man who has been asked not to speak of his feelings receives so dazzling a smile from the woman who has rapidly become the centre of his world it is both heaven on earth and sheer torture not to shout for joy and kneel to offer his heart and hand to her forthwith.

Dorothy duly saw Miss Bates to the comfort of the fire; and on finding that she preferred tea to a hot toddy went down to beg the key to the caddy from Jane to make a pot and, as she described it to the little lady, 'prigged some eats for us too which would do us more good than napping our bibs'.

It may be said that Miss Bates had very little idea of the meaning of much of this idiom beyond being vaguely aware that napping the bib was a vulgar euphemism for crying; but smiled kindly on Dorothy and delighted her with another long tale of Mrs. Jane's cleverness when she was a little girl.

Chapter 17

"I should be obliged for a word with you and Mr. Armitage, Mrs. Churchill," said Fowler quietly. "A matter arising from watching them interlopin' footmen as you might say."

"Will it wait until I have bid Mr. and Mrs. Weston 'Godspeed' when they leave?" asked Jane. Fowler considered.

"Yes ma'am; Mrs. Ketch and I have it well in hand. But if you don't mind I shall seek out Mr. Armitage; he said he was going to check over all the house just in case."

"Send Molly to look for him," said Jane. "She can leave her duties running errands for the footmen."

Fowler gave a little bow and withdrew.

"Is there a problem Jane? Should we stay?" asked Mrs. Weston anxiously, coming over to Jane.

"Oh nothing serious my dear Ma'am; just a little matter arising from the tensions between my servants and those we hired in for the day; Fowler felt I should be apprised of a potential upset. He is dealing with it," said Jane.

"He sounds an invaluable man," said Mrs. Weston.

"He is; he should be promoted to butler by rights," said Jane. "Well we shall see how the finances go when all has been sorted out. I should like to give him due recognition for his support and aid; he has risen to the occasion very well."

She saw Mr. and Mrs. Weston out to their carriage; the mews had not yet been hired out so their coachman had been able to stable the horses during the funeral. It might be nice to have a coach; but on the other hand it would also be nice to have the rent on the mews over the Season which, thought Jane, was going to bring in more than the cost of the odd hackney carriage. One had to be hard headed over these things. If she had only thought of it they could have hired out some of the unused space last season; but doubtless Frank would not have heard of it.

Well he was buried; and if the worst came to the worst she

might sell this fine house, or again, let it for the season, and perhaps rather than being a governess she might sew. The wages were lower but the abuses fewer. And with the experience she had gained copying modish gowns she might get a position with a *modiste* not merely take in sewing. If she let the house complete with Mrs. Ketch, Fowler and Molly they would keep their positions; and though it would break her heart to send her away, Frances might go with Annie to stay with the Westons. Yes, there was a way around every potential problem. And the problem would be in the way that Mr. Churchill took his nephew's death, troubles, and hasty funeral. She had written to him straight away on Monday; it must travel two hundred miles. That would take some twenty five hours; the full day round. He would have got the letter Tuesday evening. Of course he would want to post down; he had his own chaise, he would probably however hire post horses at each inn for a speedier rate of travel but he would not travel day and night as the mail did. Indeed he would almost certainly not set forth until the Wednesday; being elderly he would not travel more than six hours a day for he was not fond of the motion; and he would not travel on the morrow, being Sunday; so in all probability he would arrive on Monday. It would be embarrassing if he *did* push on hard enough to have arrived just in time to miss the funeral today; but if he did, that was just too bad. Jane was quite out of charity with Uncle Jasper, who should have apprised her that his nephew was in financial difficulties.

She might now see what difficulties Fowler had encountered whilst the footmen – one less than there should be she noted – cleared away.

She left the solicitors and clerks enjoying their meal at the expense of another and slipped away.

Caleb grinned at Jane; he and Fowler had a grimy and well trussed footman between them.

"Ah, Mrs. Churchill," said Caleb "Thanks to the vigilance of Mr. Fowler here, we have a would-be thief; whom Fowler caught creeping out of the coal cellar."

"What did he think to steal in there, Mr. Armitage?" asked Jane.

Caleb chuckled.

"Ah, not so much to steal nowise," he said "But dahn in the dark he found a certain trapdoor, with certain bolts on it which he thought to loosen and draw back; so later his villyunous friends might come in to prig anythink wot took their fancy, ain't that so, Jimmy boy? James Ripon is what this 'ere dubber of jiggers, that's an opener of doors, is called; account o' how Mr. Fowler has all their names to sign off that they came and did their work satisfactory-like. Which nowise this cully seems to have done; looks like he's definitely on the ken-slumming lay."

"I don't understand all that cant," said James Ripon sullenly. "If you arsts me lidy, him wot speak the cant is the villain, tryin' to put it onto me."

"Hoh well you prize rogue, let me put you right about!" said Fowler "It being me what had followed you about sneakin' into rooms you had no business to poke into; and then into the coal cellar. And Mr. Armitage here tumbled to what you was doin' in there, me bein' innocent enough to think you had been light fingered and were hidin' stuff in there. Well, I nearly locked him in; and I'm right glad I didn't, Madam, for he'd of slipped right through the hatch!"

"What did you do?" asked Jane "And really I am filled with admiration for your resourcefulness, Fowler,".

Fowlers immobile face actually cracked into a grin.

"I 'it the b-asket on the 'ead wiv a skillet," he said, losing all pretensions to his well cultivated accent as he strove not to swear in front of the mistress of the house.

"Oh very well done," said Jane. "Have you managed to find out if he is working alone or a part of some thieving gang?"

"He *says* he's working alone," said Caleb "But I ain't sure I believe him; he ain't got the tread of a man as can crack a crib and nab trinkets, moveables and such withaht that the 'ole 'ouse wakes up. A caw-handed lolpoop he is; or he was when he was handing round eats earlier, clumsy and lazy you'd say."

"He's also the fellow who was ogling up Juliet and spoilin' her reputation so he is Madam," said Mrs. Ketch.

"Ah, apparently a new way of, er, slumming the ken," said Jane gravely.

Caleb grinned.

"And about all he's good for; *he* ain't no bowman-prig. That's a top flight thief," he said.

"Mr. Armitage, I don't think you should be teaching Mrs. Churchill cant," said Fowler disapprovingly.

"No, likely I should not," said Caleb.

"I find it quite fascinating actually," said Jane, "when you get into the swing of the argot, Mr. Armitage you might as well not even be speaking English."

"That's the general idea, Ma'am," said Caleb. "So that swell–coves and swell-morts don't understand and then they can't whiddle the scrap."

"Tell anyone?" guessed Jane.

"Precisely," said Caleb.

"What do we do, hand him over to the watch?" asked Jane.

"I think so," said Caleb "But since there's such a lot to do he might as well be locked away for now and we'll see to it in the morning…. If we can be bothered on the Sabbath. Locked into one of the storerooms you don't use much ma'am, he won't be able to cause any harm; Fowler and me will search him as well in case he has any bessies, that's lockpicks. Unless he feels like being a milch-kine to give up his chums? No? Ah well," as Ripon shook his head.

Then the prisoner spat an epithet at him and Caleb cuffed him, roaring in anger,

"You slubberdegullion; Mrs. Ketch, I pray you some soap for his filthy mouth," whereupon, when that worthy promptly handed over the jar of soft soap he proceeded to well soap Ripon's mouth until no epithet could arise from it.

"Effective," said Jane.

"*Army* tactic," said Caleb "Not that we was a mealy-mouthed bunch nowise; but them as swore in front of orficer's wives, well that were different; and thought themselves lucky if the swell mort didn't know what they was saying, account of that'd mean a flogging. C'mon you; Fowler and me will see you abram and check your duds and anywhere else fer that matter like the northwest passage," he added ominously to Ripon, pulling the false footman to his feet and propelling him firmly out of the door. Fowler took off his jacket meaningfully and started rolling up his sleeves as he followed Caleb.

"Dear me," said Jane to Mrs. Ketch, "I believe I shall be glad to remain in ignorance of what they intend."

"Well Madam, that's what I feel too, but I can't say I feel much sympathy for that nasty piece of work," said Mrs. Ketch.

"Nor I," said Jane, reflecting that Ripon was either the result of a very long coincidence or was associated with those who had tortured and killed her husband. And whatever her feelings about Frank it was a matter of principle.

Mr. Chorleigh was looking around for Jane when she returned to the reception room.

"Ah, Mrs. Churchill; I wondered where you might be," he said. Though it was a statement it was almost worded as a question. Jane bridled.

"Mr. Chorleigh, when a lady who is, as I wrote in my last communication to you, in a delicate condition and who has been burying her husband, leaves the room for a short while I consider it ill-bred of anyone to make comment or draw attention to the fact," she said coldly. "As it happens I had also to deal with a small domestic crisis; one of the hired footmen was caught stealing. My man Fowler and Mr. Armitage are seeing to the matter but correctly Fowler felt I should be apprised of the occurrence. Which is, frankly, nothing that needs discussing with you either as the Churchill solicitor nor as Frank's employer. You are of course wishful to take your leave; thank you for coming to attend the funeral, your support has been appreciated. One of the footmen here will get your cloak," she made a sign to one of the men in attendance upon the guests who ran off.

Mr. Chorleigh had intended to lecture Mrs. Churchill on a number of matters – not least leaving her guests – but dubbed ill-bred and effectively nosy he could only gasp and take the firmly proffered little hand to kiss, by which time he was being enveloped in his cloak and his beaver and cane handed to him by a footman and Jane had carefully drifted away.

Mr. Chorleigh made her itch to do something unladylike.

StClair Despard grinned at her.

"Nice handling of the old man, Ma'am," he said.

"Why Mr. Despard I fail to grasp your meaning," said Jane demurely.

He gave a crack of laughter which he hastily turned into a cough; laughing at a funeral, and before the widow at that, was not at all the thing!

"Why Mrs. Churchill, I would say that you are a complete hand; had you any ideas about the writing your husband was doing?"

"Mr. Despard, that is a matter for the officer of Bow Street; and not to be generally discussed," said Jane "I appreciate your curiosity; but unless Mr. Armitage is prepared to share information with you, you must, I fear, learn to curb it."

"I shall be dished in that desire then," said Mr. Despard gloomily. "He's close-mouthed; for I already asked him."

"Then to try to gain information from me was highly improper," said Jane.

"Of course it was, ma'am; I'm in training to be a solicitor," said Mr. Despard "No trick too low; *fiat justiciam ruat caelorum* or as we mistranslate it, so justice be done however low the worms under the sky may crawl."

"You are a witty man Mr. Despard," said Jane "But if you will take advice, do not permit wit to outweigh judgement."

He looked at her thoughtfully.

"That is a most profound statement ma'am; one I shall endeavour to always remember," he said. "I shall be relieving you of my presence now; your servant," and he carried her hand to his lips for a briefly punctilious salute.

"That young would-be black-box kept you amused," said Caleb to Jane as the other clerks filed out in rapid succession. "Did you tell him anything?"

"Only to apply to you as the proper person to know what to tell him," said Jane with a modest, downcast look. "He is an amusing rattle; when he grows up enough to learn discretion and tact he will perhaps make a good solicitor."

"Oh," said Caleb. "I was going to warn you that he was a little immature; but I see you realise that."

"Why Mr. Armitage, did you think I was *flirting*?" said Jane. "And on the day of my late husband's funeral?"

Caleb flushed.

"I – I do apologise," he said.

Jane laid a hand on his arm.

"I should not tease you my dear friend," she said "But I feel I do need a touch of levity to deal with this awful day; and I should apologise to you for doing so. For in other circumstances one might have read your behaviour as showing jealousy."

"I'm damnably jealous, Jane-girl," said Mr. Armitage "And all I want is to protect you from unctuous chaw-bacons like Chorleigh. And please forget I spoke, on this day of all days."

"Mr. Armitage...." said Jane, feeling a little light headed, "I think we should discuss other, safer topics."

"Yes ma'am," said Caleb.

But she had not given him a set-down for using her name.

Chapter 18

Jane was extremely glad to get to bed; it had been a tiring day, and made more so by Frances, who had sensed, in the way small children do, the tension in the atmosphere. In the end Jane had asked Annie to fetch Mr. Armitage to the nursery to bounce Frances about until she was giggling wildly; and then the baby was happy enough to take her bath without screaming and going stiff and went to bed readily. Jane had apologised.

"She knows I feel tense and blue-devilled; I expect it makes her fear I will drop her in the water," she said. "Annie does most things for her; but she is my daughter and I wanted some time with her; I have not seen her all day with this miserable funeral."

"Why Mrs. Churchill, consider the impropriety of a *merry* funeral," quipped Caleb with a perfectly straight face.

She had laughed a little and sighed.

"In truth, though I am glad it is all over, I fear a little what Mr. Churchill might say about my not waiting for him," she said.

"Tell him to go to the devil; if he'd been a decent father-figure to his nephew he'd have posted down to find out why the cub was in such debt in the first place and put him right-about," said Caleb forcefully.

"You are quite right, Caleb....Armitage," said Jane. "Oh *how* I loathe confrontations; still if he cuts Frances and me off without a penny, we might raise enough to rent a small house and enough to live on just by letting this house; and I can always sew."

"You will not sew, Mrs. Churchill," said Caleb forcefully. "I will not see you be a slavey to those damned supercilious old crows!"

"Mr. Armitage; it is not right that we should discuss yet the alternative that you are on the verge of suggesting," said Jane. "And I am far better able to keep my self-respect by sewing than as a governess. I thank you for the aid with Frances; and I bid you good night for I too shall retire early."

He bowed and left her; and thus Jane was lying in bed, extremely glad of the soft goose feather mattress and the sweet fresh aroma of the lavender-scented linen sheets caressing her tired body.

But she did not sleep.

The big, ungainly figure of Caleb Armitage would insist on intruding before her eyes when she closed them; and the errant and shocking thought that his strong arms would be extremely comforting.

Jane dozed fitfully; but was awake in an instant when she heard a noise downstairs. Her bedroom was at the front; Frank liked to be on the street and she had given in, though she would have preferred the quiet of a room overlooking the garden that would remind her of Highbury. And she had had far better things to do than to worry about changing her sleeping chamber. She pulled on a robe and thrust her feet into her dainty slippers and hastily sparked the flint and tinder to light her candle.

Caleb Armitage was coming down the stairs as she emerged from her chamber. He held a finger to his lips and indicated that she should return to her own room. Jane stood back to let him pass, but she shook her head.

"I need to see," she whispered.

"Then stay well back you brave little idiot," said Caleb.

Somehow the adjective brave outweighed being called an idiot; and somehow Jane knew that he was paying her fortitude a compliment in not insisting – and he could force her – that she return to her room.

Caleb ran silently down ahead of Jane on noisless, stockinged feet, not missing a stair though the darkness was profound in the stairwell. There were sounds of a tussle; words that Jane hoped she had not understood correctly; and then a sudden detonation, which echoed!

"*Gawdstrewth* Fowler you nodcock, you've been and shot *me*," said Caleb's voice.

"Not me, Mr. Armitage, I saw the candlelight on that other feller's barking-iron; It's him I done shot and he have put a ball in you!" cried Fowler "Don't you go and stick your spoon in the wall now, or Missus'll have me guts fer garters fer lettin' of 'im shoot yer!"

"Stubble it and help me with this fellow then!" said Caleb. "It's a flesh wound. I ain't about to turn up me toes."

Jane, horrified and working on not screaming, terrified for Caleb's life, came down the rest of the way. One ominously still figure was lying in the doorway to the kitchen; Caleb was sitting on the other. His assailant was wriggling hard. Fowler was shaking like a blancmanger, the pistol still in his hand. The scene was like something from a melodramatic book like 'The Castle of Wolfenbach' in the flickering of the two candles, one in Fowler's other hand and one in Jane's. There was a solid pewter candlestick on a table by the doorway however so Jane set down her own chamber candle, picked up the heavy candlestick and hit the man under Caleb over the head.

"Oh *very* well done Mrs. Churchill," said Caleb, a trifle faintly.

"Fowler," said Jane "Light more candles; then truss up this – person. And check if the other is indeed shot dead and if there is any chance he is not, truss him up too. Mr. Armitage you are all over blood; pray go and sit in Mrs. Ketch's chair by the fire and I shall attend to your wound as soon as we are certain these two present us with no further problems," she spoke in a far crisper tone than her sick horror at so much blood would have permitted her to do had she not been sensible to the fact that Caleb Armitage needed her to be strong and deal with his wound.

"Yes ma'am," said Caleb "The mistress of the house is in charge and in fine fettle."

"There's a time and a place for facetiae, Mr. Armitage and I'll reserve judgement on whether now is it when I have seen to you," said Jane crisply.

"Mrs. Churchill! You cannot order a man around like that and then not marry him!" Caleb's voice was weak but he could not resist teasing.

"I can and I shall do as I see fit in my own house," said

Jane ambiguously.

She screamed suddenly as a smaller figure landed on her back knocking her over and putting out her candle very effectively by snuffing it beneath the weight of her body; this figure had hurtled down from the dresser where presumably it had taken refuge when it became clear that Fowler and Caleb were attacking the two larger men; and escape was its main priority.

Fowler yelled; and Caleb swore. There were sounds of a chase and the gritty, teeth-setting sound of coal on coal; and then a bang.

"Cove got out through the coal hatch," said Caleb "Strewth, I must be losin' me touch…,"

"I don't know about losing your touch, Mr. Armitage, but you are most certainly losing blood," said Jane a little breathlessly as she got to her knees, checking herself mentally for any worse wounds than a crop of bruises and being winded. "Fowler, light a candle and go bolt that door before we go any further. I will have yours to see to Mr. Armitage's wound; mine is I believe quite broken."

"Be aware," said Caleb "Coal dust can explode…. Besides, the door won't bolt. They've sawed the bolt because Ripon was not there to let them in…. That's what I heard. It must have woken you too, Ma'am."

"What I'll do Madam is to lock the door from the coal cellar to the kitchen," said Fowler, "aye, and pull the table across it too. And to think I told my brother the army was too exciting for me!"

"You're loving it Fowler," said Caleb.

"Mr. Armitage, I will not say that the exhilaration is not an interesting change but I should not go so far as all that," said Fowler. "If, however, you was finding yourself a part of the household and needing a man, I should not say that valeting might not be an interesting way forward."

"You are moving too fast on too many fronts Fowler," said Jane "And any more would be impudence."

"Yes Mrs. Churchill ma'am," said Fowler.

The ball had fortunately not lodged in Caleb's arm; it was as he had said, a flesh wound, as Jane found when she cut away the stitching of the seam of his shirt; but he had lost a lot of blood and the sleeve of his shirt was soaked in it and it had dripped down onto his buckskins too. Jane sighed.

"Mrs. Kemp is going to have to do more to them than go over with a lot of buffball," she said "They'll need salt to take the blood out, and then the stiffness from washing them will take some working with warmed beeswax and vegetable oil. Ah well, you'll be confined to your bed for a day or two so you shall not need them."

"Mrs. Churchill, I will not," said Caleb. "I need to be up and about to be ready for any reinforcements that fellow has gone after."

"If you don't sit still, Mr. Armitage," said Jane tartly "The level of reinforcements you will need yourself for causing yourself more harm will be General Blücher and all his Brunswickers. Now instead of marching to the sound of the guns I pray you will sit to the sound of my bandaging."

"Yes Colonel Ma'am," said Caleb in a deceptively meek voice.

Jane washed the wound – a neat hole right through the flesh of the upper arm – and packed it with basilicum powder and put on a linen bandage from the strips Mrs. Kedge kept against emergency. The linen was good; the sheet from which it had come had been as new as any in her bottom drawer but Frank had ripped it across because he declared that he could still scent the stench of her giving birth on it.

It had been a totally different sheet to the one she had birthed on, that had still been being laundered; but Frank had been like that. Had he only torn it lengthways it might still have been serviceable sides-to-middled; but he would rip it from side to side, and with the centre seam necessary to make a full sized sheet, a seam the other way was impractical. Jane had made two pillow slips from the torn sheet and given the rest to Mrs. Ketch to roll as bandages, for accidents can happen in the best regulated household.

Caleb grunted in relief as the bandage kept the wound somewhat compressed; and sighed in greater relief as Jane laid his forearm up across his chest to rest on the other shoulder and tied a sling to hold it.

"That should do very nicely," she said, "we can send for a doctor in the morning."

"If you think I want to see any damn sawbones...." said Caleb

"Oh I was thinking of sending for a proper physician," said Jane, "but if you dislike the idea very much we shall defer the decision until the morning; it is," she added as though in an aside to Fowler, "a necessary thing to humour the patient lest he fall into a fever."

"You're a damned managing wench, Mrs. Churchill," said Caleb. "Here, Fowler, is that fellow over there dead?"

"Yes Mr. Armitage; I fancy it must be beginner's luck," said Fowler "And I'm afeared I'm going to shoot the cat."

He certainly looked green enough to be expected to vomit.

"Rise above it, brother of a soldier!" said Caleb. "You might as well stick him in the coal cellar; here, let me have a look at his face first," he half rose.

"Fowler will lift his head for you," said Jane.

"Sorry madam but Fowler will not," said Fowler, fleeing.

Caleb got up and came over, grunting slightly.

"As I thought," he said, "this is the fellow who was torturing Dorothy. Well *he* won't do anything of the kind again."

"Indeed no; and I must give Fowler a bonus for so excellent a shot," said Jane. "He will be quite a hero with Dorothy!"

"S'welp me, better him than me," said Caleb. "This other don't look a whole lot better character; whatever else. I reckon these precious pair are the ones that did for your husband. That was quite a baste on the costard you gave him; I doubt he'll wake afore daylight. Here, let me reload the barker Fowler's left lying about so careless; with one arm useless I can't guarantee to throw this fellow in with our other prisoner and stop Jimmy the slum trying something on. You keep the barker pointed at him and I guarantees yer, there ain't nothin' so scary as a woman with a pistol."

"Why?" asked Jane.

"Because women is held to be nervous with loud noises and to shut their eyes and pull the trigger anywise; which could mean an injury a lot worse than death, especially as a woman is generally weak and can't aim as high," said Caleb. "Just take it from me that a barking-iron in the hands of any mort is a scary business," he added hastily.

He half dragged the unconscious man to the storeroom where James Ripon was incarcerated; and Jane held the pistol resolutely on the startled captive.

"Gawd, wot have yer done to O'Toole?" he demanded, shocked "Where's Smudger?"

"Well, well, quite the happy family," said Caleb. "Anyone else you'd care to name for me while you're about it?"

Ripon went green.

"No fear," he said, "they'd bloody kill me."

"Well you're for the queer ken at least and most likely dancing at Beilby's ball," said Caleb cheerfully. "And knowing what your mate Smudger did to one man and tried to do to a girl, I'd happily watch you dancing on the nubbing-cheat," and he swung the door back on the frightened man.

"And now," said Jane "You will go to bed. Fowler!" as the footman returned "All are safe bar the body; perhaps you will lock the door to the kitchen until the morning so that you might explain; and run for a constable. And on a Sunday they may not be there!" she said.

"Tomorrow, Mrs. Churchill, I will be equal to deal with anything," said Fowler majestically.

"Good man," said Caleb. "And yes ma'am, I am now going!"

Chapter 19

Jane hardly expected to sleep after the night alarums; but she woke up to Ella's cheerful voice asking if it were to be considered a normal feature of entertaining a Bow Street Runner to find bodies in the kitchen.

Jane sat up.

"Ella, you were not surely permitted into the kitchen before that horrid thing had gone?"

"Mrs. Jane I was not; and nor should you have been! You should have woken me; what is the good of me sleeping in your dressing room if not to be woken to support you? And that wretched man has taken a fever!"

"I was afraid he might," said Jane. "What has the magnificent Fowler managed to do about tea and toast with *that* on the floor?"

"Magnificent Fowler! I'll magnificent him!" said Ella "Putting on airs because he shot a common housebreaker! He went and got some street urchins and paid them to get a barrow to take the body to Bow Street with a letter in his own hand, mark you, written in Mr. Armitage's name that they were to take it in charge and send a constable to collect the prisoners. Hah!"

"I wager at that it was at Mr. Armitage's suggestion," said Jane mildly, "feverish or no. I must go and look at my patient; write a note for me to Doctor..... no, I did not like Doctor Wingfield. Dear me, how very provoking!"

"Mrs. Jane dearie, there's nothing wrong with Mr. Armitage that we can't cure and a doctor can't charge for killing," said Ella, "and I do grant you, though I wasn't sure at first, he is worth saving. And though I've had more upsets in the last few days than is considered proper in a decent household, well you can't complain that it is dull. Lawks, though, I'm glad it wasn't me hitting that fellow on the head!"

"Ella, you are sweet to me, but don't you think that you ought to be ashamed of your reticence?" asked Jane.

Ella flushed but laughed, glad that her mistress was in a

good enough mood to be moved to irony.

"Madam must have her little joke," she said. "Miss Bates is all agog to hear all about it."

Jane smiled.

"Dear Aunt Hetty; I fancy she is quite enjoying herself bar the strain of the funeral," she said. "I will go to her when I have attended Mr. Armitage. He will eat gruel; milk gruel but gruel. And if he behaves himself I may permit him a restorative pork broth."

Ella had her own ideas on what Mr. Armitage might think about that; she also had the opinion that her mistress would win the encounter.

"Gruel and bedrest or I get a doctor in to bleed you," said Jane, "and I'm not sure that bleeding might not be a bad idea anyway; it lets out the evil humours of a wound."

"I lost enough blood thank you," said Caleb, "if I lose any more I shall turn into a revenant and haunt your house for eternity moaning and rattling chains or whatever such unnatural wights do."

"I doubt anyone would notice the difference after last night," said Jane, "which as the rest of the household contrived to sleep through it means there would be little point to such a doleful and macabre exercise. Here is your gruel; when you have eaten it I shall check your wound. If you do not eat it I shall send for a military surgeon."

"Madam, you are a cruel woman," said Caleb "I believe I have been laid up under the sign of the cat's foot!"

"Indeed you have, Mr. Armitage," said Jane smiling at him.

"Jane-girl, if you smile at me like that, I'll eat any damnable slop you put in front of me," Caleb asseverated. Jane blushed.

"Why the poor man is feverish indeed," she said lightly. "Caleb, I wish you will permit Ella and me to nurse you without making a fight of it; I am not unaccustomed to sick nursing, though I confess never of one wounded by a bullet before."

126

"I'll try to behave Jane-girl," said Caleb, "even for Ella; for I fear if I refuse her ministrations you might withdraw yours."

"I should certainly have to consider it; for you are a contrary creature, Mr. Armitage," said Jane.

"Oh but Mrs. Churchill, I do have my faults also," said Caleb.

Jane gave permission for the servants to stay away from church if they found themselves too overset by the events of the night; or possibly too excited and eager to see the developments.

A pair of constables turned up to relieve the household of its prisoners, one of whom was sullen and truculent the other still groggy from a combination of Jane's blow from the candlestick and the bruising he had taken already from Caleb wrestling with him in the darkness. He was complaining in the idiom of Ireland that he needed a priest.

"Sure, for joy, and aren't I wounded t'death so I am; wirra that I should die unshriven loike yu pagan English!"

Needless to say the constables ignored his complaints.

"It's my dooty, ma'am, ter talk ter Mr. Armitage," said one of the constables staring at the ceiling rather than seem impudent enough to meet Jane's eye, "this bein' his case and nowise anyone wishful to push in on it; but I needs to report as 'ow 'e's still in the land of the living, see."

"Oh quite so," said Jane. These men were a far cry from Caleb's relatively gentlemanly bearing; and they were too far more bashful in the house of a...how would they phrase it, gentry mort, thought Jane. She led them both to see Caleb.

"Visitors for you, Mr. Armitage," she said gaily as she opened his bedroom door after a swift knock; to forestall any flippant and indeed flirtatious comment that might arise to his lips for seeing her enter first. She stood at the bottom of the bed while the men mumbled apologies to Caleb for disturbing him

"Listen you men," said Caleb, "them gaolbirds wot you're taking in; you keep 'em safe, see? I don't want 'em piking off because sure as eggs is eggs they'll be the next ones to end up dead and no good as witnesses if you lose 'em. Is that clear?"

"Yuss Mr. Armitage," nodded the least monosyllabic of the pair.

"Good; because while they're kept safe – and incommunicado if you can manage it, strewth I mean nobody didn't ought to be let talk to them, nor they to each other if the Paddy is conscious and as sensible as any Irishman may ever be," he added, seeing looks of incomprehension, " – then Mrs. Churchill and her household are also relatively safe. But look, Tobias!" he addressed the spokesman "You can give out that I am shot; and make as gloomy noises about it as you like. I ain't about to turn up me toes, but if there's them as think I might be, well we might get further, see?"

"Ar," said Tobias.

"Well that's a relief to be rid of them," said Caleb when Jane returned to see how he had born the visit.

"The prisoners or the constables?" asked Jane tartly "For the latter do not seem to be of your calibre in the least."

"Well they *are* only constables of the watch not officers of the law," said Caleb. "A relief to be rid of both I'd say. I feared a rescue if it became known the prisoners were here; if there is a master mind behind the jewel thefts – and I believe there is – then he could easily hire a small army of ruffians to storm this house on a quiet Sunday and either remove or silence Jimmy Ripon and his friend O'Toole. I think O'Toole and the man called Smudger – his name is almost certainly Smith, as it's a common nickname – were the strong arm men. Now such are easily replaced; but we may hope, if I am thought to be at death's door, that you may receive a visit from the nib cove himself. And if not, perhaps a visit to him might be in order. I strongly suspect that our precious birds will stand buff, refuse to talk; possibly because they fear the boss more than they fear the law. Though we might let loose your pretty eyes on the Irishman; they are notoriously tough nuts to crack but full of sentiment; a few tears over the terrible things done to your husband might do the trick."

Jane considered. She had stiffened at the compliment to her pretty eyes but what Caleb said did make sense.

"We shall see what develops," she said. "Better not to go out of my way to provoke a reaction until we see if this master mind tries to act first; for I will not go near him, nor O'Toole without you nearby and that is impractical until you are healed and will besides give away that you are not so near death's door as we wish them to think."

He nodded.

"Cogently put my dear Mrs. Churchill…. might I have a drop of laudanum? This arm throbs some'at cruel now I be better enough to notice it."

"Of a certainly, Mr. Armitage," said Jane. "I believe you refused it to Ella earlier."

"Yes; I wanted to be sensible to talk to any idiots who came to see me," said Caleb. "Well they've been; and I doubt anything much will happen before tomorrow. So I may take the opportunity to recuperate."

Jane decided to fill in her Aunt Hetty on all that was going on.

Miss Bates glowed pink with excitement as Jane revealed the whole story.

"Oh Jane! Oh if it were not that it has caused you misery and poor Frank lying dead so foully done away with – though I must say my blood boils that he has proved so false in more ways than just adultery, not that *just* is quite the word to use, for it is serious enough – where was I? Oh yes, if there were not so many horrid aspects to this, it must seem quite like a horrid romance of the kind that one might find in a circulating library, quite unrealistic of course but *such* an entertaining read as they may be!"

"It is easier to deal with if one can but imagine oneself living in a novel," said Jane. "For my own part the puzzle of untangling the villain of this piece is the way that I might more readily cope with the unusual and indeed nightmarish situation."

She had explained that she and Mr. Armitage believed one of the three jewellers to be involved at least in the jewellery thefts; and Miss Bates was torn between being thrilled at having actually been in the presence of a master criminal and a little shocked.

"Mr. Armitage did not ought to permit you to take such risks, dear Jane!" she said.

"He prefers, I think," said Jane, "to permit me to collaborate with his investigation and taking such risks, over knowing that I should probably investigate on my own if he did not; and that would put me in greater danger. I need to do this, Aunt Hetty."

"I find it hard, my dear, to truly understand why it matters to you so much; if Frank was so unkind to you, why do you care about finding his killers?" Miss Bates was puzzled.

Jane stared down at her hands, passive in her lap, willpower keeping them still.

"Because, Aunt Hetty, I feel some guilt that perhaps I might have managed to change his nature had I not turned away from him so soon, decided that as he did not love me I should not need to care for him; indeed I made life harder for him in petty revenges for his despite towards me. I do not know if I could have been a better wife to him and saved him from this; but you have taught me to view everyone with charity and so I feel I should try to find charity for Frank; and do my best to prevent these terrible people killing other men, those who perhaps are merely foolish enough to get into debt and yet have a much loved family. I cannot put it clearly; I am sorry."

"My dear, *dear* Jane!" Miss Bates embraced her "You are good to try to understand his faults; it is harder for me to forgive him for it is my dear niece whom he has hurt and it is easier to forgive those who wrong ourselves than those who wrong those we love; and it is so very like you to also consider the feelings of others hurt by these villains! But I pray you, do, my dear Jane, *please* take care!"

Chapter 20

Jane was doing the accounts in the book room on Monday morning when Fowler announced Mr. Churchill.

"Well Jane!" said Mr. Churchill "This is indeed a sad and sorry business! Frank *murdered* you write; though had he committed suicide over your profligacy I should have been less surprised!"

Jane stared open mouthed; then anger drove her to speech.

"*My* profligacy? I assure you sir it was not I who lost two thousand guineas in some gaming hell, nor I who maintained a mistress; indeed *your nephew* saw fit to chastise me when I tried to make economies! You *dare* to accuse me when I have tried my hardest to maintain the outsize household Frank considered necessary and when I have had to sew to create modish dresses when he believed me out shopping to avoid his punishment for looking dowdy? When I have had good nourishing food thrown at me because it is not the most fashionable cut? Indeed sir, I blame you in some measure for Frank's death for had you apprised me of his request to you for the sum I might, by use of the knowledge of the same, have been able to use sweet reason on Frank to accept that economies were necessary; or had you posted down *then* to find out what was wrong you might have had some influence on him; instead of which he has engaged in dishonesty to pay his debts the result of which means that his crooked friends have had him killed; and I am in no inconsiderable danger since they erroneously believe me to be in possession of something he stole from them! Yes, sir, *stole*! Frank stooped to common theft, it appears, no doubt with the casuistry that as he stole from thieves it did not count!"

Jasper Churchill had gone grey and he sank into a chair.

"Jane – no, I cannot believe this!" he cried.

"Well sir if you will call me a liar, I suggest you go through *my* accounts and through all of Frank's papers in the escritoire," said Jane "I have tried to put them into some semblance of order. I wish you joy of it; but I will not remain here with you to call me a liar."

"Jane; I apologise; I did not mean to call you a liar. I meant merely that I found it hard to believe that Frank could be so...so... lost to shame and what is due to his name!" cried Mr. Churchill. "I had assumed that a poverty stricken girl, given an allowance such as I paid Frank had had her head turned in the big city with all the shops and entertainments available...."

"Still my integrity is impugned," said Jane coldly, "and I will leave you to believe the evidence of your own eyes what may be my fault and what not. Since I saw some half of the allowance you paid Frank from which to make the household run, you will see I have very little over with which to enjoy much in the way of shopping and entertainment; since that also covered the cost of keeping Frank's horse. I shall have tea sent to you; good morning."

She stalked out.

"Mr. Churchill would like you to join him in the book room, ma'am," said Fowler some hours later.

Jane entered the book room and raised an eyebrow.

"I apologise for calling your management into question Jane," said Mr. Churchill. "I am shocked at how much Frank has squandered. However, as his wife I should have thought you would have had some influence over him. Alas, my poor sister! There is bad blood there; indeed I am wondering whether to continue the allowance at all, or whether to cut off root and branch; no scandal should attach to a Churchill of Enscombe."

"I will not diminish myself to plead for my daughter or the unborn child in my womb," said Jane coolly, "but as a mother I shall do my utmost for their wellbeing; and as I am a handsome woman I do not doubt that Jane Churchill of Enscombe might readily make her way and rapidly find a wealthy protector around Covent Garden."

Jasper Churchill spluttered in outrage and horror.

"Jane, you cannot mean it! To *ruin* yourself!"

"Why Mr. Churchill, it is not as though I am a maid unblemished; I felt very blemished by Frank's insistence on his marital rights after I had barely birthed," said Jane. "What is there to lose? Nothing. And much to gain in keeping my children in a way that I wish them kept. Of course I also have the satisfaction, should I have to take this course because you have proved ungenerous to your great niece and great niece or nephew, of making sure that the name Churchill of Enscombe is synonymous with the unfortunate calling I should have to embrace."

Mr. Churchill was almost gobbling with outrage.

"Jane, this is *blackmail*!" he cried.

"Mr. Churchill; it is," said Jane.

"You are … you are …"

"I am a mother, Mr. Churchill; there is *nothing* I would not do for my children," said Jane. "And as the unfortunate profession at its upper end – which I feel sure I could penetrate – pays vastly more than a governess' wages, who would not in any case be engaged if she had her own children, why, my duty is clear."

"You shall have the allowance continued in full," said Mr. Churchill in a furious voice.

"Thank you Mr. Churchill," said Jane submissively, "then there is no need for me to consider any further course of action concerning future employment."

That she had no intention of carrying out her threat – had only thought of it because she had been so angry – was neither here nor there. He had not dared to call her bluff. And in truth Jane did not see why he should be permitted to turn up full of censure for what was a fault in Frank's upbringing; indulged by his uncle and trammelled but mollycoddled by his aunt his weak nature had been exacerbated by a mixture of indulgence and being kept tied to his aunt by leading strings. Left to make his own way, and free of his aunt's demanding nature, he had let his inclinations towards profligate pleasure run wild, and the sudden stiffening of his uncle towards him over that outrageous debt, instead of making some push to find out *why* he needed so great a sum was, Jane felt, irresponsible. She had some anger towards herself too that she had not tried to be firmer with Frank from the first; but that of course was why he had married her; he knew she would be grateful for being rescued from the fate of being a governess and so would be compliant and ready to fall in with all that he said, being as unlike his aunt as could be. And she had been grateful; and it was no basis for love or marriage.

Caleb spluttered almost as loudly as Mr. Churchill when she reported the conversation to him.

"Jane-girl you would not ... why, I have thought about your situation and it occurred to me that letting the house would bring you almost a thousand a year, surely; and as Frank bought it with his own monies, it devolves to you, his widow, not the estate of Enscombe!" he said.

Jane smiled her demure smile.

"No Mr. Armitage; I should not take so drastic a course. Besides, I believe I should think that there is a good man who would offer me his name instead," she gave him an upward glance under her lashes, "but I lost my temper; I believe for the first time in my life, for I am generally of equable mien. I should have been faithful to Frank and tolerated his faults as a wife must when she has made a terrible mistake in her marriage; but after having been humiliated by him in so many ways – yes, I will admit it in as many words to you – to be accused of profligacy, to have Frances and my unborn child accused of being like to have bad blood, it was too much; and the worm has turned. It seems to me that upbringing has more to do with how a child may behave than purely blood and I was so angry that he condemned Frances and baby without trial, guilty without a chance of proving themselves innocent."

"Which is according to the Code Napoleon; and nothing good ever came out of France," said Caleb. "I am glad that you stood up for yourself and the children; I should have had a few things to say to this precious uncle of Frank's if I had been there."

"Yes Mr. Armitage; and I might too have leaned upon your strong presence and permitted it of you," said Jane "But I am determined that, bar the ordinary levels of gratitude for a good deed, that may be repaid, I shall never again be ruled by gratitude. And I would not accept an offer of marriage in the spirit of giving my children and myself a home and a father with income. I had rather be able to contribute to the household."

"Well, Mrs. Churchill, there we have a problem with *my* pride," said Caleb, "for if I were to offer for a beautiful woman whose house may bring in an income many times what I am paid, what then am I to do?"

"I should have thought that any woman would be glad of a father to her children, those that were and those that were not yours also, who would give them time and love," said Jane. "It seems to me that a man who is an honest family man and who will give himself as well as take is a man who is a prize beyond mere monetary measure."

"And any man who finds so generous a woman who could love outside her estate and give aid and succour to a man to the extent of darkening the daylights of an assailant with a glimmer-stick would consider her beyond the price of rubies as the Good Book says," said Caleb.

"Good; then when I am out of mourning we need not discuss any economics save how much we must needs put towards a household," said Jane. "When I am in half mourning you may commence to court me."

"I thought I already had," said Caleb.

"Indeed; but I am taking no notice of such contumely," said Jane demurely.

Jane was glad that Mr. Churchill intended staying in his own house at Richmond rather than wishing to stay with her; his presence in the house must needs be oppressive. Moreover, though he had met Dorothy briefly he had as yet no idea who she might be and seemed to be under the impression that she was some young relative of Jane and Miss Bates. Jane somehow suspected that if Dorothy's identity as

Frank's mistress were to be revealed to Mr. Churchill he would leap to the conclusion, as he seemed indeed inclined to leap from fact to conjecture without intermediate proof, that Dorothy had in some wise corrupted Jane to lead her into a path of vice rather than Jane having rescued the poor girl from a life that would ultimately end up in misery and untimely death; for Dorothy was never going to be what Mr. Armitage called a 'High Flyer'. This would of course lead to more argument and unpleasantness such as Jane disliked intensely; thoughshe was determined that she should stand up for poor Dorothy. Fortunately Mr. Churchill seemed all that was conciliatory; and Jane suddenly realised, with a flash of insight, that he had, like Frank, been very much at Mrs. Churchill's beck and call and his hectoring manner was a reaction to her death; and that Jane standing up to him had reminded him sufficiently of his dead wife's own strong will that he was, at least for the moment, behaving with the same meek manner that he had been wont to show to the late Mrs. Churchill.

She managed to smile wryly to herself and considered how diverting she might find the situation if she were watching it as an outsider; as Emma Knightley doubtless might do. She debated whether or not to write to Emma of this; since Emma had become less censorious since her marriage to Mr. Knightley; but decided against it. Emma must indeed be shocked at Jane's brazen blackmail of Mr. Churchill; indeed Jane was shocked at herself. Anger had its uses when harnessed but indeed was a dangerous emotion to carry one away far beyond the bounds of propriety!

It was however useful to know that one might have the ability to show anger and to stand up for oneself and one's children without even stammering or blushing if the need arose. It was an ability to be cherished; but kept firmly and securely in check.

Chapter 21

Jane took the 'Morning Post' and the 'Spectator' as her newspapers; and generally read one or the other over breakfast and saved the other for teatime. Her eye was caught by the headline 'Notorious Highwayman Strikes Again!' and she picked up the 'Morning Post' to read further.

"It was a sad night for the Honourable Mr – and his good lady on returning from a day with relatives to be held up and robbed on Hampstead Heath by a Highwayman believed to have been the notorious 'Sparkler Jack' so named because his invariable demand is 'hand over the sparklers'. Sparkler Jack has so far eluded arrest and this publication wishes to know what the Bow Street Runners are doing about the recent wave of jewellery robberies of which 'Sparkler Jack' is but one contributor Mrs – has lost a fine emerald necklace with good large stones and a curious and singular gold setting as well as the couple having lost between them several rings, and Mr – 's pocket watch, jewelled fob and snuff box."

The paper also carried the notice of Frank's obsequies;

"The funeral took place on Saturday of Mr F – C – who came to an untimely end last Sunday night" she checked to make sure that there had not been too many details; good, the Officers of the Law had not released too much to the papers.

Jane folded the paper to highlight the story and beckoned Fowler to her.

"Take this up to Mr. Armitage if you please," she said. "I fancy he may wish to see it."

Caleb came down to the dining room adjuring Fowler not to hover over him like a duenna with a debutante accidentally come to the Hell Fire Club.

"I wager that Sparkler Jack is a part of the gang," he said excitedly, "but now they are short a jarksman to forge new provenance. I am almost minded to persuade that clever-mouthed Mr. Despard to play a may game with them; save that I fancy his mouth is *too* clever for his own good and he may yet give himself away. If I could only catch Sparkler

Jack making the transfer to that slippery jeweller...but it will not be done obviously, nothing so simple as a visit to the shop."

"Why not?" asked Jane "Surely the bold approach is the best? For where does one expect to see jewellery if not a jeweller's shop? It conceals by being obvious!"

Caleb laughed, and then pulled a chair to sit down rather suddenly and shakily.

"Mrs. Churchill, it is as well that you have never decided to go in for crime; for it is quite plain that you have a talent for boldness that would surpass most of our peevy and timid criminals," he said. "Those who are on the bridle lay – the high Toby, highwaymen, call it as you will are tedious shy about their transactions; they do not risk having their faces seen. I would doubt that our shy friend Sparkler Jack is even known by physiognomy to our Froglander."

"I thought he was Dutch," said Jane.

"He is," said Caleb. "It is a name by which the Dutch are known; perhaps because they caved in so readily under the Frogs to become part of their damned republic and then empire."

"I see," said Jane, "and though they must trust each other to gain their dubious living, the one does not trust the other to see his face?"

"Do not for one moment suppose any kind of trust, Mrs. Churchill," said Caleb. "There is mutual benefit; no trust. And fences have turned in those who bring them geegaws to sell before now; the notorious Jonathon Wilde made a career of buying stolen property to return for what he described as a 'finder's fee' and if the thieves displeased him he would write a cross by their name; if this occurred twice then he would turn them in. It has given us a new phrase, the double cross, to cheat or betray someone from a position of supposed trust. No Bridle Cull would consider trusting a fence without other considerations being involved, familial connection for example; though these cullies would many of them sell their own brothers. The word 'chum' which is used to describe confederates may be translated as 'friend' but I assure you 'crony' would be closer. Sparkler Jack will wait for a good opportunity to hand over the baubles in the darksmans. And probably to a third party at that; maybe that spry little fellow who got away from us the other night, who strikes me as a bene cracksman; probably also a sneaksman. He has the build, from what little hand I had on him, to get in small places, and to readily hide all day in small places until the household is asleep no doubt too, though that's a specialist piece of crookery. And of course here we are being led by the usual maundering of a newspaper into assuming that the Bridle-cull is going to sell to the head-cully; or is even aware of him. There's more than one fence around."

"I suppose what needs to be determined," said Jane, "is whether or not any of the items stolen by Sparkler Jack have ever been recovered or whether they have disappeared into the underworld. If the latter, is it not indicative of them being reset by our Dutchman?"

Caleb slapped his thigh and winced as the movement of his body jarred his arm.

"You're right; and *that* was why I'd got Sparkler Jack associated with our other little bit o' lay here," he said "Because nothing he has ever stolen has been identified – save one dubious identification that was held unproven where a snuffbox had a cameo set in it and the cameo may – or may not – have been seen and recognised set into a necklace. Gold and silver are readily melted down of course; and stones are anonymous enough in a new setting. Fobs may be re-carved, the tops of snuffboxes, *etuis* and
vinaigrettes cut down or set in a setting the original owner is unlikely to notice them. And tattlers – pocket watches – are often sufficiently unremarkable or may have covers switched or new ones put on, to change them sufficiently that anyone claiming to identify them may be readily confused."

"It is indeed a large and enterprising industry; but I imagine that the loss of the Avon Necklace must still have been a significant loss," said Jane.

"More to the point, Jane-girl, it's dangerous. It's identifiable. And Dorothy will get her reward from Her

Grace of Avon; but I have asked that it not be made public nor any reward given until our man is caught; and I spoke to Her Grace and she is amenable to that," he nodded to Dorothy who was listening wide eyed.

"'Ow much will I get?" breathed Dorothy.

"Never you mind, my girl," said Caleb "Or you'll go shouting your mouth off about it. Enough to make it worth your while handing it over see!"

Dorothy pouted; but did not press the issue.

"Oh Mr. Armitage, you will help Dorothy not to spend it unwisely?" asked Miss Bates.

"That I will, Miss Bates; for I suggested that it be invested in the funds for her, that will give her enough to live on if she is not extravagant and any sewing she does may supplement it," said Caleb.

"You are wise and kind," murmured Jane as Dorothy discussed how much she might get excitedly with Miss Bates, "for she is quite feckless about money and would spend it all in one day if given the chance; this way it does not matter if her earnings are never good if she may have enough for subsistence."

Jane had forbidden Annie to take Frances out to the park at all for the immediate future but to permit her to take the baby only into the garden, which was fully enclosed. She did not tell Annie that it was for fear of Frances being abducted, her return perhaps conditional on handing over the Avon necklace; but permitted the nursery maid to think that with sudden showers prevalent at this time of year returning once a shower started might risk the health of little Frances. Which indeed it might; but Jane did not think Annie stupid enough not to keep an eye on the weather. However it served as a good excuse; and the outing each fine day was quite brief and Jane too attended. Frances was not much impressed by the great out of doors and protested being bundled up in warm outdoor clothes; but Jane felt that fresh air was essential for healthy lungs on warmer days. Having been a sickly child herself, she did not want to see Frances suffer childish complaints if she might help it, when the day was neither windy nor damp that the child might benefit from the mildness of the better days that held some promise of spring to come.

"My dear Mr. Armitage, tell me truly if you think I make a great to-do about nothing over the safety of Frances?" she asked him, when a locksmith had been procured to repair the bolt on the coal hatch and indeed to add a second bolt.

"Mrs. Churchill, I believe you very wise to take such precaution over your precious baby," said Caleb. "These people will stop at nothing to get what they desire. And whilst I believe that the villain may only come to threaten at first, yet I must recall that Dorothy was not merely *threatened*. This was why I suggested that it be well not to take her to the park. That you go out with her too is but an added precaution that I do not consider unnecessary; Annie is just a young girl likely to lose her head if any would-be abductor climbed over the wall. Indeed I am minded to watch out of the window too if you will apprise me of when you will be out with her. ,"

"I pray you will indeed keep close watch and employ Frank's pistol if need be," said Jane, "and if any snatch up my baby I had rather she died shot at your hands than carried off into who knows what slavery."

"Jane-girl, I'm a tolerable shot; it will not come to that," said Caleb gently. "My barking-iron suffered a flash in the pan that terrible night; I hurled it at the one Fowler shot and wrestled with the other for want of anything better to do. When my ball discharges I may expect to be as accurate as any man living that does not make a living duelling. I will kill any man who tries to carry off Frances to indentured slavery or any such fate."

"You are very good," said Jane softly; reaching out a hand to lay on his good arm. He smiled at her and the world stood still for a moment that was also an eternity.

The locksmith must be paid however, and meals ordered and all the other little tasks to oversee in a busy household; and if Jane busied herself with more minutiae than she required it was as much to prevent her heart hammering in fear over what might happen at the hands of the Jeweller as to ignore its hammering over the close proximity of Caleb Armitage.

She could not communicate her fears to Miss Bates who stood in the place of a mother to her; for the good woman would be quite paralysed with fear if Jane told her but a tenth of all that she herself feared and imagined; nor might she speak to Dorothy, who was turning out a biddable girl but not long in understanding and just pleased that her own nasty burns were healing well and that she was somewhere safe. Whether or not it was safe, Jane could not guess; what she had heard on the subject of what Caleb called 'cracking a crib' suggested that no house, hall or palace in the land might be said to be truly impervious to penetration from the cleverest of crooks.

It was almost a relief that Fowler came respectfully into the parlour to tell her that a Dutch gentleman wished to see her and that he waited in the book room.

Chapter 22

"My dear Mrs. Churchill!" Poul de Vries attempted a smile. Jane considered it about as friendly as the grin of the crocodile that was held in the menagerie at the Tower of London. The possessor of the smile was doubtless about as genial and safe to handle as the crocodile too.

"Excuse me; do I know you?" Jane let her eyes be limpid pools and smiled in a tentative and fluttery sort of way.

"Why yes, Mrs. Churchill; you bought a piece of mourning jewellery from me," said Mr. De Vries.

Jane made a moue.

"What you are come to tell me that it was on display by mistake, that it was already ordered for somebody else?" she said. "I really do not think that I am wishful to hear such excuses."

"Oh no my good lady; not at all," said de Vries, "I merely mentioned that as I hoped to jog your memory concerning my identity. No, it is that I am wishful to purchase from you a piece of jewellery that your husband had in his possession; I suspect it may have been intended as a gift for you when he believed it real…. A trumpery piece of paste which he passed on to a young woman of his acquaintance…. But I know someone who would like to buy such a piece of well made paste in case of highway robbery….. there are so many violent thieves about these days, one hardly knows where one might be safe."

Jane hid a shudder; that was a threat. Really she should be almost thankful that the tedious days pretending with Frank in Highbury had prepared her to hide her true feelings and present a bland and slightly puzzled countenance to this horrid man.

"Paste? Jewellery? Oh, Dolly did mention that she had been given a necklace; unfortunately my husband was very good about buying gifts but less good about paying bills; she pawned it, for colourless stones were not to her taste in any case," said Jane in a careless voice.

The sight of him changing colour to purple and then white

was quite priceless.

"She – she has *pawned* it?" he looked ghastly "But – but – where? Which pawnbroker?"

"La, I have no idea," said Jane, "and I doubt she has either; the girl is quite half-witted, I felt I had to take her under my protection; I expect she has already spent the whole five pounds she got for it; and it is as well if she has forgotten, for if the pawnbroker finds out it was paste and she has cheated him I should think he will be cross as crabs. I am sorry; but if you are a jeweller, then making paste pieces is easy enough for you is it not?" she smiled brightly.

"F-five pounds? That stupid girl got rid of it for *five pounds*?" he cried.

"Outrageous, is it not?" said Jane. "But perhaps he was sorry for her. I only hope he does not come looking for her to complain. I am sure though that she cannot have been stupid enough to have mentioned my late husband's name to him that he come here; she prattles artlessly in her odd argot, but nobody would bother to listen, even if she was indiscreet. But anyway, I am sorry that I cannot help you; the necklace is long gone. Are you all right? Do you require a doctor? For you look most unwell….."

"I am perfectly well," snapped De Vries. "Thank you; I can see myself out."

"Oh Fowler will not mind," said Jane knowing that Fowler was waiting.

De Vries exited all but spluttering.

Jane smiled to herself. Two men she disliked that she had brought close to apoplexy in as many days; really there was an intoxicating quality to this.

Caleb entered the bookroom through the door that communicated with the parlour.

"That was a clever play," he said, "though I fancy he will work out that it was a play."

"But the necklace is not here; that was no less than the truth," said Jane. "Did I do wrong to divert his suspicions from the household? I fear his attacks on Frances or Aunt Hetty or Dorothy. I thought if you wanted him confessed it might do to go to his shop and tell him that I have obtained the necklace back and ask him if he had lost it and if he will make me an offer.... In light of my husband's allowance dying with him. And be on hand to arrest him when he identifies it if I might borrow it to that end."

"I fancy that the Duchess of Avon will not let it out of her sight again," said Caleb dryly. "I do not know that I can let you risk yourself in a spot of ladylike blackmail however; he might seize you and threaten your person," he frowned, "and I suspect that he will decide that if Dorothy *had* mentioned your name, that meant that you, and Dorothy and all your household were a risk..... first he will send agents to every pawnbroker in Pimlico and around. That will take some of his time and energy..... then I fancy he will send in agents to murder every one. It has not taken the risk away but has bought some time. Fowler shall run errands; I have a few of the First Regiment of Foot Guards – they are the Grenadier Guards since Waterloo – who owe me the odd favour, who would quietly join the household for a day or two for a bit of milling."

"Poor Mrs. Ketch!" said Jane, "she will be most put out! Still, better put out than dead."

"Quite so," said Caleb. "I have friends enough who will not let anything happen to you or your household; I can arrange to protect Frances."

"And let us now go and spend some time with her; I have had enough of villains and I want to hold my daughter," said Jane.

As he appeared to be invited to go along, Caleb was nothing loath to join in the exercise of entertaining Frances, who had taken to him; and Jane was entertained too by the sight of the tall figure of the Bow Street Runner on his hands and knees being a horse neighing and pawing the ground and doing his best to canter for his passenger.

Jane smiled. *What* a good father he would make!

It were best perhaps not to even think along such lines, she told herself severely. Not at least for the time being.

Three slightly disreputable men drifted down into the area and were duly presented to Jane and bowed awkwardly assuring her that they would remain perfectly invisible and do their best to help with any heavy work Mr. Fowler and Mrs. Ketch set them. One was wearing an eye patch, another held his arm a little stiffly and the third seemed to be simple. Jane asked Caleb about them.

"Plenty were demobbed after the war that can get no honest work," he said, "a few days with food and a roof over their heads will suit these boys fine in return for guarding the house."

"Why I must pay them too, to be sure," said Jane. "I would not think of anything else; we shall have to see about what may be done for them for a longer period; is it because they were wounded that they cannot get jobs?"

"Partly, ma'am; partly that there are not enough jobs to be had. Mechanisation has taken many jobs, and those now released from the wars have no jobs to go to, and desperate poor because of these Corn Laws that set the price of bread so high; those with pitiable wounds like peg legs can often make their way by begging. Which leads to soldier-mawnds, beggars that pretend wounds for sympathy, giving a bad name to the many who really have lost legs and the like."

"How could you pretend to have lost a leg?" said Jane, bewildered "Is it not a little obvious?"

"Bless you for an innocent, my dear Mrs. Jane....that is what they call you in the servant's hall, so I am not too free to use that.... " he said, giving her a half shy, half defiant look. "They do it by strapping the leg up, bent at the knee and seemingly lost from the knee down; some will wear a stump and others push themselves around in a cart as many genuine legless beggars do; and some of those will too wear clymes, false sores made by bruising crows-foot, spearwort and salt and binding it to the skin to make an angry looking but not too painful sore; they may pick at it and use powdered arsenic on it to make it look worse. If they can seem more injured they get more from sympathetic coves, or more often the morts."

"Dear me!" said Jane, "there is a lot more to beggars than I had realised; I may have to peer more closely before I give to any."

"It will make you no friends with the canting crew though it will earn you their grudging respect," said Caleb, "but genuine beggars will love you for your discernment. I keep in touch with beggars, genuine ones; vail them well and they are my eyes; one of the messages Fowler ran for me was to ask a couple of beggars to shift their patch to keep an eye on Poul de Vries. Nice that we *were* correct in our determination of which one it was!"

"Well once that apprentice called him Mynheer *de* Vries, so we had the initials PDV, *and* he twitted me about not being able to wear diamonds or other stones, so it did seem obvious," said Jane. "Catching him out will be the thing. Well, if there is a reward from Lloyds of London, that may help me to find permanent positions for these three friends of yours, even with Frank's debts to sort out. And they too might run errands and be your eyes on a salary from me; if that would not dent your pride."

"To be honest I would welcome the chance to do my job better; we are underfunded and undermanned," said Caleb.

"Have you been talking with Fowler's stone in your mouth?" asked Jane "You are being all refined today, save your canting words."

He grinned sheepishly.

"Mrs. Jane Churchill should have a man whom she can introduce to her gentry friends and not be ashamed of his speech; it may take me the whole year but I am determined that none shall have cause to complain."

"You know that I am indifferent to such outward signs," said Jane.

"Yes ma'am; but many are not; and would see it as a reflection on you. Besides, I will also get the swell jobs which means in general a higher reward; which makes me more able to hold up my head to you. I know it does not matter to you; I cannot help it mattering somewhat to me," he said.

She nodded.

"It could not be otherwise with a proud man. Frank would hang happily on the sleeve of a wealthier wife; but he was weak. You are not weak in any wise," and she blushed scarlet. "It may be that when I remarry, my allowance from Mr. Churchill will be cut; or at least reduced. I plan to lay aside what I may, and so put that into the funds to give an income for the future."

"You are wise Mrs. Jane; and I will in that case definitely advise moving to a smaller house and letting this one; that way you may have both income from it and hold property."

"I do hate money," admitted Jane, "or rather I hate having to consider every farthing and how to best use it. Still, I am far better off than many and should not complain. And relative penury with love and happiness would still be an improvement on the sham of high society I lived with Frank. And if it should come to it, I have lived in relative penury with my aunt and grandmother; I am not some useless woman who does not know how to manage a household."

"My dear, that I had already realised; and we were not going to discuss economics!" said Caleb. "Let me tell you more about Will, Jackie and Daniel."

"I should like that," said Jane. "I expect each of them has something of a history!"

"Yes and I don't say I know it all either," said Caleb. "Will was a weaver; decided joining up was better than dying of weaver's lung. As you see he's not a big man though he's tall and lanky; bending over the looms must have hurt something cruel and contributed to his decision.

Tall is good for a Foot Guard; so he did well, lost his eye in the last half hour of Waterloo, which is cruel bad luck. A spent ball lodged in it; one of those unlucky accidents. Jackie, who may be muscular but isn't tall got in by blague and a big personality; he'll do most of the talking for them. London boy; not as low class as me, he's the son of a fishmonger down Billingsgate. One of the other men in his company used to call him 'The Fish' until Jackie lost his temper – he had had words before but you can drive a man too far – and he picked this other fellow up bodily and dumped him in the river, and held him under long enough to start worrying; and asked him 'who's the fish?'. I was a corporal then; I confess I turned a blind eye to the business."

"I suppose there are times when one has to do so," posited Jane.

"Yes, when there's hazing, the men do best to sort it out for themselves," said Caleb. He went on, "Jackie took a bullet much the same way I did the other night; only he didn't have so fine care as me, and that took infection. We cut it to let the poison out, but seemingly it never quite healed right. He reckons we saved the arm cutting the poison out, and when it's better weather he can use it more; and he can use it, it's just a little stiff and clumsy. He guts fish for his pa when he can't get other work but he hates it. Never eats fish if he can avoid it!"

Jane nodded in sympathy.

Caleb went on,

"Daniel, he's from Essex; a bit slow he was to start off with, which he got teased for, being a country boy; he was right by an artillery piece when it went off premature; got knocked right over and his ears bled. He was deaf for weeks, though it comed back to him. Only we don't rightly know if he's still a bit deaf or if the concussion of the blast knocked him sillier; he don't always seem to mind what you say the first time, and if that's account that he don't hear or don't understand I don't know nowise; and he never was smart enough to understand to answer if he was asked. Jackie looks out for him; gets him work carrying boxes of fish. He's strong is Daniel; and as gentle as any unless people he counts friends are in danger. Best thing for our Daniel is to put him under Annie's orders to guard the babby; he'll understand that. Nobody won't hurt Frances with Daniel on guard."

Jane nodded.

"Well I shall leave you in charge of the – dispositions, I think you call it – of your troops," she said.

Chapter 23

When Dorothy arose next day she looked quite pale and woebegone.

"Oh Mrs. Jane, please don't cast me orf aht into the world!" she cried.

"Why, Dorothy, why should I do that?" asked Jane putting an arm about the girl. Dorothy sobbed noisily and clung to Jane for comfort.

"B-because me flux 'as come, and Molly said if I weren't carryin' the master's child I weren't no better than her, less account of her bein' virtuous!" sobbed Dorothy.

"Dear me; a little unkind of Molly," said Jane. "I will speak to her quite gently. I will not cast you off; but really, you know, as you do have to make your way in the world, it will be easier for you to *not* have to have a baby. Keeping a base-born child would be very hard; and giving a child up would be very hard too, even knowing that it is best for that child. Better that you should have children with a loving husband, do you not think? You are young Dorothy; and soon the time you have had to spend at Covent Garden will seem just like a bad nightmare that you can put behind you. Though," she added "It is my opinion that honesty is always best with any man you love. If he loves you he will know that it was not by your contriving that you fell from grace and will accept it and praise your honesty. You shall stay in the household and learn as I have promised to be a seamstress or milliner and I shall see to getting you a good position."

"You are so *kind* Mrs. Jane!" cried Dorothy, embracing her.

Jane might have wished she did not embrace with quite so much enthusiasm as she still fought the morning nausea; but she said nothing. She sent Dorothy to lie down and had Ella take her a hot brick wrapped in a blanket to help her with the pains associated with the distressing monthly proof of womanhood.

"What you should understand, Molly, is that when

Dorothy was no older than you she had her virtue taken by force; and lost her position because of it," said Jane, "which is grossly unfair. She has had little choice but to embrace an unfortunate profession; but she also gave my husband affection and companionship and for that I look upon her also with affection. She is learning to speak as a lady to be able to work as a millliner one day; you might listen to her practise her speech, and help her if you wish to improve your own speech; for you and Annie do not have so far to go. If you too work hard and take the training that Mrs. Ketch gives you, it may be that you will learn enough to be housekeeper one day to a great house; where you will have surpassed Dorothy's position as a milliner. Our lives are what we make of them; Dorothy has been ready to learn to forget her terrible ordeal as one of those kinds of women. You should thank the Good Lord that you do not know how terrible that may be and have sympathy for one who has been in some respects enslaved by circumstance. You should also give thanks that you are fortunate enough to be cleverer than Dorothy and so, if you are as industrious as you are clever, have every opportunity of rising."

"Oh Madam I *will* work hard!" said Molly flushed with pleasure.

"There's a good girl; and I should like you to apologise to Dorothy for being short with her this morning; that I expect she took more amiss because we do not feel well at such times and more inclined to take offence," said Jane.

"I am sorry Madam; it just seemed she give herself airs because she might be carrying the master's child and when I saw the implement all bloody….."

"I see; but gloating is not very nice, Molly," said Jane. "Poor Dorothy! The thought that she might have a child was all she had to remember the master by; and he was very kind to her."

"Well she's the only one what misses him then," said Molly, "he were that demanding! And he frightened my sister, putting his arm around her!"

Jane sighed.

"He was worried about money; it made him short with people," she said, "and you should understand, Molly, that men become easily out of sorts over worries that women can manage to solve. I am sorry that Annie was frightened; I am sure that he did not mean to do so."

Molly considered telling the mistress that she suspected that the master expected Annie to fall into his bed like a ripe fruit but decided to leave her in ignorance; poor lady, she had to be married to him and had to stick up for him.

Jane hoped fervently that Molly did not understand too much of what Frank may have hoped of Annie and hoped the girl had not been too upset. Of course Annie was a pretty girl; Frank always had an eye for a pretty girl. And it was interesting Annie, Dorothy *and* the girl Juliet were all blonde like Emma….. Frank revealed his tastes very clearly. It left a nasty taste in the mouth to realise that she was just the compliant wife, chosen for domestic management and that perhaps she was not even particularly physically attractive to him at all; there because his allowance was increased for being married, and to be kept in her place as a housekeeper with entertainment skills on pianoforte and uxorial rights.

Jane dismissed Molly who went off with reasonably good grace to apologise to Dorothy.

Jane decided that as she had little that she could do save wait for de Vries to make a move, she might as well be engaged on domestic matters, and that she would start with clearing out the pianoforte music that had been Frank's choice not hers.

She might perhaps give it to some indigent young woman who yearned for new pieces; Jane did not wish to play them again. Some indeed had words that turned to ashes in her mouth at the thought of how Frank had given them significance in his courtship of her. She caressed the keys of the instrument, revelling in having possession of a grand piano, whatever the reasons Frank had held for wanting it, that had replaced the box piano he had bought her before they were wed and that now stood in the nursery for when

Frances was old enough to learn. She permitted the music to take her away as she sat and played. Miss Bates was there listening – Jane knew that her Aunt Hetty always liked to hear her play, even if perhaps she was not sufficiently discerning to know good playing from bad. That Caleb had slipped into the room to listen too made her heart race as she looked up from her playing.

"Mrs. Jane, you are excellent," he said. "I am no real judge of course; and beyond that you are out of practise and hesitated once or twice I could not presume to make comment that would help. But if I may make one small criticism?" his eyes were laughing at her.

"There is nothing to criticise in dear Jane's playing!" cried Miss Bates.

"Oh there is plenty; you are correct, I hesitated and chose a simpler chord pattern when memory failed me," said Jane. "What else troubled you?"

"Oh, it is not a trouble quite yet; but though music be the food of love, Fowler has laid the table for luncheon and is expecting us to repair to the dining room," said Caleb. "We have all forgot the time in the pleasure of hearing you play."

"My goodness! Is it indeed so late? I do apologise!" cried Jane. "I must have become quite carried away!"

"And we duly carried with you," said Caleb "But I fear that Fowler will become quite overset if we do not remove instantly to his snowily linened domain of culinary excellence."

Jane chuckled.

"Caleb Armitage you have the most wordy conceits!" she declared.

"I'm also hungry," said Caleb.

Jane was surprised to have a visitor announced in the afternoon; she was playing from music for the pleasure of Miss Bates primarily, Caleb having gone to lie down for the weakness that was still in his arm; and Dorothy lay on the chaise longue looking a little pale but evidently enjoying the playing.

Jane looked at the piece of pasteboard Fowler had brought her.

"Sir Richard Marjoram? Why I do not believe I have ever heard the name," she said.

Fowler raised an eyebrow and rocked his hand and cupped his ear.

Jane nodded. If he were nearby and listening it might be as well.

She went along the landing to the book room; the door from the parlour was in a recess and not immediately apparent; if this man had not poked around she preferred not to advertise that there was a second door into the book room.

Sir Richard Marjoram rose from the Hepplewhite shield-backed chair in which he had been taking his ease and held out his hand. Jane let her fingers brush his conventionally as he bowed over her hand; and sat in her own accustomed chair indicating with a wave of the hand that he should seat himself again. He seemed to be a gentleman in his attire; Jane was not so ignorant of male attire that she did not recognise the hand of Schweitzer and Davidson of Cork Street in the cut of his dark blue merino coat nor the touch of Hoby to his boots; and his biscuit coloured inexpressibles were impeccable and skin tight. If his waistcoat were a little gaudy for her liking, well there were those gentlemen – Frank among them – who chose waistcoats that were not as sober as might be pleasing.

"Sir Richard; I do not believe I have had the pleasure of meeting you before," she said.

"Alas; it has been my loss," said Sir Richard bowing from the waist in his chair. "I have come to pay a courtesy call to give you my deepest commiserations on the death of your husband; poor Frank! Who would have thought that he would meet so untimely an end?"

"You were then acquainted with my husband, Sir Richard?" said Jane.

"Indeed; a charming companion," said Sir Richard. "A great loss; I am sure that you find yourself inconsolable."

Jane viewed him with a faintly jaundiced air. Here was a

man whose mouth smiled constantly; and whose eyes held very little warmth. If anything one might see derision in their depths; and a smiling mouth and sneering eyes she was well used to from Frank. A man too who would wear a waistcoat with rather more silver thread woven into and embroidered onto it than was strictly tasteful was a man like Frank who was too careful about display of his wealth for it to be necessarily genuine; the hand full of rings and three carnelian and crystal fobs on the watch chain and silver mounted cane were also just a bit too much.

She gave a small, tight smile.

"Oh I believe, Sir Richard, that I bear up tolerably well," she said.

"Ah, you are brave; and too with a small child I understand," said Sir Richard.

Jane raised an eyebrow.

"You know of my daughter? I am surprised."

He smiled deprecatingly.

"Ah, a proud father will always speak of his offspring," he said.

"Yes; but this is my husband Frank of whom we are speaking," said Jane. "I find it hard to believe that he would have mentioned my daughter; since he was quite indifferent to her save when he found the wails of a small child intolerable. I do not believe you are a friend of Frank's at all; if you are a creditor of his I wish you will come right out and say so; it is not, after all, something that will cause me great surprise since I have been going through my husband's papers. I shall however expect you to have proof."

Sir Richard displayed his teeth in an ingratiating rictus that was hardly improved by having black notes amongst the white of his ivory display.

"Oh my dear Mrs. Churchill, you *quite* misunderstand; perhaps poor Frank found it hard to display any affection to a small baby, not knowing quite how to handle the same; but he certainly spoke of her! Which is why, as his dearest friend, I have come on this errand," he went on smoothly, rising, bowing and going down on one knee "It is my desire to take into my protection the poor bereft wife of dear Frank and to be a father to his daughter. I could hardly do less!"

Jane stared.

"Sir Richard I beg that you will rise and sit upon the chair in a civilised manner instead of making so ridiculous a declaration to one who has been in mourning for less than a fortnight! It is indeed most unseemly!" she said.

"Mrs. Churchill; I confess that such a declaration cannot be anything but bald and cold; for we do not know each other; but I can have no other wish, my heart not being otherwise engaged, than to undertake to get to know you where if not love then affection might spring from a mutual affection for poor dear Frank who would surely wish his dear wife taken care off after being so foully felled and thrown into the Serpentine."

Jane frowned briefly then schooled her face.

"Sir Richard, flattered as I am by such an offer I cannot possibly contemplate courtship until I am at least in half mourning; and moreover I should need to find out the legal position of my unborn child," she said. "I am not about to jeopardise his succession – should it prove a boy – by even contemplating remarriage until after I have birthed! You will not speak of this again for the nonce; I must bid you good day!" and she rose.

Perforce he rose too.

"Permit that I may call upon you again!" he said his hand on what he obviously fondly believed to be his heart.

Jane sighed.

"Very well, Sir Richard; provided that you will undertake to behave with perfect decorum," she said, ringing the bell.

Chapter 24

Jane sent for Jackie, the spokesman of the soldiers.

"Suppose you wanted to get hold of newspapers several days old, would you be able to do so?" she asked, bluntly.

"Yes Ma'am; what was you wantin'?" asked Jackie, looking interested and curious.

"The Monday editions of every different paper you can get hold of and any Sunday paper too if that is possible," said Jane, "for I want to check something in each of them. How much money do you need?"

"Should manage it gratis; but if you gives me a sow's baby – a half borde – sixpence – that oughta cover anyfink," said Jackie. "Reckon I can pick most up in coffee 'ouses and inns and fings."

"Well take a shilling; and what you save, you earned," said Jane.

Jackie grinned.

"Fanks Missus Churchill," he said.

Jackie was gone about an hour and a half and came back with a veritable pile.

"'Ere y'are," he said "Gazette; Spectator; Times; Mornin' Chronicle; Mornin' Post; Observer; Cobbetts dirty little Political Register; and the Globe. Reckon that covers most on 'em. Unless you wants the radical papers or specialist magazines?"

"No, these will do fine," said Jane. "I have never seen the Political Register; it seems to be more a pamphlet than a newspaper."

"Yerse, well, it avoid the tax that way," said Jackie, considering spitting and thinking better of it. "I don't say 'e's *wrong* ter criticise the government but 'e's a bit confrontational-like; and where's that gwine ter get 'im? Banned an' in the coop if y'arst me and how's that gwine ter help them as is those 'e claims to be speakin' up for, you tell me that?."

"Perhaps he feels that nobody will listen if he is not confrontational," said Jane.

Jackie sniffed.

"That's as maybe, Ma'am; but it'll only put the backs up o' the government and landowners and where does that get the common man? Looked at wiv more despite by them in power, wot'll see us as nuffink but violent protesters account o' Mr. Cobbett's big mouf, that's what!"

"I can see that it is a tricky question to consider," said Jane, "how outspoken to be in order to be heard whilst not causing too much enmity towards those one would champion."

She gave Jackie a nod of dismissal; his political views might prove interesting but there was something she was looking for; and she perused each paper in turn.

None of them gave any more information than the Morning Post she took herself.

Mr. Armitage found Jane examining the relevant passage that she had clipped out of each of the papers that carried it – which was not all – frowning.

"I may be being stupid," she said.

"Unlikely," said Caleb, "tell me about it."

Jane had an excellent and retentive memory; and relayed the conversation with Sir Richard including the tones and facial expressions.

"Sounds a dashed queer cove to me," said Caleb. "What's all this stuff?"

"I asked Jackie to get me papers, all the ones he could, that were printed on Monday or Sunday," said Jane "Read these; you'll see why."

Caleb read through them and his eyebrow gradually elevated. He whistled.

"Very clever of you Jane-girl," he said.

"Unless anything was reported before," said Jane.

He shook his head.

"Bow Street don't let out anythink – any*thing* – but the barest and baldest of facts; a robbery took place such-and-such, a body was found so-and-so, identified as so-and-so; no details just in case, see? Especially with robberies account o' finding the baubles. 'cept a list is circulated to jewellers and 'opes the expensive ones at least is honest. I dunno if you were right to say he might come back; but then if he's got somethink – something – to do wiv all this….. 'course he could say he were Sir Richard Malodorous or whatever, but how do we know he is?"

"Marjoram," said Jane mildly. "We do not; how pleasant it would be if somebody would but make a complete list of the peerage to check such things! However if one might follow him when he calls again, the size and location of his lodging might be some indication as to the veracity of his claim. Bearing in mind his blatant lies I can but assume that he is one of the same stamp as that footman James Ripon; a butler perhaps who has learned to support the manner of a peer. Not that I have much idea how a 'Sir' or a 'Lady' might be in any wise different to any other of the gentry if indeed they are."

"Well the odd few I've tangled with vary from bein' gents through and through to bein' arrogant and stiff rumped," said Caleb. "Which ain't any guide nowise. Well I don't say someone born in the purple ain't necessarily not goin' to be a wrong 'un; look at Frank. Who might have been half flash half foolish but a fly cove who's weak enough to need a quick way to the readies….. yes, he shall be followed. I don't like to ask, but a bit of blunt to throw about would help."

Jane unlocked the small chest in which she kept cash.

"Take what you need," she said "There's a mix of coin in there."

"I will write you a receipt for it," said Caleb.

"Very well; it will make you more comfortable and will mean I keep track," said Jane.

Caleb took a selection of coins, and counted them out to write a reckoning.

"I don't know that I shall use all this but it is useful to have more than you need rather than less," he said.

"I have noticed this also with household accounts," said Jane demurely.

"And you keep them with such a neat and pretty hand," said Caleb, "no man would feel he had to stand over a woman keeping such excellent accounts but he might decide to do so anyway just to breathe the scent of her hair and admire her neat and well shaped hand pursuing of its most efficient endeavours ..."

"Mr. Armitage you are flirting again," said Jane in a tone of reproach that her flushed cheeks and sparkling eyes belied.

"Why Mrs. Churchill! I'm afraid I am!" said Caleb not sounding in the least bit apologetic.

"And why I should accept it from you when I would not accept it from Sir Richard Marjoram I am at a loss to consider!" said Jane with an attempt at severity.

"Because I'm sincere about it and that havy-cavy cove is deucedly smoky and too false by half," said Caleb. "Besides you don't want nothink – anything I mean – to do with him."

"Implying of course that I am willing to flirt with you? You are a presumptuous man, Mr. Armitage," said Jane.

"Not half as presumptuous as a fribble who thinks you'll fall into the arms of someone you don't know for the waving of a title at you," said Caleb, "and has me wondering what his lay might be!"

"Indeed; it is puzzling," said Jane, "and you have managed to turn the subject from my ringing a peal over you!"

"Adept at it, ain't I?" said Caleb. "A skill I picked up in the army."

"Mr. Armitage you are a most complete hand," said Jane sternly. "And you have work to do in collecting your army of beggars to follow Marjoram!"

Caleb brought a filthy small boy to see Jane some hours later. The child had a lopsided face and a withered arm under which was jammed a rude crutch to compensate in some part for the atrophied and dragging leg.

"This yere is Simmy; he's as sharp as the taste of Norfolk mustard," said Caleb, "and he already knows something about our Sir Richard."

"Strite up I do," said Simmy, "see, when I heered that Mr.

Armitage was stayin' 'ere, wot finds jobs for me, I hopped up as fast as I could toddle, see, Lidy, bein's as 'ow nobody don't take no notice of a kinchin-zad, wot Mr. Armitage find dead useful right? So I'm hangin' abaht, and this plum-voiced servant come aht an give me a half-bord wot she say is from the lidy – that's you, right?"

"Kinchin-zad is a cripple child," explained Caleb.

"Indeed," murmured Jane, who had standing orders to Ella to give largesse to any deserving beggars she caught sight of, and feeling faintly ashamed that she had been too caught up in her own troubles to have noticed this pathetic scrap of humanity for herself. "Ella is my dresser; she is a kind woman."

"Ar, she gimme a groat from herself," said Simmy, "which I took most kindly; and she didn't make no condition that I should make meself scarce neether. Wot some swell morts and their servants do see?"

"Get to the point Simmy," said Caleb, not unkindly.

"Yerse, well, I seen this swell cove come out and I fink t'meself, 'Ullo Simmy, I seen him somewhere. And I knows where it is; 'e goes ter cocking and dog fights where vere's good pickin's fer a beggar – better for a diver but I ain't got the agility t'pick pockets. 'E know a few rum coves too; but 'e is a gent, account 'e knows uvver gents wot are famous enough ter reckernise, though I don't say that 'e's no bosom-bow o' any on em. 'E ain't wot yer call the demi-monde but 'e do know plenty wot are if you arsts me, though 'e do go out o' 'is way ter make sure none o' the swell coves 'e goes arahnd wiv don't notice. But maunders – that's beggars in your tork, lidy – maunders see everyfink. And it pay ter know 'oo yer might touch fer a few coppers and 'oo might scrag yer; and reckon 'ed be one as would scrag yer. 'E 'as bang up prancers though! I kin find out 'oo is reelly is if it ain't what 'e says 'e is," his eyes glittered.

"Well Simmy, if you would do that, I should be well pleased," said Jane "Go first to the kitchen however and Mrs. Ketch will give you a square meal and will pack you up a veal pie and some bread and cheese to take on your investigations;

but you are not to take risks! Do not ask questions of anyone who might, er, scrag you! And here is some payment for your information and some on account in case you need to grease a palm or two," she took two shillings from her reticule, looked at them, and felt around to find instead two sixpences and three groats. She looked up to see tears in the child's eyes; and knelt beside him to put an arm around his filthy shoulders. "Why Simmy, what have I said to upset you?"

"Oh *Lidy*! Mr. Armitage, 'E says ter tike care, but even 'E aint never told me direct not ter arst questions o' dangerous coves!" said Simmy. "And yer gwine ter feed me *and* pay me?"

"I ain't never forbid that, because, little kinchin, I give you credit for not bein' stupid enough to do so," said Caleb. "Strewth, the brat's napping his bib in earnest!"

Simmy was quite clinging to Jane crying and she lifted his pathetically light body into her lap, cradling him to her. At first he stiffened then leaned into her bosom, every line of his body begging caresses.

"Oh Caleb, anyone would think nobody had ever even embraced him before!" she cried in distress, stroking his filthy hair.

Caleb shrugged.

"I don't suppose they ever have, Jane-girl; as I understand it he was abandoned on the doorstep of an orphan asylum at birth, and was too crippled to be indentured either at the mills or as a climbing boy, and ran off when he was about five. I feed him from time to time and he does errands for me.... He's such an independent little sprout, which I admire, I never quite liked to offer to adopt him though I'm fond of him; he's brave and still as gay as a grig with all his troubles. I ruffle his hair; but ... I guess he ain't never had a female what hasn't made the sign of the evil eye; some believe that even lookin' at him can make the same cripplin' effects happen to an unborn child. I didn't think you'd be superstitious like that."

"Quite right; I am not. How ludicrous! Well you shall

adopt him as soon as you may be publicly alive again; and in due course he shall have a stepmama," said Jane firmly. "Simmy, you shall have my handkerchief but you must promise to learn to use it properly. Would you like Mr. Armitage to be your father?"

"Strite up, Mr. Armitage?" gasped Simmy

"Straight up, Simmy; but for now I'm pretending to be dead because I'm working against a very dangerous cove and this Sir Richard might be associated with him. So for now, you're just a kinchin-zad and *no boasting* because that could lead to you, me, and Mrs. Jane here all being scragged, right?"

Simmy nodded. He understood; and Jane's heart went out to a pathetic scrap of humanity not ten years old who understood too well about violent death. He blew his nose ecstatically on Jane's delicate linen handkerchief and Caleb took him off for some food.

Jane reflected soberly that this business was bringing home to her how well off she had always been; and that the bonds of extreme poverty and physical deformity were more profound than those of being a shabby genteel person like a governess. Simmy was fairly repulsive to look at; but cleaned up and fed up a bit she had no doubts that she would get used to his odd appearance with the drooping right hand side to his face. If Caleb had been married before and had already had children, crippled or no, she would accept them as stepchildren; so it was untenable that she should not be a mother to one Caleb had considered adopting without realising that the independence was but armour against the world. Of course Caleb saw poverty and misery every day; had grown up with it. He could be fallible in reading people; and how typical that he should err on the side of not wanting to take the child's self respect and independence!

Chapter 25

"I meant to tell you about Simmy and see if you wouldn't find him a spot to sleep at times," said Caleb. "A man is shy of adopting a lad when there's no woman's hand in the house and equally shy of asking the best woman in the world to see her way to giving any kind of affection to a child not even a blood relative of.... I am losing myself here; you know what I mean don't you, Jane-girl?"

"If you have an affection for the child then you should look on him as your son; and it argues well that you will readily accept another man's children as your own," said Jane. "How could any woman not warm to that poor child? He is a loathsome creature at the moment, but it is hardly his fault! Cleanliness and good food will do wonders; but my dear Mr. Armitage, he must learn to speak in a way that will not leave Frances and baby picking up bad habits. To learn cant for the fun of it when they are old enough to use it only in play and not as everyday is one thing; but I will not have them use it as a matter of course."

"No; and I will engage to teach Simmy the same," said Caleb. "Had you thought of a name for baby?"

Jane sighed.

"It would be politic to call a son 'Jasper' for his great uncle," she said, "for he will be the old man's heir. For a girl I thought perhaps Henrietta for Aunt Hetty. I felt I should try to appease Uncle Jasper; he will have found out that Frank made a will leaving the house to me, which will not please him that it does not automatically entail to Frank's son should baby be one; nor does my blackmail of him to have the jointure in full please him any the better. When he dies the property of Enscombe will pass to baby if he is a boy or to the crown if not; so I am hoping that he should be a boy for why should the crown profit? I doubt I shall have any monies of the estate as I brought nothing to the marriage; but I shall lose no time in getting Mr. Weston, as Frank's father, to arrange guardianship of baby in that case. I cannot dare remarry until he is born; for that would probably forfeit his right to inherit.

And to do so would be unfair to baby. I can only be grateful that Frank laughingly made out a will naming me as heir to any house in London he might own; which was before he bought this house. It is unfair that women should not be permitted to inherit property! And if uncle Jasper saw fit to contest that will, it would probably be decided in his favour, to be held in entail for any son of Frank or as dowry for his daughters to the benefit of any husband they might have!"

"It is unfair," said Caleb, "and by law, which troubles me, I shall have ownership of the house when we wed."

"You might however if you prefer agree on a secured settlement to give me full rights to leave the house as I choose," said Jane. "And how sordid that such things should have to be discussed! Particularly since I have not yet even given you leave to court me and we are discussing marital finances!"

"Sordid indeed Jane-girl; and perhaps premature; but with children in the case, finer feelings must be laid aside for sordid financial consideration."

"Oh yes, I do agree; else I had not acted so towards Uncle Jasper. I was disagreeably surprised that so meek a man should be so unpleasant towards me; and it gave me the bravery of a lioness in defence of her cubs," said Jane.

"And quite right too," said Caleb. "I have noticed that men who live under the sign of the cat's foot may, when released by widowhood, run quite counter to what one might have said was their nature, either behaving with impropriety or becoming very hectoring bullies. And you are quite right to put your children first. Mr. Weston seems a good man to consult; what little I saw of him I liked, and firmly suppressed the regular soldier's contempt for a militia man."

"Why is there contempt for the militia?" asked Jane.

"Because they are toy soldiers who join up for the uniform and are never posted anywhere more dangerous then Bath where only the designs of moonstruck young girls may pose them any danger," said Caleb.

"You *are* a complete hand!" giggled Jane.

Simmy came back late in the evening and was not too pleased to be firmly bathed and dressed in cut-down clothes that were clean by Mrs. Ketch before he was permitted to go and report. He did get rewarded with a bowl of stew and a good chunk of bread however; all of which mixed indignity and largesse he told Caleb before any kind of report might be extracted from him.

Caleb laughed.

"Well lad, when you're my son you'll wear a clean mish every day, and wash every day too; and you'll thank me for it! It's the dirtiest as catch Gaol Fever first, as well you know! And you'll eat three times a day too."

"*Gawd*!" said Simmy "Well fer eatin' free times a day reckon the scrubbin'll be worth it!"

"It is," said Caleb sympathetically. "I know; for I found out when I joined up. Now what have you found out?"

Simmy grinned.

"Well the cove is Sir Richard Marjoram like wot 'e say 'e is; that's strite up. Got *that* off the footman cove what gimme a baubee, skinflint owd....."

"*Language*!" barked Caleb "And if you spit in here I'll tan your jacket!" he then added to Jane "A baubee is a ha'penny; not much of a vail."

"No indeed," said Jane "If I catch you spitting, Simmy I will make you clean it up and I will wash your mouth."

"Sorry sir, sorry lidy," said Simmy more impressed by the cruelty of women than the idea of a whipping. "Any roads, this Sir Richard, he come by the title in the army seemingly for bravery in action; 'swhat the footman say. 'E's the third son of some Earl or uvver – that's this Sir Richard, not the footman," he explained "Wot's disin'erited 'im fer some sort o' kick up over someat. I dunno! Didn't make no sense t'me."

"You did well Simmy," said Jane, "and when you are Simon Armitage you shall be properly educated so you do understand and then you may help Mr. Armitage even more."

Simmy blinked.

"I ain't averse t'be Armitage, Lidy, but why won't I be

Simmy no more?"

"Why, because Simmy is but a shortening of the name Simon; it is a name you might think more a man's name than a boy's as you grow up," said Jane.

Simmy considered this.

"I ain't never been nuffin but Simmy," he said "But stand to reason; the 'sylum christened all the boys in rotation after disciples and all the girls after all the morts in the Bible which ain't as many. I've allus wonderd, Lidy, 'course they learned us Bible stories, if there weren't no morts, 'ow did they….." he caught Caleb's eye on him and amended what he had been going to say to, "……'Ow did they marry and 'ave brats?"

"Why Simmy, if anyone wrote an account of history of our own time, there would be a great deal about the men; those who fought Boney and those who make laws; when it is men who write history it is merely that they do not bother to mention the women unless they cannot help it," said Jane. "It is not that there were fewer women in Biblical times; just that they were not mentioned."

Simmy digested this.

"Reckon it's account of 'ow once you lets morts in you bain't never shut o' vem," he opined.

"And when they cook and mend and care for you, that's not such bad thing young shaver," said Caleb firmly.

Simmy was provided with a blanket to sleep in the kitchen with Caleb's small army; and went to sleep more comfortably than he recalled ever having been in his short life before.

"What I want to know is," said Jane to Caleb, "why, if this Sir Richard is involved in the killing of Frank, would he want to offer marriage to me? I can see why he might want to question me to find out what I know – I confess when I became wise to him I almost became sick with apprehension – but marriage?"

"You sweet and green goose," said Caleb "*That* part of his lay was plain from the start; what but that a man owns his wife, and her possessions, and that as they are one in law she cannot testify against him?"

"I could not in any case; I know as yet nothing to testify," said Jane.

"Unless you know of the necklace – and to get it back, and quiet your tongue on it, do you think any man is going to find it a hardship to wed a beautiful woman who has besides this elegant town house and potentially a fortune too? Recollect he does not know that all the dibs were on Frank's side; indeed he may even believe that Frank married the fortune he ran through so successfully, since he suddenly appears on the town with money and a wife. You know, and because you have told me, I know that he married you only because his aunt had died; and that she had obviously also had a secured settlement to leave money directly to him. But to all outward appearances he has a new wife and blunt to flash to go with her."

Jane paled.

"Does that mean I shall be the butt of all the gazetted fortune hunters in town?"

"More than likely," said Caleb cheerfully. "I'll darken their daylights for them though if you want me to."

"I should prefer to use tact in the first instance and if that fails a bucket of cold water as one uses on amorous curs," said Jane sedately.

He gave a shout of laughter.

"Jane-girl, the suggestion is delightful; and spoken in that prim tone of yours, one might take you for the governess you never had to be dealing with some embarrassing cur in the park when out with your charges!"

"Well it is a deal better than falling into hysterics and merely dragging interested little eyes past and hoping that the children do not ask loud question with the unfailing clarity of tone that always occurs for such inappropriate queries when their mama is listening," said Jane.

"You have no illusions I perceive," said Caleb.

"None whatsoever," said Jane. "So he prefers to *own* me than to kill me; I suppose that it makes sense. A drab like poor Dorothy being murdered would, I am sure, elicit less interest than a widow of respectable birth living in a neighbourhood such as this. Should I encourage him at all?"

"I should say your tone of censure about his unwarranted hurry was about the right tack to take," he said. "Do not *dis*courage him; but permit my friends and me to do a little carpentry."

"What are you about?" asked Jane.

"The bookroom and the Parlour run back behind the stairwell to have a deep alcove on each that has the connecting door in it. Doubtless he noticed the alcove; but made a little shallower and lined with books, that there might be a concealed doorway, I might construct a small secret room, that he not, I hope, notice the difference in the depth. If a piercing is made to the stair well for fresh air and some modicum of light from the skylight above the stairs it would be a place in which to listen to conversations in either room at need. And a better choice than the little parlour across the landing from the bookroom."

Jane nodded. The bookroom was a long narrow room permitting a second room at the front that was best described as cosy; the deeper rooms lay at the back, the parlour and the dining room, the dining room running across the stair well.

"Yes; you do what is needful," she said half reaching out to him "Indeed I would that you will start first thing in the morning; for I fear this Sir Richard and I would be happier to know that you are indeed nearby."

"Don't worry, Jane-girl; I won't let the fellow hurt you," said Caleb taking her hand and pressing a gentle kiss on the palm.

Chapter 26

Caleb was still not recovered from the bullet wound by any manner of means; Jane cleaned and dressed the wound twice daily, and though he mostly scorned to lie abed he did lie down on the chaise longue to direct the efforts of Will, Jackie and Daniel who seemed to take a positive delight in a little bit of constructive demolition, as Caleb put it to Jane.

"You are an infuriating man with a propensity for making contrary comments," said Jane surveying the mess and concealing her dismay.

"Well if you are disposed to compliment me so well, Mrs. Churchill….." said Caleb who was rigorous in his propriety over terms of address in front of others, especially underlings if not in the outrageous things he said..

"What, you thought it a compliment Mr. Armitage? I fear you must be feverish again," said Jane.

"I could make a few comments about the fever you create in me but I fear I should only make you blush. Like that," said Caleb.

"Impossible man!" said Jane, more irritated with herself that he could bring colour to her cheeks so easily.

He grinned at her.

"Break your fast, Mrs. Churchill; and *then* comment," he said.

Jane went in to breakfast with Miss Bates who wanted to discuss all that the soldiers were doing in great detail; Dorothy agog to know what the purpose was; and Jane murmured that they were employed usefully as seemed fit while they were about the place setting up a chamber that might comfortably house a patent flushing water closet on this floor rather than the more primitive arrangement of the close stool in the little room off the dining room.

"Why what an excellent idea!" cried Miss Bates "The Bramah closet downstairs is a most excellent contrivance; Mr. Woodhouse has one too at Hartfield to prevent his servants having to go down the garden in the cold for emptying things; and the Coles have one on *each* floor in their house, only fancy!"

Jane murmured that she was glad that the idea suited and added that it did not seem quite the conversation to go with toast and conserve of apricots even if there were no gentlemen present at the moment.

Miss Bates fluttered an apology and turned the conversation to the sewing Jane was engaged upon.

Jane happily answered all her Aunt Hetty's questions on her plans and Dorothy, feeling better this day, joined in happily and the ladies planned sewing endeavours to take up their day while the men sawed, hammered and converted.

They were thus engaged, Miss Bates having started Dorothy on the long seam of the centre back of her gown, having completed the two side seams, and Jane gathering ruffles for her own gown, when Fowler came in.

"It's that fellow Sir Richard again," he said, "and I've left him downstairs in the salon next the reception room; couldn't think what else to do with him, Madam, with the work in the book room and in here."

"Dear me, how very precipitate of him!" said Jane. "You had better show him up here to the parlour; or no, perhaps that will not answer; unless, Dorothy my dear, do you mind repairing to the nursery to play with Frances for a while? Annie shall bring her down in a quarter of an hour. You may be in danger if he sees you. Aunt Hetty, I beg you say *nothing* of Mr. Armitage to this man; he may be an enemy; I pray you might talk of dear Highbury to him and how much we miss it. Caleb shall go through to the other room and direct from there; the men, setting up a Bramah closet shall continue working."

"Oh Jane!" gasped Miss Bates "I know I talk too much; it is a fault of mine because I so much like company; can you trust me not to say anything untoward?"

"*Dear* Aunt Hetty, you should think only that you do not want to discuss this nasty business; think about Highbury and its excellent people. I will not let him question you," said Jane.

Dorothy, at the word that this was an enemy took herself

off without further bidding; she had no desire to be burned again! The burn on her face was nicely crusted over but she feared she might bear a scar all her life and the thought of the men who had been prepared to go to such lengths filled her with horror.

Caleb nodded at Jane's dispositions and quickly explained to the three soldiers what Mrs. Churchill was suggesting was their supposed purpose.

"Ain't a half bad idea at that," said Jackie, thoughtfully, "and explainin' wot you was doin' in there too if you gets found listenin' any time,"

"And the plumbing might be installed at a future date; never mind that for now!" said Caleb.

Sir Richard bowed over Jane's hand and permitted himself to be introduced to her Aunt Hetty.

"You are having work done to the house?" he asked, wincing at the banging.

"Indeed yes!" said Jane with a look of fatuous enthusiasm "My husband had wanted a Bramah closet for a long time; and as it was all fixed up that they should come I could hardly say them nay; and indeed such a modern feature is an advantage, do you not think?"

"We live in such exciting times!" added Aunt Hetty "With such wonderful inventions; fabric woven into such pleasing patterns or printed with complexities no loom could make and wonders like the Bramah closet; why in no time at all the clever little machine Mr. Trevithick built might even be made big enough and fast enough to carry people as fast as a post chaise, and never tiring the way horses do! Mr. George Knightley – he resides in Highbury where I generally live, you know – considers that it may be ultimately possible for steam powered carriages to reach an average speed of as much as fifteen miles per hour! And just imagine the luxury to travel so fast and cut the time of travel by so much!"

173

"Perhaps Sir Richard is a noted whip who already knows the thrill of travelling so fast, at least over short distances," said Jane. "Do you drive, Sir Richard?"

"I do; and I like to ride," said Sir Richard. "Would having a phaeton and pair help to make up your mind, Mrs. Churchill?"

Jane copied the irritating titter of false laughter that Augusta Elton was wont to utter.

"Fie Sir Richard!" she said "I have told you I will not even *think* of this matter until I am out of black!"

"What matter is this, my dear?" asked Aunt Hetty.

"Why dear aunt, Sir Richard has a mistaken idea that his friendship to Frank means that he should make me an offer; *most* ineligible until I am out of mourning."

"Oh indeed!" cried Aunt Hetty. "It cannot be thought about! Sir Richard, you are at fault!"

Sir Richard smiled his mirthless smile.

"It has been known for a widow to put off her weeds early for the sake of a father to her children," he said.

"Oh quite impossible," said Jane, "and moreover there is the matter of the entail on Frank's Uncle's property; if I remarry before my child is born and it should be a boy, I shall be disinheriting him; you must recognise that, Sir Richard, that family matters must stand above everything. I did mention this yesterday when first you mooted this foolishness."

There was a tic in his cheek.

"Ah, quite, yes, I see that," he said. "But what of your own fortune, Mrs. Churchill? Might not the entail be broken if your own fortune was to be added to the estate?"

"Oh but my fortune is all you see in front of me," said Jane deciding to equivocate over owning the house. "My face is my fortune, sir she said, as the song will have it. Everything else was Frank's. The house is mine as long as I care to stay in it; and if I dislike my grandchildren, why I might have myself embalmed after the Egyptian fashion and insist on staying on display in the reception room to irritate them," and she smiled brightly enjoying the effect of letting foolish whimsy rule her tongue in trivial inconsequentialities of so absurd a nature.

"*Jane* dear!" protested Miss Bates.

"It seems a trifle macabre," said Sir Richard looking startled.

"It is the Egyptian touches that some architect has put to the pillars and sconces in the reception room has put the idea into your head," said Miss Bates. "*What* would Mr. and Mrs. Weston say?"

"I do not know, Aunt Hetty," said Jane demurely, "but I should think that they would probably say nothing as I might expect them to predecease me unless I die young. But there is no reason to suppose that like Cleopatra I should fall victim to any poisonous asp; wherein are such to be found here?"

"There are adders on the downs near Highbury," said Miss Bates seriously.

The conversation was interrupted by Annie tripping in with Frances in her arms.

"Precious darling!" cried Jane taking Frances and almost thrusting her at Sir Richard – taking care that she had tight hold of the child – "Isn't she just adorable?"

Sir Richard actually recoiled.

"I, er, I do not know much about small children," he said, "I had been expecting to see you alone."

"Oh now *that* would have been ineligible," said Jane. "I saw you alone in the book room yesterday because I assumed it was business that brought you; but in light of your rather improper proposal I would not see you again without my duenna. And if you *were* to consider any serious courtship in due and proper course I should fail in my duty as a mother not to be absolutely certain that I present to my daughter any men who would wish to be her father. Though I must say that I am not sure that I am wishful to consider one to whom I had, for the time being, given his congé; for I will not be out of black for another five and a half months. And I have to say that I believe I must give Fowler orders not to permit you entry until August."

"But my *dear* Mrs. Churchill!" he looked angry but

schooled his features as Frances' lower lip came out and she started to cry, turning from him, "my dear Mrs. Churchill; a moment's reflection will show you that a woman cannot undertake to deal with business matters; and I am ready to stand as your helpmate in that respect without pressing my suit; to deal with any paperwork that should arise!"

"Oh dear Jane is *quite* equal to dealing with paperwork!" said Miss Bates.

"Poor sweetheart! Do not cry!" crooned Jane to Frances then smiled brightly at Sir Richard. "And such things as require a gentleman's touch can be far better dealt with by Frank's father," she added. "Oh Frances, didn't you like him then, precious?"

"His *father*? I understood that it was his uncle who held the purse strings and he many miles away in Yorkshire!" said Sir Richard scowling at the infant who was taking Jane's attention.

"Oh his uncle is usually to be found on the estate in Yorkshire," said Jane, "but Frank was adopted by his Uncle and Aunt because his father was a widower; his father lives just two hours from town you know and might come up to conclude any business I require and return the same day. SO fortunate is it not? You will not need to trouble yourself in the least!" and she smiled brightly again.

"For so lovely a woman I should not think it any trouble at all; besides being closer at hand," said Sir Richard.

"Oh to be sure; but it would not be proper of me to place my family business in the hands of one who is to me at least a stranger," said Jane, "for my Father-in-law would be most put out.   And if I have any immediate trouble, why I might doubtless rely on Mr. John Knightley who lives in London – he is a barrister at law – who was long a neighbour of mine and known to my Father-in-law as a most reliable man. I would not worry over putting yourself out on Frank's behalf; for it will be news to me if he ever put himself out on behalf of anyone but himself. Now, Fowler will see you out; and I shall be ready to receive your card in August, Sir Richard," and she rang the bell.

Fowler was hovering; he had taken Sir Richard in dislike being, as he told Mrs. Ketch, too free with his vails and expression too veiled to be free, which witticism pleased him so well he stored it up to repeat to Mr. Armitage who was, as Fowler also said to Mrs. Ketch, more the gent in his manner than this supposed knight may be.

Chapter 27

"Of course, Jane-girl, now you've told him to shab off it might have queered the pitch," said Caleb, "if he really is any good at playing the waiting game he *will* wait until August and we lose the Dutchman and we lose him."

"He doesn't play the waiting game that well," said Jane. "He won't wait; I fancy he will report to the Dutchman and we shall find ourselves either invaded by ruffians or a housebreaker infiltrated into the house; who will not, of course, find any such thing as the Avon necklace so I do not actually fear the same; since the orders must needs be specific."

"You reason so very well," admired Caleb, "I thought I was pretty long headed; but you have me beat!"

Jane laughed.

"Oh perhaps I can help you by being moderately good at understanding people too; together we cover most things," she said. "I was wondering…. Concerning a future that we were not going to discuss…."

"*Your* rules, Jane-girl," said Caleb.

"Yes, my rules; and bad of me to break them," said Jane. "But I was wondering, hypothetically, whether a wife of an Officer of the Law might be permitted to help him in other cases….."

"Well in such an hypothetical case of course no rules of conduct of speech have been broken," said Caleb with a perfectly straight face. "Now the rules for an Officer of Bow Street do not permit an Officer of the Law to discuss his cases with anyone else; but," he held up a finger and grinned as her face fell, "a wife is held to be one body with her husband in law; and indivisible; so if an Officer of the Law spoke to his wife of his cases and obtained her advice, why then he will not have violated the rules for he is merely cogitating in another part of his indivisible self."

Jane laughed.

"Mr. Armitage, you are a philosopher; a Sophist!" she declared.

"It seems to work," agreed Caleb cheerily.

Simmy had been busy throughout the day too and returned in triumph to tell Caleb and Jane that he had set up a whole network of informers watching every move that Sir Richard and Poul de Vries made.

"And vis Sir, 'e ain't of the sort wot get vouchers to Almacks," giggled Simmy as though this were a tremendous joke, "'cos apparently 'e go out on Wed's'd'y an' also on'Sund'y, though vat ain't an Almack's day, to a low dive aht 'Ampstead way, place called 'The Spaniard's Inn'!"

"Hampstead? Why is that name familiar?" wondered Jane, "ah, was it not the place of residence of William Murray, Lord Mansfield the judge who famously ruled that slavery was against English law? It was an early step towards abolition and I read a 'life' of his in a magazine after I felt so oppressed by that wretched Elton woman and her boasting about her brother-in-law whose family made their wealth on the backs of slavery."

"Indeed Mrs. Churchill, I have heard of Judge Murray too, though you are more knowledgeable than I; but it may be that you recall a more recent reference, for there was an article in the Tattler that the poet Mr. Keats is to remove there for the good of his health since the city air makes him unwell," said Caleb. "You read out his poem 'On first looking into Chapman's Homer' to Miss Bates when it was printed in the ladies' magazine you take; I was much struck at the time that by his suggestion one might read these old Greek tales and feel like a gallant explorer and adventurer."

"Indeed perhaps the air outside the city may improve his poetry also; for I cannot admire his writing so well as that of Lord Byron, for all that one might deplore that man's lifestyle and scandalous behaviour," said Jane. "I do not believe it was in connection with either Mr. Keats or Lord Mansfield however that I connected the town of Hampstead; how vexatious! Perhaps it was mentioned in stray conversation by someone recently!"

Simmy sniffed. Discussion of queer-cuffins, as his idiom designated judges, or poets, whom he apostrophised as bennish lolpoop chaunter-culls, bored him.

"Well reckon if Sir Richard want some lolpoop to write rhymes for 'im, 'e don't need ter go aht ter 'Ampstead," he said firmly. "The Spaniard's Inn is a place where cocking and the like take place, see?"

Caleb laughed.

"Oh I don't have any suspicion that Sir Richard has any literary bent, nor any desire to oppose slavery, Simmy; but there is a former resident of Hampstead as may tickle your imagination; Dick Turpin was said to have drunk in your very Spaniard's Inn in his heyday."

"*Cuh!*" breathed Simmy, awed. He went on, "That feller Deevrees or whatever 'e's called, 'e don't go out much; and 'e's a skinflint too so nobody 'as took much notice of 'im. Seemingly 'e does go to clients 'ouses though, like some milliner; so we'll find out 'oo 'e visits in a brace o' shakes! Can I 'ave one o' vem little veal pies wot Mrs. Ketch make? Cuh vey aren't 'arf tasty!"

"You most certainly may if there are any over," said Jane. "Mr. Armitage will make it all right with Mrs. Ketch. And Mr. Armitage, if it means we are to be one short at the table tomorrow why then, Mrs. Ketch shall slice them and serve a platter with slices and a salad arrangement in the middle. It will look quite pretty and will go round quite well enough."

"Yes ma'am," said Caleb. At least he would be able to flatter Mrs. Ketch into accepting such an idea; and the good woman had fortunately taken Simmy more as a challenge than a nuisance.

Jane spent the rest of the evening playing dance music and counting out the measures to teach Dorothy to dance; and for that matter Caleb, who learned fast enough listening to her explanations. By pushing the furniture back they might manage Sir Roger de Coverley and some of the less complex country steps.

"It is hard to show you how to go on without three couples," said Jane, "so many dances require the triples to be made into the patterns of the set; and it helps to create the serpentine movements that are so necessary for a pretty effect. Still, if you will learn the steps it will stand you in good stead; for then you may just watch the leading couple at any dance and follow what they do."

"Will yer learn me to waltz?" asked Dorothy eagerly.

"I will *teach* you how to dance the country measures that are danced as waltz-time dances," said Jane, "but to dançe the actual *waltz* is extremely fast you know; it may be danced at Almack's as they say, with the express permission of the patronesses, but High Society is a trifle ramshackle in its morals you know. Why even Lord Byron is said to have disapproved of the waltz and nobody can call his morals anything but a trifle *lax* whatever you may believe of some of the wilder gossip about him."

"What is the wilder gossip abaht 'im?" asked Dorothy, interested.

"You are too young to know," said Jane primly, "and despite all your unfortunate experiences, too much an innocent. It would shock you."

She had no intention of disclosing that it had been hinted that Lord Byron had fathered a child on his own sister; that was a deeply shocking idea that Dorothy might have difficulty coping with. And as for some of the suggestions that he liked *men* in a certain fashion as well as women, why she preferred not to even contemplate that herself! And she certainly had no intention of repeating any of these shocking whispers in front of Aunt Hetty who would be much upset! Ella associated with too many high class dressers when out shopping. And she, Jane, should be firmer with her dresser over what gossip she repeated on her return to the house, for what she had heard was often quite scandalous. Ella had too much of a taste for the salacious.

And at that, such a taste in one's servants might yet be an advantage to the wife of an Officer at Bow Street. Jane coloured slightly at the turn of her thoughts and gave her attention to what Miss Bates had to say.

"Dear me, he *IS* a rather unsatisfactory character, to be sure!" said Miss Bates of Byron, "but he writes *such* evocative poetry; dear Jane has read out loud to me from some of his works and I enjoyed it excessively until I heard that he was a womaniser!"

"No doubt when he is dead, the test of his work will be whether it endures because it is well written, and his peccadilloes forgotten, or will fall into obscurity because the scandal sells it," said Caleb cynically.

"I believe it will endure," said Jane. "One may prefer not to think of the scandal attached; but one cannot help enjoying the cadence and rhythm that makes his poetry exciting. Though his central male roles would doubtless be very uncomfortable for any real woman to have to actually live with; one cannot imagine asking the Corsair to see to ordering a Bramah closet."

Caleb gave a shout of laughter.

"Why Mrs. Jane how very practical you are to be sure!" he said delighted. "Is that your measure of a hero – to be able to arrange so fundamental a domestic article?"

Jane considered.

"I should say the ability to procure a Hackney carriage rapidly, to be ready to deal with housebreakers, and to take with equanimity a breakdown in domestic arrangements due to a crisis in the kitchen provide a true measure of a real man," she said, "also the ability to think and improvise in any crisis and to be ready to notice the indisposition of his wife or any of his offspring."

"Why Mrs. Jane, I do believe that you have a far more pragmatic state of mind than those who would sigh over a romantic figure," said Caleb, not displeased in having already managed to cope with all the examples she had cited. "But then, the romantic heroes in poetry and lurid novels are there to be sighed over by romantic young females that may imagine clandestine embraces with a figure who is, when all is said and done, made merely of paper and ink and therefore of no real danger to their virtue until they may meet a more realistic ideal."

"Indeed; if only the silly widgeons may not reject the ideal man for them for failing to recognise that he is a reality and does not need to live up to some fantastic and unrealistic ideal," said Jane. "And alas! I was such a silly widgeon to have my head turned by one who seemed every semblance of a romantic hero whose lustre wore off when I realised that he was but a man of straw if not a man of paper and ink."

"*Ooo*, Mrs. Jane, was that some cove you knowed before Frankie?" asked Dorothy.

"No my dear; I spoke of Frank. You saw the generous and heroic side for he visited you; living with him was not always easy," said Jane reflecting that she spoke in understatement. "If he had not been a weak man he would not have told them that you had the necklace, opening you to being hurt. Nor would he have got into such straits that he worked for such villains in the first place," she added then went on with some bitterness, "and if he did not care to humiliate *you* when he was with you then he treated you well enough that you are fortunate not to have seen his other side."

"Cor Mrs. Jane, did 'e do it to you too?" asked Dorothy who was fingering the rove on her burned face in resentful memory "'E never '*urt* me, so I figured, I could of 'ad worse, and 'e allus apologised."

"Then, my dear, I fancy he respected *you* more than he respected *me,*," said Jane, "and we speak out of turn before a gentleman; which was my fault for permitting my feelings to be carried away in so unladylike a fashion."

"Oh my poor dear Jane!" cried Miss Bates, "and poor dear Dorothy too! I could not ever imagine such things of Frank!"

"He hated strong minded women," said Jane. "And did not want me ever to be in the situation his aunt held regarding *her* husband; because like his uncle he was weak and could not perceive that a strong man likes a woman to be strong also as his helpmate, not his possession."

"If I may say so, hear hear," said Caleb. "Would you like me to withdraw so you may speak more freely?"

"Not in the least, Mr. Armitage," said Jane firmly, "it is an episode that is behind us; and I need you to walk through and then dance a cotillion with Dorothy."

Chapter 28

"Will we sew again today, Aunt Hetty?" Jane asked at breakfast next morning.

"Oh my dear, that would have been pleasant, but it is so vexatious!" cried Miss Bates, "I am afraid you miscounted the number of yards of black ribbon we should need for you neglected, my dear, to calculate the knots of ribbons the servants must wear, *and* the ribbon trim for bonnets! We are *quite* running out! I shall need at least six yards of threepenny width and four of sixpenny width and it would not be amiss to get some fourpenny width against need too."

"Then it is best that we step into town for some more," said Jane, "see, it is a fine day to day; and that we may not guarantee if we wait until tomorrow. I cannot think that the house would be attacked in broad daylight; no ruffians are *that* bold. And come what may they could not persuade any group of Luddites to believe that our house was any kind of mill or manufactory to be attacked to burn machines; nor is it a part of London in which mill owners tend to reside, so using a riot as a cover seems unfeasible. We shall be safe to leave the house for a couple of hours shall we not, Mr. Armitage?" she asked.

"I do not see why not," said Caleb, "though I should avoid getting into speech with anyone; and I shall have Fowler find a Hack that has a driver he knows too. One cannot be too careful."

Miss Bates gave a little scream.

"Oh my dear Mr. Armitage! Surely you cannot be serious? That is a suggestion from melodrama! Can these villains be so bold? Surely we shall be safe in broad daylight on the streets of London?"

"More than likely, yes," said Caleb, "but I would prefer not to take any chances with Mrs. Jane's safety, as I am sure you will agree."

"Oh *indeed* Mr. Armitage!" agreed Miss Bates.

It was indeed a fine day, if cold; the sun shone thinly and

burned away the last sullen strands of haze that would have veiled its face in the half-mourning of the late winter for the summer that was no summer of the previous year. Frost sparkled on the ground and Jane knew better than to touch the cold iron railings about the area, even with gloves, for the cold would strike through the thin leather. Young Molly had left washing on the line the night before and had run out after dark, absently placing her bare hand on the decorative iron surround of the kitchen garden and had a nasty frost burn in consequence. This winter was not over, despite the meagre promise of the half-hearted sun and the brightness of the sky around it, the colour of tarnished silver, bright against pewter clouds. The air was sharp; and tasted of sleet or snow to come. It was wise to shop now, not wait to see what the morrow would bring; and since the clouds were already beginning to form into the serried ranks of mackerel skies then wind was promised. If the crocus spears that speckled the garden came to flower too soon the blooms would be destroyed in the frost; though the single clump of brave snowdrops seemed immune to the cold.

Jane pulled her muffler closer because unlike the snowdrops she felt the cold keenly and it made her feel nauseous if she breathed in the chill air; hence a muffler to cover her mouth more warmly than a veil. It was bright blue and not conventional mourning at all; but it had been knit for her for Christmas by Patty, the little maidservant in the Bates home; and Jane had been much touched and would not discard it for convention. It was besides warm, of wool from the Donwell sheep, sent to be dyed and spun; and it was a reminder of what was, in many ways, home.

Fowler had found a hack; and was returning sat beside the driver, the clop of the horse's hooves ringing loud in the still frosty air, the metallic ring of the horseshoes on the road a musical note like the striking of hammer on anvil. But the sound of the sedate pace of the horse harnessed to the hack was drowned out by the sudden fusillade of galloping feet from another vehicle; which careered up the street, a closed carriage, a berlin, pulled by two fine bays. The coachman was muffled; not unreasonable on a cold day, but his face might as well not have been there for all one might see of it, thought Jane, wondering what the fool was doing driving so recklessly in a town street.

The bays were pulled up short, almost sitting on their own haunches, right beside her and Miss Bates who was clinging to Jane in some terror that the horses might be runaways and might mount the pavement.

Instead the door opened and a man, also muffled, leaped out and pushed Miss Bates so hard that she fell away from Jane to sprawl on the ground. Jane turned to her with an exclamation of horror; and found herself grabbed by the upper arm. She twisted to get away; but the grip was cruel and was dragging her towards the berlin.

Jane went to hit her assailant; but he only laughed.

She could not escape.

She could however hope to be followed; and she went limp as though fainting. He gave an exclamation of disgust and went to pick her up; and Jane used the opportunity of having both hands free to loosen and pull off her muffler, gasping as if feeling short of breath; and as she was about to be thrust into the carriage clung suddenly to the door, long enough to loop the brightly coloured muffler round the handle outside, unseen by her abductor who was trying to manhandle an unwilling female inside the coach before reinforcements should arrive.

She heard Fowler's voice.

"Don't shoot you Bedlamite! Nah then cully, give up; you can't get away wiv this in the middle of London!"

The coachman laughed and his muffled voice replied

"I think we are – cully."

Jane was now inside and as the door pulled to her assailant rapped on the coach. There was a stomach lurching moment as the horses doubtless shied and came down running following the crack of a whip.

Jane, who was still queasy in the mornings, promptly lost her breakfast on the floor.

"Well I shan't feel like kissing you now awhile," the voice was familiar; and as he took off the muffler so was the face.

"Sir Richard! What is the meaning of this?" demanded Jane, "if you plan to abduct me and force me to Gretna Green I assure you I shall not be a compliant prisoner!"

"Gretna Green? What maggot have you in your head?" Sir Richard sneered.

"What else am I to think?" said Jane, "you called two days running making much of the idea that you wished to wed me; I can only suppose that you still persist in the idea that I have some control over the monies that are in entail for my children and have some idea of gaining control over it by wedding me; I assure you that by marriage I stand to lose every last penny of the jointure I have. It is a ludicrous idea of yours and if you were at least even *born* a gentleman whatever manner of coxcomb you have become you would offer me a drink to wash out my mouth!"

He gave a sneering laugh and handed over a hip flask.

Jane took a drink, making a face at the taste of the brandy, rinsed her mouth around and looked for somewhere to spit. He pulled a silver chamber pot from under the seat and she spat thankfully.

"Though as you have already defiled the floor of my carriage, your need to spit in an utensil seems a little nice," he said.

"I had very little choice in the matter," said Jane. "Had you been a man of any delicacy and sensibility you would have left the utensil ready, bearing in mind that a lady in a certain condition is inclined to a degree of delicacy in her digestion. Or as is proved, the incomplete action of digestion," she added with a grimace. "But of course a man of delicacy and sensibility would not resort to abduction. If we are not bound for Gretna, where may we be bound?"

"You have no need to know *that,*," said Sir Richard. "but believe me, you *will* be begging to marry me before much longer; the alternatives would be very much more unpleasant. And if you do as you are told and make me a pleasant wife, you will have a pleasant enough life; a little confined perhaps, but I shall make sure you have every comfort."

"But I do not understand *why*!" said Jane opening her eyes ingenuously. "I do not have a sous of my own; nothing in the funds, no income, no expectations; Frank married me and rescued me from the humiliating penury of becoming a governess; my father was a penniless lieutenant in a foot regiment! What then can be the attraction in marrying me?"

"Apart from allowing that you are an attractive and spirited wench, the matter is your silence my dear; that you shall not be able to speak against your husband," said Sir Richard.

"Excuse me? Why should I wish to? Surely you have not *defrauded* my late husband?" asked Jane.

He gave a bitter laugh.

"You ninny! It is the other way round; are you not aware of that? You know about the necklace; and it has not been pawned. You lied to Poul; you *will* tell me the truth!"

She stared.

"The necklace? Are – surely you cannot mean the trumpery paste necklace my husband gave to his mistress? This is all very confusing; I cannot think; why the world spins!"

Artistically Jane put her hands tremulously to her head and permitted herself to sink back in the seat.

Had the floor not been covered in vomit she might have considered casting herself on the floor but in fear of her life or not she recoiled from such a recourse; not least because the proximity of the smell might have brought up more which would have spoiled her pose as quite insensible.

Sir Richard gave vent to a blistering oath.

"Stupid piece!" he muttered, "she *has* to know!"

Jane moaned gently. She could only continue to lie and hope that the blue scarf was seen by enough beggars to bring Caleb and his men to her rescue before she was tortured badly enough to cause her to miscarry. Jane had every belief in her own stubbornness to make her last longer than Frank had done; though her belly turned to water in fear at the very thought.

"Oh, this is surely a bad dream!" she murmured thickly, her eyes still shut, "I shall open my eyes and I shall be back in my own bed!"

"Not a chance I'm afraid, Mrs. Churchill," said Sir Richard's sneering drawl.

She opened her eyes wide to stare at him and began to scream.

He slapped her; which she had expected, though the pain of the hardness of the blow was more than Frank had ever managed.

She started to sob hysterically; it was guaranteed to make men nervous though it was a tactic she had scorned to use on Frank, scorned to let him have the victory of making her react at all.

But her victory here was to stay alive and hope that she might do so long enough for rescue.

Caleb would not leave her.

Chapter 29

Caleb came running out on hearing a commotion and Jane's voice raised in distress; he was in time to see the berlin turning the corner of the square towards the Pembridge Road by which the vehicle might go left into the city or right towards the north. Fowler was arguing with the driver of the Hack.

"Foller that bleedin' carriage!" shouted Fowler, beside himself.

"You're 'avin' a laugh, Mr. Fowler, strite up you are!" said the coachman "Swelp me, my poor nag can't keep up wiv even one o' them prime prads, never mind two!"

"He is correct, Fowler," said Caleb tightly as Fowler made a move as though planning on leaping up and taking the reins. "However we shall need the services of this good man to take us to see if we cannot get clues as to which direction this carriage has taken. If it only had any distinguishing features!"

"Well there can't be many berlins wiv – with – a blue muffler on the door handle," said Fowler with satisfaction, "not bereft of her wits, Mrs. Jane ain't not by a long mark!"

Caleb heaved a sigh of relief.

"Miss Bates!" he said kneeling beside the poor woman, who was sobbing, still on the ground "Are you badly hurt? I should have asked immediately!"

"Oh Mr. Armitage, you are everything that is good," cried Miss Bates, "I am not hurt….a little bruised perhaps but an application of arnica will soon set me rightabouts; oh, my poor Jane! What is happening? What will become of her?"

"Nuffink if I have any say in it," said Caleb, grimly, "my dear Miss Bates, permit me to assist you to rise; ah, here is Simmy. What news Simmy? Did you see what happened?"

Simmy nodded, sobbing in fright himself.

"Oh Mr. Armitage, that loverly lady, will vey sell her inter slavery?" he cried.

"It's generally the province of those who abduct children," said Caleb as Miss Bates gave a little shriek and swooned. "Here you silly young fellow, get in that Hack – here's a purse – and see what you can't find out. Mr. Fowler says there's a blue muffler on the door."

"I seen it," said Simmy. "Reckon I know the prads too; but I'll be back in a brace o'shakes. Onward my man!" he put on a false society accent as he mounted into the Hackney Carriage painfully and awkwardly but proudly.

"I'll Onward you, you little scamp," said the coachman without much rancour. The boy had been given money; and this was a guaranteed fare for most of the morning. It could be worse though if the brat showed any signs of putting on airs to irritate, he'd get a clipped ear for his pains!

Caleb carried the swooning Miss Bates within and up to the parlour where he laid her tenderly on the chaise longue. Dorothy tripped into the room; she had not wished to join the shopping expedition and had gone instead to play with Frances; but she was beginning to wonder what the commotion was about.

"Eoow, poor Miss Bates!" she cried, "what 'appened, Mr. Armitage? Where's Mrs. Jane?"

"She's been abducted," said Caleb grimly, "now you be a good girl Dolly….. strewth!" he added as Dorothy set up a screech.

"Eoow, eoow, eoow, vey'll murder 'er and sell 'er to ve resurrection-coves if vey don't sell 'er inter slavery!"

Caleb looked around and picked up Jane's floral arrangement of greenery and snowdrops and threw the water, flowers and all in Dorothy' face. She sputtered in shock.

"Right my girl; pick up them flahrs and stems and put more water in 'em or Mrs. Jane'll be disappointed when we gets her 'ome," said Caleb losing control of his vowels and aitches a little. "Then you shall see to a hot brick for Miss Bates and a shawl to wrap herself in and a cup of tea. You make yourself useful to her and leave me to worry about Mrs. Jane, see?"

"Yes Mr. Armitage; sorry Mr. Armitage," said Dorothy, subdued.

She was rather in awe of Caleb; but he was kind too, and most men would have slapped her. Dorothy got about the task of picking up the scattered snowdrops and greenery, mostly rosemary, lavender and bay from the kitchen garden, there not being much in the way of plant material at this time of year. Dorothy was not an expert flower arranger though she liked to watch Mrs. Jane at the daily task of keeping pleasant bowls of what Dorothy's uneducated idiom called 'erbs in the parlour and dining room, with such flowers added as might be in bloom. Jane had shown Dorothy the green shoots that would be crocuses and bluebells over the next couple of months and had suggested an outing to pick hazel catkins on Hampstead Heath. Meanwhile Dorothy enjoyed the scent of the lavender and rosemary as she poked the plant material back into the pretty bowl Jane had chosen to arrange them in, and stood it near Miss Bates so the scent might help revive her. She ran for a carafe of water and a glass too, to water flowers and give Miss Bates a drink at the same time; for Dorothy was a thoughtful enough girl even if not particularly clever. And if Mr. Armitage said he would get Mrs. Jane back, he would get Mrs. Jane back! And so she assured Miss Bates!

Caleb knew that Dorothy would look after Miss Bates well enough once brought out of hysteria; and ran back down. The three soldiers were waiting for him, much upset.

"I'm not sure we might of stopped it 'appenin' nowise," said Jackie, "but one of us might of leaped that rattlin'-cove afore 'e fired on Mr. Fowler, or one of us might of stopped the nags, or at least leaped on the back and hung onto the boot!"

"Oh I doubt you might have stopped it," said Caleb, "it was over too fast; I sent Simmy to get word from beggars which way they went. He ought to be back before long, so get your barking-irons primed and ready and check the sharp on your cutlasses and we'll be off, I hope, presently."

"We have a sharp on our tooth picks; you don't need to worry about *that*," said Jackie. "Good naval ones they be; got them cheap. Purser on the make; less ways to feather their nests now the war's over, see."

Caleb saw; he had heard much about the depredations of crooked pursers at sea, and they made the shenanigans of the Royal Waggon Train look quite honest by comparison.

He was however quite relieved when the Hackney Carriage returned bearing Simmy and a disreputable looking beggar with one leg and scabs and sores all over his body. Caleb eyed the newcomer with mixed feelings.

"If you think I'm introducing you into the house where I'm staying looking like that you maundering fermerdly-cove you can think again, Billy Blue!" he said "Simmy, you take him down the area steps and clean orf all them sores and scabs so he look half respectable and you can let down that leg o'yourn too," he added.

"There's rhino in this right?" said Billy Blue.

"Mr. Armitage will give you a quid; di'n't I say?" said Simmy shrilly.

Caleb raised an eyebrow.

"He has information worth that much?" he queried.

"'E's seen that carriage afore and where it go," said Simmy in great excitement.

"All right; when he's respectable," said Caleb.

Billy spat, and undid a strap allowing the leg that had been held up behind him to be released, and shook it to restore the feeling.

"Fer gelt I'll take orf all me artistic finery," he said.

"Bring him to the book room when he's fit to be seen," said Caleb hoping that the information was good; and knowing that a guinea was a small amount to pay for Jane's safety.

Miss Bates had shown signs of wanting to hear what Simmy's acquisition might have to say but Caleb had dissuaded her from leaving the parlour. Billy Blue was a beggar of more colourful language than Miss Bates' delicate nerves would be able to stand, though Caleb grinned at the thought that Jane would have found him more fascinating than disgusting. Jane was a remarkable woman! And he must make shift to rescue her as soon as possible; at least that blasted Hackney coachman was ready to be held as long as need be. Of course he was used to waiting on gentry-morts doing all their shopping; it was probably all of a piece to him.

Caleb tried not to sigh with irritation as he waited; and hid his impatience as he heard Simmy on the stairs with Billy Blue.

"I went down and found beggars to say what route were took, see," said Simmy, "and seeminly 'e was 'eading *Norf* so I finks, Gawd, is 'e takin' Mrs. Churchill ter Gretna? And when we was on the Great Norf Road startin' up 'Averstock 'Ill well I fort that were it! Ven I seen Billy yere, in Camden so I says to the jarvis to stop, see?"

"Camden?" queried Caleb.

Billy started to hawk, caught Caleb's furious eye and swallowed, choking horribly.

"Big bully," said Billy.

"Gawd, Bill, 'E ain't nothin' on Mrs. Jane, *she'd* make yer clear it up *and* scrub yer mouf aht wiv soap!" declared Simmy.

"And yer wants 'er back?" Billy was incredulous. Caleb took a single panther like pace and grasped him by the throat with one big hand.

"One word contrary to Mrs. Jane and you might not live to enjoy your guinea; and I'm beginning to wonder if Simmy ain't made a mistake and you don't know nothin'! Why Camden?"

"Stand to reason, don't it?" Billy said. "They just got the Regent's canal as far as Camden; and there's new 'ouses goin' up. Gawdstrewth, bein' the first on the grahnd fer the pickin's is worf a mort o' rhino."

"That follows," said Caleb, "touching the navvies too I suppose with sporting tips, spurious or otherwise, while they extend it towards Limehouse?"

"Well, mebbe," said Billy looking shifty. "Few good fibbing-matches take place out Primrose 'Ill way. Vere's one termorra night, cove called Charlie the Miller against....."

"I am not interested in bare knuckle fights," said Caleb waspishly. "Did you see the carriage with the blue muffler?"

"O'course I did!" said Billy "Struck me as right queer t'see Sir Richard Marjoram's berlin bedecked like a dell in a milliner's shop; so I was able to tell Simmy yere what I knows; and I'd like ter see yer gelt, no offence, Mr. Armitage, afore I whiddle the scrap."

Caleb laid a guinea on the table.

"That's for identifying the berlin," he said. "There'll be a brother to it if you have any more."

Billy started talking very rapidly.

Chapter 30

The drive was not long for Jane; that they had left the metropolis she was able to gauge by the cessation of the noise of frequent traffic and the shouts of itinerant peddlers and traders; they appeared to travel up hill for some way then the carriage turned sharply left and came to a halt.

"We have arrived," said Sir Richard, "and if we should encounter anyone and you kick up any fuss I shall smile and inform them that you are my unfortunate cousin released from Bedlam to be under the care of a private doctor. Screams of abduction would be disbelieved I assure you!"

"Oh I don't know," said Jane, "you look sufficiently like a loose fish to me that I shouldn't mind putting it to the test. Shall we try it? After all the worst that can happen is that people think I am mad and pity me; at best someone might run you through which I should find vastly entertaining."

Sir Richard stared like a stuffed cod; then slapped her resoundingly across the face. Jane was knocked sideways on the seat but managed to give him a brittle smile.

"Why thank you Sir Richard," she said, "the bruise and the cut on my cheek from your ring immediately tells disinterested passers by that you are violent and will make them more inclined to believe me over you!"

He gaped.

The door was opened by his footman.

"Problem, Sir Richard?" he asked.

Sir Richard glared.

"Make sure the coast is clear; this little virago believes she can call my bluff; and I would rather not try her and see," he said.

"Yessir," said the coachman, "here's a muffler on the door; you want that out of sight."

Sir Richard rounded on Jane who ignored him and cried out in delight.

"Oh my muffler! Why I made sure I had lost it when this horrid creature grabbed me; it was knit for me by a maidservant you know, all with her own hands!"

"Cease your prattling woman!" cried Sir Richard, grabbing her by the arm again to manhandle her down the steps. Jane fumbled with her skirt, glad that fashion decreed more width in skirts this season; and took a flying leap for the ground. She stumbled slightly but her arm was free for Sir Richard lost his balance and fell ignominiously to the ground. She found herself in the yard of a coaching inn, which was open and not in an enclosed courtyard; there was some kind of structure on the other side of the road down which they had presumably come, and beyond the hard gravely sand that made up the yard was some kind of heathland, with short rabbit-cropped earth and gorse bushes. Taking all this in at a glance, Jane lost no time in setting off towards open country at a run.

Her freedom did not last long; with a yell the coachman flung himself upon her and pinioned her arms.

She bit his wrist.

Then Sir Richard was there with a wicked looking knife.

"If you don't want me to cut your face off you'll behave," he said.

Jane considered her options. There was no guarantee he might not do so anyway to keep her at home when he married her by force as such was his intent; and that if she got hurt she might at least remain free. But Caleb would come; the main thing she must try to concentrate on were delaying tactics so she might not have to hold out against torture too long.

"How can I be certain you will not cut my face off in any case to make me a compliant wife?" she countered, "it might be worth my while to take my chances," and she bit the coachman again. He howled satisfactorily.

"By Jove it is an idea," said Sir Richard. Jane bit harder.

"Please guvnor, guarantee the zantippy so she stop bitin' me!" howled the coachman.

Sir Richard touched the knife to Jane's nose and she felt a sharp pain and hot wet blood.

"I *may* not spoil your face in any case for I like the look of

198

it," he said, "but I *will* slit your nose if you do not stop biting right now."

Jane stopped biting.

It had taken up some time at least.

They dragged her to the coaching inn, an unprepossessing building that looked to be two hundred or more years old, three stories high and the plaster covering what was doubtless a timber frame painted white, though there was precious little white to it now, being quite uniformly grey and grimy. Plaster had fallen from the wall in places and Jane was reminded of the women who haunted Covent Garden when daylight came at the end of their working day, the white lead paint too many of them wore cracking after the exigencies of their nightly activities.

She let them manhandle her in a back door and upstairs. There were some semi-clad females up here too who laughed and talked raucously. That should be no surprise; it was plainly a low dive. There had been some sort of sign at the front which looked to be a man in armour of some description; though it looked more like a lobster with a strange looking helmet.

Jane received a jolt of revelation. A man in lobster armour and a morion helm. Well that told her exactly where she was!

She was pushed into a chair; and the coachman left. She suspected that he would be standing outside the door. One of the other chairs was already occupied by Poul de Vries; Sir Richard took the other.

"I really am still most confused about why you have abducted me," said Jane, "for my nerves were quite shattered in the coach when you made me cast up my accounts and I was unable to take in anything save that you are not dragging me to Gretna. And this is that Jeweller; the one who came to see me. Why is he here? Are you acting as a pawnbroker, Sir Richard? You said something about Dolly's wretched necklace; did she pawn it to you? I really cannot be held accountable for my husband's mistress cheating you and in my opinion five pounds was a stupidly high price to give for it even if you did feel sorry for her, and surely recourse to the law would be a better way to recoup...."

Sir Richard hit her across the mouth.

"Shut up!" he said.

She had at least half expected it having copied her aunt's way of rattling on inconsequentially; and Frank had once said that he longed to slap Miss Bates across her stupid mouth. It was something Jane would never forgive; true he had been half in his cups, and she had been suggesting leaving him and returning to Miss Bates because he was being unreasonable; but the outpouring of how hard it had been to make up to Miss Bates without losing his temper had been vitriolic. It had been the point at which she had told him that as he did not like garrulous women he need not expect her to speak or react more than was needful.

Expecting it, she rode the blow a little; but it hurt.

Well if he was as easy to manipulate as Frank she would be as passive as with Frank. She sat limp in the chair, trying to relax.

"What did she say in the carriage? Have you questioned her without me that you made her vomit?" asked the Dutchman.

"She cast up her accounts because of having a broken ankle," said Sir Richard.

"She seems to walk quite adequately," said de Vries puzzled. Sir Richard gave him an impatient look.

"She's pregnant you stupid Dutchman," he said. "It is a euphemism.....And all I did was to tell her that we knew she was lying about that prime piece of goods pawning the necklace. She made that she did not understand."

"So? Vell she must understand or she vill not like the consequences," said de Vries. His cultivated accentless speech slipped, Jane noticed, quite as much as did Fowler's under stress. "Mrs. Churchill, you vill tell us all about the necklace that we vant to know or it vill not be pleasant; first ve can hurt you vith much more subtlety than poor Smudger managed with the trug; and ve can also arrange that you disappear into a brothel yourself and be most unhappy when you will be villing and ready to tell us all and to marry Sir

Richard for his and your protection, no?"

Jane stared.

"Well?" demanded Sir Richard.

Jane transferred her gaze to him, looking mildly puzzled.

He struck her.

"Are you going to talk?" he asked.

"Oh I do not understand!" cried Jane, "first you say to shut up now you say to talk! What do you wish me to talk about?"

"What do I wish......why you stupid woman I want you to answer questions as de Vries has asked you!" ground out Sir Richard

"He has asked me something? I do not know Dutch though; I could not understand what he said at all, it was like a dog barking," said Jane "And moreover why would I answer questions of a nasty little mushroom like him? I do not have conversations with cits you know, Sir Richard, especially those who cannot even speak the king's English!"

De Vries looked angry; Sir Richard was quite purple.

"Richard you have better ask the questions," said de Vries in a low voice"If the *verdompt vrow* cannot understand my accent; ach, it is true I am agitated enough that I do not have command of my voice!"

"I agree," said Sir Richard, also in an undertone. "She is not faking; she did not once blench when you told her the consequences; I thought it odd."

Jane heard him well enough; the ears of a musician were quick to hear. Once again she was grateful that she had learned to mask her expression during that secret engagement.

Sir Richard schooled himself to impassivity of manner and explained in detail the consequences of failing to talk to Jane who assumed an expression of worried horror.

"So; what do you know of the necklace?" asked Sir Richard.

"Oh I am so confused and scared!" cried Jane, "you are a cruel and ungentlemanly man; why should you care so much about that wretched necklace? I *told* de Vries that Dolly told me she had pawned it; what can anyone care for – good God! Are you saying that Frank picked up the wrong one by accident when he bought it, that it was *real*? Why Sir Richard, was it then yours and you ended up with the paste necklace? Why then you have every right to be testy but surely you could have been honest with me about that, and not act in so hole-in-the-corner way? If I thought for one moment that Dolly knew, I should have gently persuaded her to tell me where then it might be; but you are not going to think that I shall ask her now you have behaved so shabbily towards me; for I shall not be in the least co-operative over helping you to find the wretched thing and I hope it was sold to some Mill Owner's wife for a fraction of its value!"

"Does that *onnozelaar wijf* not have any kind of speech that is not like your *dombo* horse that can only gallop or stay still?" cried de Vries.

"Apparently not," said Sir Richard. "Are you trying to put over me the tarradidle that you had no idea that the necklace was anything but fake? Any woman who has seen real diamonds knows what they look like!"

"Oh yes! For I have real diamonds in the necklace that Frank's uncle made me wear at our wedding, and I was never so disappointed in all my born days; for they were so dull and shabby and the rubies quite unprepossessing too, and Frank said that they should have been cleaned, though I do not know how to clean such things and there was not time to take them to a jeweller because they arrived so soon before the wedding. If I had seen Dolly's necklace I should have known at once it was real because diamonds are such ugly dull stones and not in the least bit as exciting as the name of them seems to suggest, for is there not something evocative in the very *word* diamond?" said Jane. "At least coloured stones have something to them other than the dull grey look."

"Dull? Grey? That wench has never a diamond seen never!" cried de Vries "Much less the Avon necklace! That sly little piece Frank was keeping has held out on her also; you will have to get hold of that one, Richard and put *her* to the question!"

"I am still tempted to run a needle or two up under her nails to see if she continues to tell the same tale," said Sir Richard.

"Lock her in; and give her time to contemplate that you will test her," said de Vries.

Sir Richard nodded; and seized Jane's left hand, withdrawing a needle pinned to his lapel.

He pushed it a little way under her middle fingernail.

Jane cried out; the pain was considerable.

"It can go a lot further than that," said Sir Richard, "and it will. Because in an hour I shall come back and test whether you still tell the same story. And if you wish to change it either speak now, or the minute I return; because that wasn't even starting."

"I don't understand," Jane nursed the abused hand, "how can I change what I have told you? You asked questions and I have answered them. Do you want me to *lie*?"

"I just want to make sure that you do not, you little gabbster," said Sir Richard.

He and de Vries exited the room and she heard the lock turn and Sir Richard's peremptory command to the coachman to keep guard.

Jane heaved a sigh of relief; that bought more time.

And then she might, on their return, spin some fictional tale and let them realise it was fictional with false details; and then sob that she did not want them to hurt her so had made up another story as they seemed to want one. They would still hurt her but the longer she spent talking rubbish the less time they would have to hurt her before Caleb arrived.

And besides she would also spend the time seeing if she might escape.

The window opened inwards; but when she opened the casement she found that the poor quality glass in the narrow leads concealed bars. They had already thought of that.

She turned her attention to the chimney; they would never suspect a lady of quality trying to climb a chimney. In truth, Jane was not too sanguine about her chances of succeeding herself; but where needs must she might make some shift to try. The trouble was, deciding which flue to take if she *did* get up the chimney; coming down ignominiously in a pile of soot in the room where her enemies were would not be a good idea. And when they returned to this room they would see a soot fall and guess; and a fire lit under her would be as bad as any other torture. Jane sighed; she must pin all her hopes on Caleb; but then Caleb was a man on whom one might pin one's hopes.

And Caleb might be helped by having some clew to follow like the thread of Ariadne....

Chapter 31

Caleb, Will, Jackie, Daniel and Fowler were ruffianly looking enough to frighten any villain, as Miss Bates said with half admiration and half trepidation.

"Are you sure your arm will take not hurt, Mr. Armitage?" she asked anxiously.

"Miss Bates, if I knew it would cost me the use of it for the rest of my life you know I must still go to rescue Mrs. Jane," said Caleb gruffly.

"You *dear* man!" said Miss Bates. "I have my salves if we are ready."

"Beg pardon ma'am? I was not expecting you to be coming....."

"And who else will see to my dear Jane if I do not come?" said Miss Bates, "she may need a woman's hand; you and she might very well be smelling of April and May but there are some things that are not seemly. I shall not get in the way."

"Why Miss Bates, I believe I see where Jane gets her indomitable spirit!" cried Caleb in admiration. "You will do well though to stay back; we shall not be playing a gentlemanly game of cricket."

"Mr. Armitage, if you plan to save parliament the price of rope by killing them not saving them to be hanged I shall not grieve; these monsters are ready to harm poor helpless women!"

"Ar, and half-women too like Mr. Churchill was," Fowler muttered, fortunately too low for Miss Bates to hear.

Caleb agreed with Fowler; he strongly suspected that the villains would find that Jane was a far less helpless proposition than her husband!

The drive was not accomplished as fast as the berlin and its two fine horses might have managed; but it was done with as much despatch as the driver was able to manage for the promise of gold if he might do so. The horse, poor creature, was sweating profusely; but it might rest once they got to 'The Spaniard Inn'; where the jarvey would rub it down and see it fed.

Miss Bates was to wait in the Hackney until called; the three soldiers and Caleb stood as though arguing about something, and pointing much at the tollbooth built on the other side of the road, a gate barring any further progress north without payment of the required toll.

Will walked around the inn towards the back, supposedly to relieve himself and came back grinning.

"Single blue strand o' wool danglin' from a winder," he said; and proceeded to describe in detail where the window was and exactly how far along the back of the inn, and up on the second floor under the eaves.

Caleb grinned. She would not have got away with using the whole muffler again; his clever Jane.

They walked into the tap room; still apparently quarrelling.

It did not take much in the way of contentious comments about Government and taxation – leading from tolls to the Corn Laws – with one supposed apologist for the government, before a full scale brawl was in progress with other interested parties joining in. Dealing with incidental locals was going to be something that needed to be done first and hard fists and the butts of pistols soon saw these possible reinforcements laid low, while Caleb went up to mine host, smiled, put his pistol to the man's ribs and required him to turn around.

A heavy pewter tankard knocked scientifically against his head ensured that the man lost all further interest in the proceedings; and Caleb tied him up expertly. The soldiers, having subdued the half dozen or so locals, kicked, dragged or persuaded them to sit in a circle, and proceeded to cross their hands behind them to tie in a ring one hand to the hand of the fellow next to him. It had been a method they had used to deal with French prisoners requiring a minimum of twine to keep a relatively large number of prisoners immobilised.

They were then ready to proceed upstairs.

And there would be little notice taken of a bar room brawl in so rowdy an inn.

"Beg pardon I'm sure, ma'am," said Caleb, lifting his

beaver to the almost naked prostitute whose door he had just kicked in.

"Strewth! Charmed I'm sure," said the lightskirt half ironically, wriggling provocatively as a matter of course.

"And sorry about this too, ma'am," said Caleb, whipping the key from her side of the lock, pulling the door to and locking it.

He hastened away; the language was indescribable. He had a grim look on his face; this, the second floor, was where Jane was apparently held; and seemed to be given over to prostitutes. They had ignored the first floor as well as the ground floor to get Jane out first; and hope that she had not been taken to some other chamber. Well, he had miscounted; and yet … there was no other room further along …

Caleb peered at the panelled wall at the end of this passage; and pounced on what appeared to be a knothole.

There was a click of a latch; and then the concealed door swung open, revealing a villainous looking fellow in the livery of a coachman standing outside another door. He went for a pistol; and Caleb shot him without compunction. thrusting the discharged weapon back in his belt and pulling the second as he turned the key, still in the lock, and kicked the door in.

"Good morning Mr. Armitage; I am afraid I cannot offer you any refreshment," said Jane.

Her face was white and strained; and much bruised; and Caleb jerked her into his arms.

"Oh yes you can," he said and kissed her hard.

Jane had never been kissed like this, with this longing need and passion; and her legs felt quite weak as she surrendered to the embrace of her wonderful Caleb who had no sense of propriety at all to kiss a widow with quite such ruthless abandon.

And since he was irredeemably abandoned in any case, Jane kissed him back with equal fervour since he had plainly run mad and one should always humour a madman.

He lifted his lips from hers.

"Jane-girl, they have hurt you ... *where else*?" he demanded terribly.

"Only a demonstration with a needle under one nail," said Jane in a whisper, "you are come in the nick of time; I have heard a church clock strike the quarters from somewhere; and I was to be left an hour to contemplate. Oh Caleb! I fear I am close to swooning!"

"Here, Jane-girl, you can't do that yet awhile," said Caleb firmly, "you keep behind me, see; and we'll take in the precious villain what took you – Sir Richard Malodorous as I do believe."

"Yes; and oh Caleb! I believe that he may be Sparkler Jack; for knowing this inn near Hampstead Heath; I recalled why it was familiar, because of the highwayman attack."

"Yes and that tallies with what an informant has told me too," said Caleb "And what's more I am hoping to find some of the baubles here that may even convict him of that; I want that …..man……to go to bed with a hempen collar!"

"De Vries is here too," said Jane.

"Is he begawd!" said Caleb, "well he ain't stirred out since the robbery on the heath…. And I must say, with losing you I weren't about to be ready for reports if they'd come in of him stirring today; so there's a good chance of finding all that got took. And if I'm not mistook that's them a-comin' t'see why a shot was fired."

Sir Richard was in the fore and De Vries's voice was to be heard behind him yelling hysterically,

"If dot *dombo* coachman of yours has shot the wench he vill be in trouble isn't it!"

Sir Richard came face to face with Caleb as he came round the top of the stairs.

"Mornin'," said Caleb, "I am an officer of the law and you are under arrest. Are y'comin' quiet-like or do I get the pleasure of hurting you?"

Sir Richard recovered quickly.

"Why – what can you mean?" he said, "an officer of the law? Why should you arrest me? I have committed no crime.

I am Sir Richard Marjoram; you are making a big mistake my man."

"Well abduction in itself may not be a crime, cully, but torture now, that's a different matter," said Caleb "'Old out yer fambles; I got darbies yere for them."

"Why, a hysterical woman of good family but hardly high degree is scarcely going to have her word believed over mine," said Sir Richard, "now do yourself a favour, fellow, and accept a gift to make it worth your while to just forget this nonsense."

He reached towards a pocket.

"Sparkler Jack is going for a pistol!" shouted Jane from behind Caleb.

The shock of the use of his soubriquet made Sir Richard freeze momentarily; and in a stride Caleb was beside him, kicking his feet out from under him so he fell down the steep, narrow stair, taking the Dutchman with him.

"Take them, lads!" shouted Caleb.

There were brief sounds of a scuffle and a yell from Jackie "Gottem!"

"Good; tie them securely then search their rooms thoroughly. Daniel, fetch in Miss Bates and see about making tea for her and Mrs. Jane," Caleb called back, turning just in time to catch Jane as she swayed and would have fallen had not his strong arms been there to catch her.

Chapter 32

Jane came to with the awful smell of burning feathers in her nostrils; Miss Bates' kind, anxious face swam into her vision, waving the smouldering feathers.

"Oh Aunt Hetty!" whispered Jane, "Caleb did not bring *you* surely?"

"Only after I insisted that he did so, my dear Jane," said Miss Bates, "now if you feel ready to sit up there is a cup of tea here for you; the tea is stale but Daniel at least knows how to make a tolerable brew."

Jane sat up – no easy task for the sofa on which she found herself was an overstuffed thing of too many curves that appeared to attempt to frustrate any move save rolling off it – and took the cup of tea that Miss Bates held out to her.

"They are taken then?" she said. "Is Caleb certain he can get a conviction?"

Caleb's own cheerful voice answered her.

"I am now I am able to make deposition that I found the baubles that bridle-cull prigged last Sunday in the room which also has items in it provable to belong to Sir Richard Marjoram; and his change of duds in which he plays at being on the High Toby. You knocked him all of a piece calling out about him being Sparkler Jack; I had been going to shoot him and deprive the nubbing-cheat of some ripe fruit. But that will be a fine prize award to you for Sparkler Jack as well as De Vries. And I'll get my reward too; he sang like a canary. I only had to hint that Frank had already informed and that you were a furious virago out for revenge and that you knew his doxy – I presume he must have one – and he caved in, cursing and blaming the Dutchman for bringing in Frank in the first place. It turns out that someone Sir Richard robbed had vowels from Frank, among others, in with his money; and De Vries hit on the idea of using forged provenance just as you guessed to pass off jewellery changed enough to disguise it. There should be a nice haul of the same, partly broken up, at his workshop; which is where I shall be going next. It's done, Jane-girl; no more danger! And you have found out who killed Frank; you wanted to do that, didn't you?"

Jane nodded and she laid aside the tea cup.

"I did," she said, "oh! Does it always feel so flat when you have succeeded?"

Caleb came and knelt by the sofa and took her hands. Miss Bates tiptoed tactfully out of the room to leave them together.

"Jane, Jane! It only feels flat because you have swooned!" he said, "tomorrow you will be elated!"

"No I shall not," said Jane sadly "For you have no more excuse to stay with us."

Caleb paled slightly.

"No, Mrs. Churchill, I do not; and now of course what happens depends on whether you will receive a low creature like me socially or whether the excitement of the chase has brought about feelings you prefer to forget and all who are associated with it," he said.

"If you mean to abandon me without coming to court me properly when the time is right after kissing me so hard upstairs, Caleb Armitage, then you are nothing but a flirt!" said Jane.

Caleb grinned.

"Why Mrs. Churchill, if it is your wish, then I shall most certainly visit you.....every day if my duty permits. But I shall remove from your house so that nobody might say anything improper is afoot. And you and Miss Bates shall visit my more humble abode, that Sir Henry Wilton arranged for me; nothin' fancy you know, but snug."

"Why if it is not too snug to rear children in then I fancy it may do well enough," said Jane, "and you must take Simmy into your home right away!"

"Yes, bless the brat; he found us the one beggar in all London Town as knew where Sir Richard was a-takin' you; and that he stables a horse there that some might say was similar to the one Sparkler Jack rideo. So I had my information too. How did you come by the conclusion?"

"I fear merely by that uncertain route of female intuition," said Jane, "for he is known to have excellent horses and to ride and drive; and to visit this inn that was famous for having once harboured Dick Turpin; which is close by Hampstead Heath where Sparkler Jack was known to operate. That a horseman should be associated with jewellery thieves made a connection in my thoughts and I took a leap of faith in the matter. That is all."

"Well it is to my mind an astute assimilation of what little we knew – and a good working guess," said Caleb, "and on that information I'd have felt safe to raid this inn I have to say, even if I might not arrest Sir Richard or search his town house. Which now I might do," he added in satisfaction. "And take this precious pair to lie right-and-tight in the lock up; and once it is known that they are caught, then their confederates might be induced to talk to get transportation instead of hanging," he grinned suddenly, a savage grin, "and the queer-cuffin – magistrate to you, Mrs. Churchill! – might have been unwilling to give credence to arraigning a noble knight without the overwhelming evidence we have here; but once one of their own class turn bad, they get mighty peevy about it. There'll be no mercy for Sir Richard; and as he's entitled to a jury of his peers, he won't be able to browbeat no low class types with his rank neither," he winked at her "They'll only be impressed, and not favourably either, at how rank he is!"

"Oh Caleb you are so very handy with words!" said Jane. "And I should put aside my mourning and marry you tomorrow but for one thing."

"Indeed; you must not do Frank's brat out of his property if it is a boy," said Caleb, "and I support you in that with all my heart; and I shall fight for my stepson's rights too."

Jane gave a sigh of contentment.

This time she had made a good choice in a future husband!

She put up her mouth for a kiss; and Caleb obliged her with a heady and passionate embrace that almost caused Jane to swoon again from the sheer excess of emotion and anticipation of what was yet to come!